"I'm sorry. Did I hurt you?"

The guy quickly set Violet on her feet and steadied her. "Seriously, are you hurt?"

"I'm fine," Violet managed to say, looking up into worried gray eyes. Six feet, she guessed, lean and athletic, tousled tawny hair.

"Well, don't I feel like a moron? Plowing right over a woman isn't the usual ploy for making a good impression." Then he grinned, and strikingly handsome became breathtaking. He stuck out a hand. "JD Cameron. How am I doing so far? Wowed yet?"

Charming, too. Her first instinct after everything she'd been through was to go icy, but that would be giving Barry's betrayal too much power. Plus, Sophie said he was the next thing to family and she could trust him. She would try. "Let's just say I won't forget our meeting." She slid her hand into his and smiled.

Oh, yes, clever and charming in addition to his good looks. She wondered what he'd think if he knew that what actually tempted her about him was the hint of shadows in his eyes. For all his good-natured banter, she sensed more depth to him than his manner revealed.

Dear Reader,

A number of you wrote me after *Most Wanted* to tell me how much you liked JD and thought he needed his own story. Well...okay, so it took a while, but...here he is! He was such a tease and a cutup (as well as a gorgeous hunk) in that book, and he was also very young. His reputation as both a fun guy and a lady-killer continues to this day, but JD's been through the fire since you last saw him, and I enjoyed exploring both his sunny side and his shadows.

It was fun to revisit Hotel Serenity from *A Texas Chance*, too. Its location bears a resemblance to a very cool hotel in Austin, Hotel St. Cecelia, in the fun and funky SoCo district, but that's where the resemblance ends... except in the draw the actual hotel holds for the hip crowd. The beautiful city of Austin itself is a character in this series, much changed in recent years but still retaining its unique flavor of college town and music lovers' paradise, with a little gloss of high-tech heaven and big-city glamour lacquered over it.

Next up in The MacAllisters miniseries is the story of the youngest MacAllister, Jenna, out in June. I hope you'll enjoy it.

Thank you, as always, for letting me share my stories with you. If you'd like to get in touch, you can reach me through my website, www.jeanbrashear.com, or at www.Harlequin.com, as well as on Facebook or Twitter.

From my heart to yours,

Jean Brashear

On His Honor

Jean Brashear

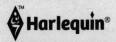

TORONTO NEW YORK LONDON
AMSTERDAM PARIS SYDNEY HAMBURG
STOCKHOLM ATHENS TOKYO MILAN MADRID
PRAGUE WARSAW BUDAPEST AUCKLAND

Recycling programs
for this product may
not exist in your area.

ISBN-13: 978-0-373-71775-0

ON HIS HONOR

Copyright © 2012 by Jean Brashear

This is a work of fiction. Names, characters, places and incidents are either the product of the author's imagination or are used fictitiously, and any resemblance to actual persons, living or dead, business establishments, events or locales is entirely coincidental.

This edition published by arrangement with Harlequin Books S.A.

For questions and comments about the quality of this book please contact us at Customer_eCare@Harlequin.ca.

www.Harlequin.com

Printed in U.S.A.

ABOUT THE AUTHOR

Three RITA® Award nominations, a *RT Book Reviews* Series Storyteller of the Year and numerous other awards have all been huge thrills for Jean, but hearing from readers is a special joy. She plays guitar, though, knows exactly how it feels to have the man you love craft a beautiful piece of furniture with his own hands...and has a special fondness for the scent of wood shavings.

Jean loves to hear from readers, either via email at her website, www.jeanbrashear.com, or Harlequin's website, www.Harlequin.com, or by postal mail at P.O. Box 3000 #79, Georgetown, TX 78627-3000.

Books by Jean Brashear

HARLEQUIN SUPERROMANCE

SIGNATURE SELECT SAGA

*The MacAllisters

Other titles by this author available in ebook format.

For all those who put their lives on the line
to protect others

And, as always,
for Ercel, my own hero and protector

ACKNOWLEDGMENTS

Many thanks to Dr. Kalin Kelso and his
wonderful staff at Austin Orthopedics,
Meggan Delvecchio, Amy Jackson,
Mandy Villanueva, Karen Kelso and
Brandon Williams—thanks a million for
working your magic on my shoulder woes so
I could finish this book in time!

Great appreciation to Nicole Cunningham,
Regina McCarley, Shawn Sabo and Linda Bullock
of St. David's Rehabilitation for getting me back
in fighting trim after the surgery (and special
thanks to Nicole for playing what-if with me
regarding JD's injuries and recovery).

A huge shout-out to my fabulous author friend
(and former Oklahoma City PD civilian crime
analyst) Maggie Price and to Lt. Bill Price,
OCPD (Ret.) for emergency answers that kept
me moving forward—a million thank-yous!

Any errors made or liberties taken with all this
valuable information are completely my own.

PROLOGUE

Los Angeles
Golden Screen Awards

"VIOLET, OVER HERE!" cried more voices than Violet James could count.

"Awesome gown!"

"Man, you look hot!"

Then, in one slice of silence, "Violet, I love you!"

The crowd tittered at the heartfelt declaration. Violet paused on the red carpet and pivoted on her sky-high stilettos, smiling when she spotted the young man in the stands. She blew him a kiss, to which he responded with a shout and an ebullient fist pump. The crowd cheered loudly for America's Sweetheart.

They loved her.

And East Tennessee's favorite daughter loved them right back.

"We're going to be late, darling, and we still have to face the dragon." Her husband of four months, British actor Barry Marsden, placed his palm on the small of her back and guided her gently toward the waiting fashion reporter.

Violet turned up her palms toward the bleachers. "Gotta go. So sorry," she called out, then blew another kiss to encompass all of them. The screaming rose to a fever pitch.

Then, with a sigh, she headed for the has-been actress who'd breathed life into a dying career by carving up other actors for fun and profit.

"Hello, Violet. Who are you wearing?" asked Sally Stern, her face permanently frozen by countless surgeries. Sally's verbal knives were already sharpened and eager for her flesh, Violet had no doubt.

"A brilliant, exciting new designer, Adam Cutler." Violet smiled brightly and executed a quick runway twirl to give the television cameras a complete scan. The figure-hugging silver garment with the modest front neckline skimmed her collarbone in a boatneck, the long fitted sleeves widened at the wrist to drape in an elegant trumpet nearly to her knees. The gown followed every curve of her body so faithfully she hadn't eaten anything but low-cal protein shakes in a week, then it belled out below her knees to pool gracefully on the ground.

The dress was the picture of restrained grace—until she revolved, giving the camera a glimpse of her back, bared by a scoop nearly to the cleft of her derriere. Down her spine spilled a single line of pearls and silver rosettes, linked by a chain so delicate it was invisible to anyone not right next to her. The only other jewelry was a wide silver cuff bracelet studded with pearls and diamonds, and at her ears the diamond teardrops Barry had given her for a wedding gift. Her jet-black hair was styled after the legendary glamour girls like Jane Russell and Veronica Lake—a smooth fall turned under at the ends and dipping over one of her famous turquoise eyes. Her lipstick was killer red.

Violet's curves might be more modest than Jane Russell's bombshell proportions, but she knew she was pulling off quite a look with the striking contrast of milky skin, silver gown and raven hair. Sometimes being a girl was too much fun.

"Stunning, darling, simply stunning." Violet's eyes widened in wonder as Sally touched her with surprising gentleness on her arm. "You're going to win tonight, I'm certain, and you'll deserve it for your courage."

The diva reporter dished out praise so sparingly, Violet had to work hard not to faint.

Or throw her arms around the woman, as her basic nature urged her to do. Even after twelve years as an actress, five at the top of the box office, she couldn't completely stamp Southern warmth out of her, nor did she have any desire to. It was hard enough to remain human—or sane—in the artificial Hollywood environment in which she lived.

So she gave in and hugged Sally, smiling as the dragon's cheeks turned rosy. "Thank you, Sally. That means a lot."

One genuine squeeze of the hand from the older woman, then Violet all but danced away. What a night this was!

And the icing on the cake was her handsome spouse by her side, escorting her with his usual panache. She was grateful for the evening together, even if too much of it would be spent in public and on alert. Juggling two busy careers meant they didn't have nearly enough time alone with each other.

But that was part of the package, so Violet smiled and smiled. Stopped to sign autographs all the way into the auditorium, once even forcing the security guys to allow a preteen girl to come down from the stands to present her with a teddy bear she'd made just for Violet.

Because she adored her equally talented husband who, by all rights, should be up for an award, too, she took less time with her fans than she normally would, waving goodbye and heading inside.

Now to endure the hours until she would learn if the role she had defied her wholesome image to play would, at long last, garner her the respect of her peers.

Just as they reached the doors, Barry dipped her into a romantic kiss that sent cameras flashing and would have her fans sighing over the fairy tale that was her life.

It reminded her that this was what was truly important, the love they shared, the life they would build. Whether or not she won mattered much less. She had everything she'd always wanted.

Her first marriage to the director who'd made her a star had ended after four years, and she'd grieved over the loss of a dream. No one in her family had ever been divorced, and beneath the star patina beat a very ordinary heart, one that only wanted to love and be loved. Trouble was, she loved her work, too, and she was good at it. When her marriage had ended, she'd decided that perhaps love wasn't her lot, and she'd told herself to be grateful for all she had.

Though she'd thought she'd never marry again, three years later, Barry had charged into her life and swept her off her feet. She hadn't believed the on-set love affair cliché could ever happen to her, but Barry and she were no cliché. He loved her to distraction, and she loved him.

She had been given a second chance, and this time she would get it right. She and Barry would be Joanne Woodward and Paul Newman, with a dash of Ward and June Cleaver thrown in. They'd grow old together gracefully and, with luck, die in each other's arms.

So what if she was a hopelessly middle-class small-town girl, as her best friend Avery had teased? She didn't care. Her parents were still in love after thirty-six years, and Violet's two brothers had growing broods themselves.

She laid one hand over her flat belly as Barry ushered her inside. Before too much longer, she hoped she and Barry would begin a brood of their own.

Life was so good it was almost scary. She pressed her lips together and sent up a silent plea.

"What is it?" Barry asked her.

She shook her head. "Just…I love you so much. I'm so happy."

He smiled and led her inside.

CHAPTER ONE

Three months later

"VIOLET, OVER HERE!"

"Have you talked to Barry? Have he and his latest conquest emerged from their love nest?"

"How does it feel to have him cheat on you barely six months into your marriage?"

Cameras flashed, television cameras rolled, the gleaming shark teeth of entertainment reporters menaced as the crowd closed around her.

Oh, God, she couldn't do this. What had she been thinking, trying to show up on the set as though her world hadn't been shattered into a thousand pieces?

She hadn't slept at all the night before, not after she'd seen the photos splashed all over the internet and the tabloids, photos of the man she'd trusted with her heart and her dreams caught with a woman he'd apparently been involved with even before he'd met Violet.

She knew she looked like death warmed over, her eyes too scratchy for makeup, her unwashed hair scraped back in a ponytail. But she was two days away from wrapping her role in this film, and she was determined to be the professional she'd always been.

Though she had no idea how she was going to play a romantic role with the slightest trace of sincerity when she no longer believed in love. All she wanted was to be alone, to climb under the covers and hide, to never speak to another soul.

Before she'd been caught in the storm of scandal, she'd accepted that lack of privacy was the price of success, and had done her best to get along with those she told herself were only trying to make a living.

But now, witnessing the undisguised glee on their faces, the avid curiosity to see how soon she'd break… the people she'd cooperated with once now showed her no mercy, not even when her heart was breaking and she wanted to crawl into the nearest hole.

"Violet! His lover's not even that pretty! How does that make you feel?"

She whipped around. "How do you think it makes me feel?" she yelled. "Why are you doing this?"

For a second, the only sound came from the cameras. Even hardened reporters were shocked.

What am I turning into? The depth of her bitterness stunned her.

I can't breathe. Frantically, she scanned for an opening as the crowd surged closer and the shouting resumed. Her heart pounded. Her vision blurred. Blindly she pushed to get away.

Just then, two beefy men shoved through the crowd, and she recognized them as part of the security crew for the production. The yelling only mounted as security whisked her away. The cameras never stopped whirring.

Once out of sight, she half collapsed against one of them.

"It's okay, Ms. James. We've got your back now. Sorry we weren't here. No one expected you today."

I shouldn't have come.

Desperately she tried to get a grip on herself,

though she was trembling. "I don't know how to thank you."

"Miss James, those bloodsuckers will never leave you alone, not after—" the second one halted in mid-sentence. "Um, sorry."

He might as well have said it: *after you and the rest of the world found out that your husband had been cheating on you from the first. When your marriage—your second marriage—turned out to be a lie.* But none of that was anyone's fault but hers.

"It's…okay." But it wasn't. Barry had made their marriage a freak show. Had made a fool of her.

She wanted to carve out his heart with a rusty spoon.

Her shoulders sagged. She didn't understand why this had happened. What had she done? What hadn't she done? How had she failed? Was she only lovable from a distance, only as an image, not a real person?

Then she realized the security guys were staring at her. "I'm…sorry. I'm just…" Sick at heart. And so very sad.

"Can't trust anyone in this town," the second guard muttered. "Folks will sell their own grandmas to get ahead."

She knew he meant well, but she couldn't handle sympathy right now. She would break.

She shouldn't have come to the set, but the madness was worse at her house. Her housekeeper had helped spirit her out the back of the property in disguise, but it hadn't been enough.

She didn't know what to do. Where to go. How to live with this. "Excuse me. I have to…" Vaguely she waved toward her trailer.

"Sure thing. You need anything, Ms. James, anything at all..."

"Thank you." She dug deep for strength. Tried hard to remember who she'd been only yesterday. She cleared her throat, composed her features. "Would you please tell Mr. Forbes that I'll be ready for makeup in fifteen minutes?"

"You're going to stay?" The guard looked incredulous.

"I am. It's my job." She pulled herself up very straight, composed her features. Somehow she would gather herself, shake off the miasma of grief and shame and humiliation blanketing her like a filthy fog. She made her way to her trailer.

Just as she got inside, her phone rang. She nearly hit the button to reject, but when she glanced at the display, she seized upon the lifeline.

Avery. Her dearest friend. He would understand.

"Hello?" she answered.

"What the hell happened? I was out of pocket, so I just heard. Where are you? Are you all right?"

For a second, she couldn't speak.

"Violet? Talk to me."

"No," she whispered brokenly. "I'm not all right."

"I'm going to kick that bastard's ass."

They'd never been lovers, but in some ways they'd been closer than she'd ever been to her romantic partners. Avery Lofton had saved her life. She'd dropped out of college and made her way to L.A. from Tennessee against her parents' wishes, a naive, headstrong Southern beauty who'd grown up in the bosom of a protective, loving family. She'd had no grasp of the world's darker realities, and she'd believed all those people who'd sworn she was the next Julia Roberts.

One week in California had taught her some hard lessons.

After one week she'd been dead broke after falling for a bogus agent scam. She'd been too proud to ask her parents for help. Avery hadn't been much better off financially, but from the moment they first met at an audition, something had clicked for them, and she'd spent months sleeping on his sofa as he became a combination older brother and best friend. She'd learned the Hollywood ropes from Avery, and as her star began to rise much more swiftly than his, she'd done what she could to repay him. Once she'd wielded enough box-office power, she'd insisted that he have roles in every one of her productions.

His pride wouldn't stand receiving charity forever, though, and eventually he'd given up his acting dream and left L.A. for Austin. Four years later, he was now a successful restaurateur and owner of Danger Zone, the hottest club in town, but they'd never lost touch. Avery, she realized to her chagrin, knew her better than either of her husbands had.

"He never deserved you. He was just—" Avery didn't finish.

"Using me to boost his career? I know. At least now I do. I thought…" She shook her head. "It doesn't matter." She'd seen what she wanted to see in Barry's devotion.

Until everyone on the planet had been shown the evidence that she was a stupid, lovesick fool. The fever pitch, the headlines, had quickly exploded.

America's Sweetheart Duped!

Did She Know?

Fool Me Twice…

"It does matter," Avery insisted. "Look, you know your director would shoot around you today."

"This is all I have," she said. "I'm a failure at love, Avery. All that's left is my career."

"You're allowed to be human, Violet. You can take time to deal with this."

"I am dealing with it. There are people waiting for me to do my job."

"They can work around you for a few days."

"A few days? I don't know if I'll ever get over this," she whispered.

"You will," he said fiercely. "Damn, I wish I weren't halfway across the country."

"I'll be okay. I just…" *Want the pain to stop.* She couldn't go anywhere without being followed, even on a normal day, but now… To have been so wrong, so sick in love with a man who didn't love her was humiliating. Somehow she had to find her footing again, and work was the only thing she knew to do.

Before the misery could tighten its grip on her again, she changed the topic. "So what are you up to today?"

Avery all but growled. "Don't do that. Your Mary Sunshine bit won't work on me."

"Fake it 'til you make it, my mom always says."

"You know I love your mom, but—" He snapped his fingers. "That's it—you should go home."

"My folks are on a month-long second honeymoon. I hope to heaven they haven't seen any of this."

"They adore you. They'd want to be there for you. And frankly, right now you could use some babying."

"They've waited years for this trip. I'm not screwing it up."

"What about your brothers?"

"Both of them have called."

"And?"

"I didn't take the calls. I had my assistant reassure them. I know they love me, but I don't want to have to dwell on how I've failed."

"Failed? Get real." He snorted. "Marsden's the screwup."

"In my family's world, I'm the screwup. This is my second divorce. My parents have been married forever and are still madly in love. My brothers and their wives, too. Kids all over the place. Me, I keep believing in this fantasy that I can have what they have and my career, too."

"You can. Look at your co-star, Zane MacAllister."

"Zane's a freak of nature." When he chuckled, she smiled. "I mean that nicely, but the reality of our business is that what he has—the mega-career and a solid family life, too—is almost impossible to achieve. Particularly for me, as I'm clearly a lousy judge of men. I wanted the ivy-covered cottage, adoring spouse and two point five kids, but I didn't want to give up my career to do it. I need to stop dreaming and get practical. You can't have both—well, Zane can, apparently, but the reason everyone revered Newman and Woodward was that they were the exception."

"So find someone who's not in the business."

She rolled her eyes. "When do I ever get to meet a real person? Anyway, you know how it is—actors' egos are too big and too fragile so they're lousy partners, as I've just been so rudely reminded. And with a normal man, the gap in lifestyles is too huge, to say nothing of the disparity in income—most men can't get past that. The life actors live is deadly to a relationship. Simply dealing with our schedules is horrific enough, and the issues are so much more complex than that."

"Babe, if anyone cañ make that happen, it's you."

His faith was lovely, of course, but seriously misplaced. "I'm exhausted, Avery." Weary to her marrow. "And I don't trust my judgment. I can't try again."

"Of course you're worn out. If you won't go home, then come to Austin. You have to get out of there."

"No. I know how busy you are. I'll be all right, I promise. It'll get better." Though she had no idea how.

"You need to be away from Hollywood to recover from this. Come see me. Take some time off and rest up while this dies down. Some other scandal will break soon, and you'll be old news. Austin's great, you know. It's actually a pretty terrific place to lay low, if that's what you want. People are cool about celebrities. They let you be. And Austin's got everything—live music, the lakes, great food. And I know this hotel that totally rocks, Hotel Serenity."

She was surprised that he hadn't asked her to stay with him as he always had before. "I don't know...."

"I wish I could have you here, but I'm gone too much these days. I'd be a lousy host, but you're exactly the kind of person Hotel Serenity likes to pamper. And hey, there's a bonus—the owner is involved with Zane's brother."

"Seriously?"

"Yeah, Zane helped make the opening a big splash. Everything I hear about it is impressive. It's small and exclusive, tucked in among trees and very private. The owner restored an old mansion, and she's reputed to be a tigress about protecting the privacy of her guests."

"I don't know, Avery...." Running away went against the grain, but she was so weary. So sad. So confused, and the wellspring of optimism that had nurtured her through the long trek to the top had gone bone-dry.

"Even if I can't play host, I want to help, Vee. You're my best friend. Let me do something, please."

She was too worn out and heartsore to think straight, but she had to find some way to get over this. She didn't like feeling angry and bitter. It wasn't who she was. Who she wanted to be. "I have to finish filming."

"You're nearly done, though, right?"

"I was supposed to finish my scenes tomorrow."

"You know they could shoot them at the end of production."

"No. I won't do that to the cast and crew. I'll finish." Somehow.

"I'll call your director for you."

"No, Avery, don't. I have to do this one thing right."

"That damn work ethic of yours." He sighed. "Okay, listen, I'm going to make the arrangements. Leave everything to me. I'll call your housekeeper and tell her what to pack."

Tears threatened again. In truth, having someone take care of her for a while sounded wonderful. "You are so good to me."

"You have the best heart I know. Now go lose yourself in that role and let the hours go by. I'll take care of everything else."

"Thank you so much." She wanted to cling to the phone, to the island of sanity and safety Avery had always represented. Before she got weepy again, she disconnected, instead.

She went into the tiny bathroom of her trailer and

took a good, hard look in the mirror. "You can do this," she told her reflection.

Then she turned on the shower and began the process of becoming America's Sweetheart instead of a discarded, unlovable wife.

"DID YOU HEAR WHAT I SAID?" The chirpy blonde perched on Detective JD Cameron's lap frowned. "You're not paying attention. What's wrong?"

"Hmm?" JD stirred from the haunting memories of last night's grim discoveries from his current case. "What did you say?"

"I said—" she exhaled in a gust "—I thought we were going to dance. The music's great tonight."

It is? He frowned. He loved live music, of which Austin had tons, but it was wasted on him just now. Anyway, she was only asking because it was her job. "Sorry, uh—" What the devil was her name? Brandy? Barbie?

"Bella. Like the girl in *Twilight,* you know? I mean, that's not my real name, but I am sooo in love with those books. Are you Team Edward or Team Jacob?"

"Team…" What the hell was she talking about? Then he recalled a set of books one of the Violent Crime Task Force assistants was crazy over. This blonde was just as young.

He was thirty-six. Too old to hang out with babies.

In his mind, he saw the face of another girl, her face frozen in death, another child who'd never grow old. He'd do whatever was required to nail the bastards responsible for the misery of so many.

"You haven't read the books?" She was clearly astonished. "What about the movies?"

When had he last spared time for a movie? He

couldn't remember. That wasn't her fault, however. This whole case was about making sure that sweet young girls like Barbie—er, Bella—weren't sold as sex slaves, forced to become addicted to drugs so they'd be easy to handle.

And with that, grisly images from last night rose again. Seven women, two girls. All dead because JD and the rest of the task force couldn't destroy the web of human trafficking in which those nine and countless others were ensnared.

He nearly set the girl aside and left. He was no good to anyone tonight. He should be catching up on his sleep, but sleep was elusive these days.

So he'd come to Danger Zone, one of the businesses the task force suspected of laundering money for the cartel behind the trafficking. Sometimes you could obtain information you didn't expect from people the bad guys didn't consider important. Like Bella.

He shook his head and focused. "I haven't seen the movies, sorry. Want to tell me about them?" At worst, maybe pure foolishness would clear his head and get him some distance on the case.

Blonde Bella chattered on, and JD listened. When she again suggested they dance, he didn't argue. He wouldn't pass a pop quiz on vampire movies, but maybe he'd dance this funk out of his brain and learn something useful about Danger Zone and its owners, Avery Lofton and Sage Holland, at the same time. The pair was careful not to leave any tracks, but clubs and restaurants handled plenty of cash and thus provided an ideal opportunity to launder funds. A disgruntled waitress had given the task force a tip that pointed a finger at Danger Zone, but she'd left town before anyone could find her to get details.

Blonde Bella gyrated to the music, rubbing herself against him, making it clear that she could be his for the night. Lofton and his partner were smart, seeding the audience with glorified hookers posing as dancers. Ten years earlier, even five, he'd have been much less immune to the blatant invitation.

But even if he weren't here to troll for intel, he wouldn't accept. More and more often lately he'd found himself wishing for someone to talk to, really talk to. Someone to share not just his bed but his life, to make a home with, put down roots.

But he'd need a head transplant first. The kind of hours he worked, no woman would willingly sign off on. Once considered the task-force playboy, he was in danger of becoming the task-force workaholic, instead.

The hell of it was, he wasn't making one bit of difference, no matter how many hours he put in. For every bad guy they locked away, plenty more stepped up to take his place. JD had often been accused of being a Boy Scout, someone who believed in black and white, good vs. evil, wrong against right, but ten years on VICTAF—the Violent Crimes Task Force—was wearing him down. VICTAF was made up of members from every law-enforcement agency in the Austin area, state, local and federal. He could have rotated out years ago as most members did, but Doc Romero, the FBI agent at the helm, had liked his work when he was brand-new out of APD uniform, and he'd kept him on. It was a coup for JD, but constantly dealing with the worst of the worst criminals could do a number on your head if you weren't careful.

And JD was being very, very careful. He believed in what he did, and he wasn't going to let any case, however seemingly impossible to crack, get the better of him.

Just then, a face caught his attention several feet away from where he and Bella were dancing. Why did the woman seem so familiar? Something was wrong, too—though very pretty, her face was ravaged and she walked like a zombie, hardly noticing the various men trying to get her attention. His eyes followed the woman's progress through the crowd to the edge, nearing the hallway where the restrooms were and, farther down, to two doors with special locks, purpose undetermined. Rumors, however, had him suspecting that the doors led to private areas suitable for indulging in sex and/or drugs with women like Bella.

Why did this woman seem familiar—

Then it hit him. One of the victims last night, that's who she resembled. Strongly.

"I'll be back," he said absently to Bella, pointing toward the restrooms.

She made a little moue of displeasure and trailed her fingers down his arm. "Don't stay gone long, handsome."

But mentally he had already left. He kept his focus on the woman's last location as he cut through the crowd. She looked enough like the victim to be her twin—except that she was still alive. Was there a connection? Was she caught in the same nightmare?

When he reached the crowded passageway, he swore ripely when he couldn't see her. He hoped like hell she was in the restroom and would emerge soon. He didn't want to attract attention by lingering, but she might be a valuable lead if he wasn't deluding himself about the resemblance.

Then bodies shifted, and he spotted her way back

by the two unmarked doors, her shoulders hunched to avoid a guy who was all over her.

If there was anything guaranteed to make JD see red, it was a man forcing himself on a woman. He'd been on Vice before being recruited to VICTAF, and he'd seen too many women and children victimized. He'd dealt with it, but the brutality he'd witnessed had never left him. Swiftly he threaded past the dancers, trying very hard not to draw attention to himself while still reaching her as quickly as possible.

"Hector says I can have you tonight, so don't give me any crap." The man had a brutal grip on the girl's arm and shook her forcefully.

JD wanted to cold-cock the guy, but if Hector was the girl's pimp, he'd only make life harder on her. JD used his fingers to squeeze a painful pressure point on the guy's wrist, forcing him to release her. "But my turn's not up yet, so you have to wait," JD said.

"Who the hell are you?" Clasping JD's wrist with his free hand, the guy turned his fury on him.

Again, JD had to remind himself of the endgame, restraining himself from unleashing his frustration and rage over the memories of last night on this guy. The woman had to be his focus. "Let's go, honey," JD said to the woman—girl, really—as she stared up at him with wide, terrified eyes. "It's okay," he said gently into her ear. "I'm taking you out of here." He swept her out of the guy's reach quickly, hearing the bellow at his back but proceeding onward and heading for the outside.

"No," she moaned faintly, squirming in his grasp. "I have to do what he says. Hector has my sister. If I do not obey, he will send her with the others—" Abruptly she clamped her mouth shut.

"Who is Hector and why does he have your sister?" Though he was pretty sure he knew. She shook her head vehemently. JD hustled her around the corner and into a darkened alley. "I want to help you. What's your name?"

"You cannot. No one can." She was visibly trembling.

"Just tell me your name," he said softly. "I won't hurt you."

Her face was pale as death, and sobs wracked her frame, but still she said nothing.

"I'll go first. My name is John." True, though he never used his first name, but John was innocuous enough that he could easily use it undercover. "Please tell me your name."

"I am called Candy."

"But that's not your real name, is it?" Not with that accent, though he couldn't clearly place it.

"It does not matter. There is no help— Please…go. I must return before—"

"Where would I find Hector?"

"Stay away from him. He is dangerous."

"Why?" So close… He nearly held his breath, sensing in his gut that she could give them the information they needed.

She clasped the locket at her throat with white-knuckled fingers. "My sister…I am so afraid. We were to meet—"

Sisters, just as he'd expected. She was involved with the smuggling ring. "Let me take you someplace safe."

"No!" Her head shook violently. "If I leave, he will hurt her. We were brought over together, but the other man took her away. I have only seen her once. I must take care of her. She is my only family. There is talk that some will be moved soon. I must find her first."

"Where did you come from?"

"Istanbul," she whispered.

Bingo. Not content with trafficking in Latin America, the cartel was rumored to be spreading its tentacles into the Middle East in recent months.

"When is this move?"

Her eyes narrowed, and he backtracked from the too-direct question a simple do-gooder would not have asked.

"Never mind." He grasped her arm. "Let me take you away from here. I'll help you find your sister." He didn't like lying to her—though, of course, he actually could take her to her sister, only not alive—but this case was about hundreds, possibly thousands of young women like Candy and her sister.

"No—you do not see—no!" She wrenched her arm away from him just as a shout echoed from around the corner, snagging JD's attention.

He couldn't draw his weapon here, he'd blow his cover. "Stay there," he said over his shoulder and began easing his way to the corner to see what was going on.

Too late he heard the footsteps behind him and whipped around.

But the girl was already gone.

His instincts were itching, though. She'd said they were going to move the girls, and soon. He had to find a way to get to Lofton or Holland, some means to learn their weak spots without tipping them off.

Everyone had a weakness. He would hunt until he found theirs.

CHAPTER TWO

"GOOD MORNING, GORGEOUS." Shopping bags in hand, Avery strode across the verdant grounds of Hotel Serenity and bent to kiss Violet's cheek. Of medium height, with rich brown hair and melting brown eyes, he had been quite handsome when they first met, but she could see the strains of his lifestyle in his softening jaw, the new thickness around his middle. He was only five years older than her thirty-four, but he had aged markedly since he'd last come out to see her in California.

"Avery, you don't have to bring me goodies every day."

"Okay." He shifted the bags behind his back. For her, he could always summon mischief, however harried he was.

Violet laughed and half rose from the bent willow chair. "Gimme." With a child's delight, she peered inside one of the bags. "Yes! Chocolate! How did you know?"

He snorted. "Like that's not a required part of any gift. Even when all we could afford was one Hershey bar to split between us, you'd give up a decent meal to have it."

They shared a smile swimming in memories.

"You gonna split that with me for old times' sake?"

he asked as she pried open the box and reverently inhaled the dark, delicious scent.

"Are you kidding?" She clasped the container to
her chest. "Get your own Hershey bar." With a grin,
she proffered the box. "Of course I am. You first, my
friend." After he'd selected one truffle, she chose one
for herself and took a dainty bite.

"Oh, God." She would swear her eyes rolled back
in her head. "Where on earth did you find these?"

"Second Street. A little shop where they make them
by hand."

"Yum. Serious yum." She smiled. "Between Sophie's amazing food and your goodies, if I don't start
running again soon, my trainer will kill me."

"You're getting antsy." Not a question.

"Yes…well, maybe. I'm not quite ready to brave the
world yet." She frowned. "Such a coward."

"You're not. You never have been." He placed his
hand atop hers.

If she'd felt a little unsettled because he hadn't
invited her to stay with him after all the times he'd
begged her to visit, he was here now, faithful as ever,
and that was enough. She turned her fingers in his and
squeezed. "I've lost my optimism, Avery. I always believed that he was out there, my perfect match. That
I'd be like my parents one day, that one man would
love me for who I am, not because I'm famous, but
simply for myself." She sighed and shook her head.
"No longer."

"You wouldn't be you if you weren't a cockeyed
optimist. Don't you dare change. He's out there somewhere."

"You really believe that?" Violet rose, began to
pace. "I've proven myself to be a lousy judge of char-

acter when it comes to men." And that wasn't all she was questioning about her life, which scared her half to death.

Avery went to her, held out his hand. "You'll get back on the horse one of these days. Meanwhile, I have an idea—you ready for an adventure?"

"What kind?"

"A *let's sneak Violet out of here covered with a blanket in the backseat* adventure."

"I don't know…."

"C'mon," he entreated. "I have a couple of hours with nobody breathing down my neck. Let's make a jailbreak. You haven't turned chicken on me, have you?"

"A blanket? Seriously? It's too hot."

"I have a/c. And I brought the Rover, not the Jag, so you'd have room to stretch out."

"Where are we going?"

"Are you turning into a full-fledged recluse on me? 'Cause if so, I'm calling the paparazzi myself."

Alarm shivered through her. "Avery…"

"Oh, honey, you're worse off than I thought. If you don't trust me, of all people…"

Had she become that suspicious of everyone? If she couldn't trust her best friend, who could she trust?

She refused to go down that road. "Of course I do." She sighed. "It's just been so great to feel this safe." Hotel Serenity was as advertised—better, even, since Zane had gone above and beyond and had made arrangements with the owner, Sophie Carlisle, for Violet to have the place all to herself.

Violet awoke each morning in this magical place Sophie had created—her quarters were the amazing aerie that was normally the honeymoon suite, an entire floor atop the former carriage house, with killer views of downtown Austin and Lady Bird Lake. A mocking-bird serenaded her with its repertoire as she enjoyed her own nest in the treetops, and each night the moon silvered her bedroom. The food was amazing, the ser-vice discreet and there was the added kick of a tran-quility room on the grounds, complete with massage anytime she wanted it. Violet's heart was still sore, but every day the pain receded. And the respite from her normal breakneck pace was sinfully delicious.

"And you don't think I'll protect you?" He wasn't teasing anymore. He was hurt, this man who was the only one she truly did trust outside of her family.

She took a deep breath. "I know you will. So where will this adventure take me?"

"Maybe…my house? I didn't plan ahead, but—" His cell phone chirped with a voice mail. She appre-ciated that he turned off the ringer when he was with her. He glanced at the screen and frowned. "Damn."

"Go ahead and listen."

He did, and a change swept over his handsome fea-tures. When he finished, his strained expression said it all.

"Go on," she urged. "I'll be fine here with my good-ies." Even though the notion of getting out had begun to appeal to her more than she'd expected. Maybe she *was* getting a little antsy in her ivory tower.

He bent to kiss her cheek. "I'm sorry." He shook his head. "It's great to be successful, but…"

Violet placed one hand on his jaw. "You're preach-ing to the choir, you know." She smiled past her disap-pointment. "Now shoo—I have chocolate to pig out on and, thanks to the demands of your business, no one to hang around and give me puppy-dog eyes to beg me to share."

"I'll try to make it back later."

"I'm fine, I swear."

"Sorry, kid." But his mind was clearly elsewhere already.

Violet hugged her dearest friend and watched him go.

And admitted to herself that she was lonely.

She squared her shoulders, gathered up her goodies to take them to her quarters. She mounted the steps but paused halfway up, gazing out at the lake, at the beauty of the day she was missing while she cloistered herself here. The grounds were beautiful and she'd desperately needed the peace when she'd arrived, but she'd seen nothing of the wonders of Austin Avery had described.

Was he right? Was she really ready to emerge? A part of her was restless, but another part shuddered at the notion of attracting the paparazzi's attention.

She glanced back at the house. Maybe after she put all her goodies away, she'd see if Sophie had time to visit, instead.

"OKAY, SO WHO WANTS TO GO FIRST?" VICTAF head Doc Romero's piercing gaze scanned the group gathered around the conference table at task-force headquarters in an anonymous office building in northwest Austin.

"Internet chatter's picking up," offered Doc's right-hand man, Bob Jordan.

"How would you know? You figured out how to turn on your computer yet?" teased Trini Sanchez, the group's newest member, on loan from Immigration.

Some grins, a couple of raised coffee mugs. Balding, paunchy Bob was everyone's favorite uncle and the go-to guy for anything you didn't want to bother Doc with, but his aversion to technology was legend.

"Bite me," Bob retorted. "I can read reports."

"As long as someone prints them up for you," quipped Vince Coronado who, like JD, had come to VICTAF from the Austin Police Department.

"Okay, okay," Doc said. "So brief me. What's the chatter?" Though he was asking for the sake of the group—there wasn't so much as a dust mote that Doc didn't register. VICTAF was his baby, and while most cops would have retired by now, at sixty-two, Doc showed no signs of slowing down or handing over the reins. JD was glad about that, personally. Imagining VICTAF without Doc—or Bob, for that matter— wasn't something he cared to contemplate. He'd been psyched to be invited to join the prestigious inter-agency group, and he'd been here longer than many of the others. Most rotated in and out within a couple of years in accordance with Doc's original design, but JD had found a niche where he'd felt like he was making a difference, and Doc had encouraged him to stay.

But sometimes that difference seemed too minus-cule to count. Like now. This human-trafficking case was driving them all buggy.

"First of all, investigation of this recent crime scene isn't producing much in the way of promising forensic evidence," Bob said. "And we're running out of time. Word is, Popovic is planning to deliver a shipment of Middle Eastern women and children next."

"What's motivating his change of merchandise? He usually handles Hispanics. And why bring them through Texas?" asked Mack Lawrence of the Department of Public Safety. "A lot easier for Central Americans to blend in."

"Sad statement," interjected Vince, "but thanks to the overall paranoia about the Middle East, there's an increased appetite in the sex-slave trade for women from that region."

Expressions of disgust, from hardened jaws to shaking heads and narrowed eyes, traveled the room, but this group had seen too much to be easily shocked. You had to have a cast-iron stomach to survive in the world they walked in.

Sometimes, though, JD thought, man's ability to enjoy the suffering of his fellow beings, to profit from misery, made him damn sick.

"We still think he's using Jorge Lima to get them in and out?" asked Trini.

Doc nodded. "Or whatever name he's going by now. Why mess with a winning formula?" The Brazilian had proven elusive to both his own country's law enforcement and U.S. agencies. He'd created a pipeline that shifted constantly but never ceased operations.

Assorted muttering made its way around the room.

Doc shrugged. "Lima's not in our purview, though. We have to focus on what we can do here at home."

"The money laundering," JD stated.

"Yep," Doc answered. "The money laundering. The cocktail waitress at Danger Zone, the one that gave us the intel then disappeared—any progress on finding her, Vince?"

"Nothing worth talking about. Since we have to stay under the radar at the club, I've been playing it low-key, asking around. I had a young patrolman go in, pose as someone whose eye she caught, trying to get her phone number so he can see her again. The bar back he talked to said she wasn't sociable. That she left after her shift and didn't really get friendly with anyone. No one seems to know where she lives, and she didn't show up for work yesterday. The bar guy says she'll play hell getting her job back. We've talked to her family, but she left home at seventeen and they don't care if they ever see her again. In other words… we got nothing."

"Keep tugging that line for a while. It's the best lead we've had," Doc said.

Around the table, faces echoed his frustration.

"I may have something," JD offered.

Doc lifted an eyebrow.

"I was there last night, at Danger Zone, and I met these two women…."

General hoots and catcalls. "No surprise there, Romeo," snickered Vince.

JD rolled his eyes. That whole bit had gotten old years ago, but if he let them see that his rep as a ladies' man bugged him, they'd never leave off. So, instead, he played it up. "Not my fault you're boring old married farts. Women like me…it can't be helped." He actually did get along well with women, always had, but he preferred to think it wasn't his face but the fact that he genuinely liked them back.

"I'm not old—or married," piped up Trini.

"And Chloe doesn't seem to think I'm too boring," intoned Vince.

JD couldn't refute that. Vince was part of the Montalvo/MacAllister clan by marriage if not by blood, and it was rife with happy couples. Somehow JD had been adopted by them when Jesse Montalvo had been his supervisor at VICTAF. He had attended many a family gathering since then, seeing for himself what a good marriage could do to smooth out life's rough edges. Vince's was one of them.

"Yeah, but Chloe's a shrink, and with you she's got a lifetime project," he quipped.

Vince laughed.

Doc cleared his throat. "Okay, people. Back to business." He turned a stony look on JD. "So you just, what, decided to drop in on Danger Zone without clearing it with anyone?"

"You can ask me that after the other night? You saw what they did, those bastards."

Doc only looked at him over his reading glasses with an expression that made JD feel all of fifteen, trying to defend actions he knew pushed the boundaries. "So, what happened?" Doc asked.

"The first girl was just one of Lofton's teasers, girls he hires to bring the guys. Sort of a cross between saloon girls and hookers, but they're careful not to get busted. He must pay them well, since they're so close-mouthed."

"So why is this one going to pan out?"

JD relayed what Bella had told him before he'd seen the other girl. "Her loyalty is being strained. She's got the hots for Lofton, and Sage called her out on it." Avery Lofton and Sage Holland were co-owners of the club. "She thinks Sage wants him for herself."

Bob looked cheerful. "Jealous women make great CIs."

"Sometimes," Vince said. Confidential informants, as they all knew to their peril, were unreliable by nature. "Until one takes her man back, and the case goes south on you."

Heads nodded all around the table.

"But she's not the one who got my attention. I spotted a girl whose sister is one of the vics from the other night, I'm damn near positive. She was back by those doors, the new ones Vice thinks are being used for more than private dances with clients, but…"

Around the table, people straightened in their chairs.

"But…?" Doc prompted.

JD exhaled in a gust. "I lost her. I had her off by herself, but her pimp came searching for her. When he got too close and I turned to deflect his attention, she took off."

His frustration was echoed on other faces.

"She's a key to this whole case, I know it. Scared to death of her pimp, Hector, and worried sick because her sister didn't show up to meet her. She talked about being brought over from Istanbul and a move that's going to happen soon."

"Got a name?" asked Vince.

"Not a real one. Says it's Candy, but that's her pross name, I'm sure. She's a dead ringer for a girl from the other night, so much so that they could be twins."

"That it?" Doc asked.

"Yeah," JD answered morosely.

"A slim lead, but we're not getting any good ones. I'm not ready to send someone in to get an invitation to one of the back rooms. Busting the club for prostitution or drugs, either of which is very likely going on, will dry up any chance we have of getting on the inside. Our focus is not sex or drugs—we'll leave that to Vice later. We need to find the money trail and trace it back up the trafficking pipeline. That's job one for us, people." Doc shot a glare at JD. "And no more cowboy vigilante action. You know better." His eyes locked on JD's.

JD didn't look away, though he knew Doc was right. He was just so damn tired of the bad guys getting away with so much.

Doc leaned back in his chair. "Anybody else got something to report?"

"Yeah," replied Holly Patterson, DEA agent. "Lofton's formed an interesting new pattern. Every day for the last week, he's gone shopping—"

"Holy crap," quipped Mack. "The guy's obviously gone off the deep end. Shopping? Every day?" He gave an exaggerated shudder.

Holly sighed. She was also new to VICTAF, though she was an experienced agent. "Then he pays a visit to the same place."

"Where?" asked Bob.

"This expensive hotel off South Congress, an old mansion that was turned into what they call a boutique hotel."

"Boutique?" hooted Bo. "What the hell does that mean?"

Vince glanced at JD. JD stared right back. Only one place met that description, and they both knew the owner. Had helped get it ready to open as a favor to a mutual friend.

"If you'd ever stayed anywhere but a no-tell motel, you'd know that means a place catering to a special clientele," JD explained. "And, no, I don't mean anything dirty." He looked at Holly. "Hotel Serenity, right?"

"Right. Is there a problem there? Should we be investigating?"

"No. Absolutely not." Vince was frowning.

JD could read his mind. No way would Sophie Carlisle allow something illegal to go on at her beloved hotel—and she would know. Nothing escaped her notice. Hotel Serenity was her dream, and she was fierce in her love for it.

"How can you be sure?"

JD spoke up first. "A friend of ours owns it. It's strictly aboveboard, and it's too small for anyone to be using it as any sort of front. She keeps her finger on every aspect."

"Sophie is family," Vince said. "And the MacAllisters are all straight arrows."

"MacAllisters?" Doc asked. "Jesse's family?"

JD nodded. "His brother Cade and Sophie are a couple."

"Jesse Montalvo," Doc explained for the benefit of the newer task-force members. "Former FBI. He and his wife Delilah were both on VICTAF. Delilah rotated out a few years ago. Jesse retired before that."

"How come?" asked Bo. "I mean, if it's any of my business."

"Because now he's making more money than this whole group put together," Vince said. "He's one hell of an artist, and he's getting famous."

"MacAllister…" Holly looked up. "Zane?"

"Bingo," replied Bob. "Jesse is the older half brother of Cade and Zane."

"Wow." Holly wasn't that easy to impress, but clearly she was now.

"Yeah, there's no way anything illegal is going on there," mused JD, echoing his thoughts. But Lofton's new-found love for the place was the best lead they had, and it could be just the angle he'd been searching for. "We need to find out why Lofton is visiting every day."

"There's something else," Holly said. "No guests

coming in or out the entire week we've been watching him."

"No guests?" Vince shook his head. "That can't be right. Sophie opened last September, and she's booked solid months ahead. It's *the* place to stay in Austin now. Big hit with the entertainment crowd."

Holly shrugged. "I don't know what to tell you. There have been a few food deliveries and some workers coming and going, but otherwise...nada."

"What kind of shopping?" JD asked.

"Women's clothing, books, gourmet food. Chocolate, the expensive stuff."

A woman, JD thought. *Jackpot.*

"So he's got a woman in there? Why wouldn't she be staying at that big-ass place of his out in the hills?" Mack asked.

"Maybe he's wooing her."

"Look, we can speculate all day, but it appears either of you could check it out pretty easily," he said to JD and Vince. "So who's going to find out what the deal is?"

"Not that easy, Doc," said Vince. "Sophie has a lot of guests who come specifically for the privacy she rigorously maintains. She's fired people with loose lips."

"He's right," JD added. "It's a religion with her. Guests count on that."

"So you seriously can't ask her? Or won't?"

"She's family, Doc," Vince repeated. "I mean, if I hear something..."

"But we won't," JD said, though his mind was already spinning through the possible angles.

Doc's expression made clear that he was unhappy. JD knew, however, that Doc held the same healthy respect for the MacAllister family that JD did. "Eyes sharp," Doc ordered Holly. "If you need more help, you speak up. Someone's got to come out of there at some point, whoever it is Lofton is visiting. We'll respect the hotel's privacy as long as we can, but if you get the faintest whiff that there's something illegal going on there or that those visits are more than chasing tail, we have to act." He stared at Vince and JD in turn. "I understand how you feel, but…"

JD nodded. "I know. But Sophie's a good woman, Doc, and she's had a tough road. I'd bet everything I own that nothing illegal is going on inside Hotel Serenity."

"Then how do you explain Lofton visiting every damn day?"

"I don't know. But I will." JD frowned. The problem was how without breaking Sophie's cherished confidentiality. He thought of everything Sophie had been through. Then he thought of Candy and her sister.

No contest. And an excellent place to start was at the youngest MacAllister's birthday party Saturday night, to which he was already invited. He didn't like doing it, but if Sophie had any answers… If he could explain to Sophie, she would be sympathetic, but he couldn't. Whether he liked being in this position couldn't matter, not when women were dying.

Doc didn't seem happy, but he changed the topic. "So do we have any answers from Treasury?" he asked Bob, since money laundering fell in the U.S. Treasury's purview. Money laundering was only one of the suspicions they had of Avery Lofton, but it was an angle they were vigorously pursuing.

JD tried to focus on Bob's answer, but in the back of his mind, he was strategizing how to approach Sophie and Lofton's mysterious guest....

CHAPTER THREE

"YOU ARE POSITIVE YOU'RE all right with this?" Sophie asked Violet a couple of days later. "I can cancel the party, or we could move it. Jenna would understand."

"Cancel your best friend's birthday party? I don't think so! Certainly not on my account."

"I wish you'd change your mind and attend. I promise everyone would respect your privacy. It's only family, and they're accustomed to dealing with the complications of Zane's fame. They, of all people, understand the price of what you do."

"But I'd be an interloper," Violet pointed out, even though she desperately wanted to say yes. Avery's daily visits weren't doing it for her anymore, and she had to face facts: she was a sociable person, accustomed to a great deal of human interaction every day and her haven was beginning to feel like a cage.

"You know Zane and Roan. Plus, the MacAllisters have a loose definition of family. JD will be here, for example." At Violet's lifted eyebrows, Sophie explained. "JD Cameron used to work with Jesse, and he still works with Vince. He's always invited to family events."

"Jesse is…Cade's older brother."

"Half brother," Sophie clarified. "Not that any of them differentiate. They share the same mother. Grace was widowed with two boys, Diego and Jesse, when she met Hal MacAllister."

"Zane's dad. And Cade's."

"And Jenna's."

At Sophie's nod, Violet cast back to see if she could recall others in the family. "But Vince is…?"

"No blood relation, but the eldest brother, Diego, is married to Caroline, whose sister Chloe is married to Vince." She smiled. "Your head spinning yet?"

"Pretty much." Violet rubbed her temple. "Okay, go ahead. So this JD person…"

"Vince and JD are both police detectives. Jesse was an FBI agent, and his wife Delilah came from the Austin Police Department, just like Vince and JD."

"But Jesse is an artist now." Violet seized on the one fact she was sure of. She'd seen Jesse's stunning oil paintings and intended to own some of his work herself, once she'd bought a new house with no memories of ex-husbands in it.

"He is. So are you straight on everyone?"

Violet opened her mouth to say yes, then promptly stopped. "Not hardly."

Sophie laughed. "Welcome to my world. It took months. I won't confuse you further by naming all the little kids. You'll love meeting them, though."

"I do like children."

"Me, too." Sophie had a faraway look in her eyes.

"You okay?"

Sophie snapped immediately to hostess attention. "Of course." She lifted her eyebrows. "So you'll come to Jenna's party tonight?"

Violet had to laugh at her friend's relentlessness. "Apparently I will."

And found herself almost ridiculously excited at the prospect.

JD EMERGED FROM HIS TRUCK, gift bag in hand, resolved to find answers to the mystery of Sophie's guest during Jenna's party tonight.

It wouldn't be easy, he thought, given Sophie's mania for protecting her clientele. And he didn't like being less than aboveboard with these people he so genuinely admired and thought of as the next thing to family.

But there were lives at stake.

He'd take it slow, he decided, see what developed. Kick back with a bunch of really nice people and have a good time. Tease Jenna as his honorary little sister, enjoy the hell out of her dad, Hal, who reminded JD of his own father, play with the little kids. He nodded approval at the hotel's security guard, who was rigorous in his duties, and looked around as he entered the grounds, amazed at all Sophie had accomplished since he was last here. He headed for the lights sprinkling the trees and found his spirits lifting as he heard conversation and laughter and music.

And then the answer to the mystery fell right into his lap.

Holy crap.

JD blinked once, twice. Shook his head to be sure he wasn't hallucinating.

Only one guest, he recalled.

Pretty much the ultimate one, short of maybe the president.

"What, Pretty Boy is speechless?" teased a familiar voice.

JD turned to see Delilah Butler Montalvo sauntering his way, her red-haired daughter Addie on her hip. Delilah was a knockout—too bad she'd met The Sphinx, as Jesse had been known in his FBI days, first and had never had eyes for anyone else. "You look great," he said to her.

"You look gobsmacked."

"That is seriously Violet James?"

Delilah glanced over to where the most famous actress of their time was laughing as she tossed washers with Hal MacAllister while Zane kibitzed. "Well, she's not too serious at the moment, but…yep, really her."

JD whistled softly. "I assumed it was cameras or makeup that made her that beautiful."

"Wait 'til you see her up close. She's prettier than you, Romeo. Imagine that."

"Cut it out. You know I hate that." He mock-glared at her before he spoke to Addie. "Tell her, princess. Men can't be pretty."

Addie granted him a smile that was going to be giving Jesse heart attacks in a few years. "I think you're pretty."

He threw up his hands. "And here I thought I could count on you." He grinned and kissed Addie's cheek. "Traitor."

Addie giggled.

Delilah set her down. "Why don't you go see Grandpa, sweetheart? He's right over there."

Addie's eyes lit as she spotted Hal. He was everyone's dream grandfather. "Okay. Bye, Mommy. Bye, Uncle Pretty!"

JD had to laugh. "You are so in trouble with that one."

"Don't I know it?" Delilah studied him, and JD tensed. "You look beat. Bad case?"

She would understand, if anyone would. She'd experienced one of the worst herself when she'd posed as bait for a serial killer. "Bad enough. Drug and human trafficking with the trail winding right through Austin," he explained.

"Nasty business. Man, if it weren't for the kids, I would so want to be in on stopping them." She was still in law enforcement, but she worked as an investigator for the district attorney's office now, a job with actual office hours that afforded her more time with her children. And little exposure to danger, which no doubt eased Jesse's mind. Jesse had never avoided danger himself when on the job, but when it came to his family, he was all protector, just like the rest of the men in the Montalvo/MacAllister family.

"You miss it."

"Occasionally. The juice, the gamble…" Delilah sighed. "But you can't have it all, at least not at the same time. My family's the main thing, you know?" At his nod, she narrowed her eyes. "But you are developing the thousand-yard stare, my man. You need to tell Doc you're done."

She might be right, but he wasn't ready to pack it in, not while this case was open. He'd stood over the bodies of victims whose only mistake had been wanting a better life. They deserved justice. Anyway, what the hell else did he know how to do? "I'm fine," he protested. "Just need some progress in the case."

"It'll come." She squeezed his arm then looked outward. "Amazing, isn't it, how beautifully this place came together?"

"Sophie's amazing, that's for sure. Cade made any headway on getting her to marry him yet?"

"They're taking it slow." She shook her head. "Which is just crazy. When you know, you know."

"I don't really believe in that meant-to-be stuff, but I have to say, this family can sure make you reconsider." Both Cade and Sophie had gone through a lot before their paths had crossed, but they were a walking advertisement for the hand of fate. "So there goes the last MacAllister, down for the count."

"Except Jenna," she reminded him.

"Jenna's too young to get married."

"She's turning thirty today, I'll remind you." Her eyebrows rose. "How about you, Lover Boy? Any sweet thing caught your eye?"

"All of them." When she smacked his arm playfully, he chuckled. "I'm still young," he teased, "unlike some of you, old married lady."

She didn't rise to the bait, even though she was barely older than him. "Well, for that, sonny, this old lady is not going to introduce you to America's Sweetheart. You're on your own." She tossed her mane of flame-red hair. "Me, I'm going to see if I can trap my husband behind one of these trees." With a saucy grin, she sauntered away.

JD watched her go with a smile. Instead of approaching the stranger in their midst, however, he veered off to the right, making a path toward his favorite girl, who stood with her back to him. He neared and bent over her shoulder. "Someone's making time with your man. Now's our opportunity to run away to South America."

Grace MacAllister, family matriarch, whirled. "JD! I'm so glad to see you!" She grasped his cheeks much as his own mother would and made him feel about ten years old when she put the slow mother-eye in motion and gave him the once-over. "What's wrong? Are you eating well? Sleeping enough? You're working too hard, aren't you? Do I need to call Doc?"

JD noted the amusement on the faces of the three sons standing with her. Every one of them understood her mama-bear nature. The entire family save Jenna towered over her, but she was the clear queen of the castle, the benevolent dictator who ruled with both unfettered love and an iron will.

"You sure know how to ruin a good proposal," he complained. "Here I am, inviting you to an exciting life of scandal and sin, and you completely blow me off. I'm wounded, Grace."

"Oh, pooh. You're shameless, is what you are. But since I've already chatted with my boys—"

"Chatted," Cade objected. "Interrogated, is more like it. You should get Doc to hire her, JD. The rest of you could sit around and play cards while Mom solved your caseload. Meanwhile, we'd be off the hook." He grinned at his mother, who rolled her eyes.

"There's an idea." JD acknowledged Cade with a nod. "Haven't gotten a ring on Sophie's finger yet?"

Cade shrugged. "Working on it." But he didn't look all that perturbed. He'd been at death's door less than a year ago, and JD knew he wasn't the only one who felt Cade deserved every bit of happiness he could get. Same went for Sophie.

JD glanced at the others, Jesse and Diego. "All of you dads now. And husbands. Wow."

"Your turn," Grace noted. "You're not getting any younger, JD."

He ignored the smirks and turned his attention to her. "If I can't have you, Grace…" A gusty sigh and a dramatic clasp of his chest. "I'm a broken man."

"Are you hitting on my mother again?" Jenna asked as she walked up.

"Hey, Sunshine." He swept her up in a hug, then twirled her around before setting her on her feet again. "How's it feel to be old?" He tugged at a lock of her strawberry blond page boy.

"Shut up and give me my present." Like it or not— and she often didn't—Jenna was everyone's kid sister, and she looked the part, her nickname reflecting her personality, a pretty, sunny girl who was the eternal optimist, the person who always brightened the day.

She was also every bit a worthy successor to her mother. She might not have children, but she was always taking one sad case or another under her wing, relentless about doing what it took to solve her charges' problems or make their lives better. Like her mother, she was slender and lovely, and pure steel ran through her spine.

"Don't you have to wait to open gifts until after we have cake?"

"I'm the birthday girl. I can do whatever I want."

He glanced toward a table piled with packages. An adjoining one was currently being stocked with steaming platters of food by Sophie and her chef. "That doesn't seem to be Sophie's game plan." He held his package high, far past her reach. "And I'm hungry."

"Then I won't introduce you to Violet."

"Violet who?"

She nudged an elbow into his side. "Yeah, right. You know you're dying to meet her. Who wouldn't be?"

"Well, yeah. Since I'm not stupid."

"Give me my gift, then." She waggled her fingers.

Instead, he dangled the gift bag in his hand and began to back away. "If you're so impatient, birthday girl, come and get it." He picked up his pace, his eyes on Jenna as she squealed and started after him.

"This better be a great gift, smarty-pants."

"Maybe there's nothing in here." He grinned at her, then feinted to the side as she grabbed for the bag.

"Oof!"

He smashed into someone and whipped around, using his quick reflexes to grab the falling person—

Then he realized he was holding America's Sweetheart in his arms.

And Delilah was right.

Violet James was even more beautiful up close.

"I'M SORRY. DID I HURT YOU?" said the new arrival at the party. "I was—"

"Being a brat and not letting me have my birthday present," said Jenna, approaching from behind him.

He didn't respond to Jenna. Instead, he quickly set Violet on her feet and steadied her. "Seriously, are you hurt?"

"I'm fine," Violet managed to answer, looking up into worried gray eyes. Six feet, she guessed, lean and athletic, tousled tawny hair.

"Well, don't I feel like a moron? Plowing right over a woman isn't the usual ploy for making a good impression, or at least not one I've tried before." Then he grinned, and strikingly handsome became breathtaking. He stuck out a hand. "JD Cameron. How am I doing so far? Wowed yet?"

Charming, too. Her first instinct after everything she'd been through was to go icy, but that would be giving Barry's betrayal too much power. Plus, Sophie said he was the next thing to family and she could trust him. She would try. "Let's just say I won't forget our meeting." She slid her hand into his and smiled.

"Ouch. So I need another ploy. Hmm, let's see… I'm guessing people tell you all the time how beautiful you are, so I won't bother with that. And I already know what you do for a living, so strike that one. Then there's *what's your sign* but I could find that out pretty easily online, I imagine, so that leaves…" He stared blankly then snapped his fingers. "Got it." His gaze locked on hers, his eyes sparkling with mischief and fun. "What's a fine filly like you doing in a one-horse town like this, little lady?" His voice was a perfect cowboy twang as he tipped an imaginary Stetson then stuck his thumbs in an invisible gun belt.

Oh, yes, clever and charming in addition to his good looks. She wondered what he'd think if he knew that what actually tempted her about him was the hint of shadows in his eyes. For all his good-natured banter, she sensed more depth to him than his manner revealed.

"Mostly wondering why you won't let the poor little birthday girl have her present."

He snorted. "Poor thing."

"Yeah!" Jenna stuck out her tongue at him then grinned at Violet. Deftly she snagged the gift bag from the ground and looped her arm through Violet's. "My new best friend and I will be over at the gift table if you need us."

Violet laughed and let herself be led away.

JD FOLLOWED HER WITH HIS EYES but stayed where he was for now. They'd been introduced. He'd play it cool, as he'd planned from the start.

He was surprised to discover, though, that for the first time he could recall, he was nervous around a woman. Amazing how easily he'd fallen back into being a lame jokester, as though he was still in junior high.

Real good, dumbass.

Zane strolled over. "Your fatal charm not working, Romeo?"

"Bite me."

"She's been through a rough time," Zane said.

"Like what? Her manicurist didn't get the polish color right?"

"No, idiot. Her husband cheated on her. Got caught with photos all over creation. What, you live in a cave?"

"Oh." Vaguely he recalled some buzz but he'd paid little attention to it. "Tough break." She probably wasn't a big fan of men right now. That would make it hard for him to get any information out of her.

"It was a tough break. They don't come any nicer than Violet. She's the real deal, not a fake bone in her body. That bastard humiliated her, and the press has been on her like a pack of dogs. That's why she's here, hiding out."

Wow. She was so larger-than-life onscreen, it surprised him how delicate she actually was. She seemed…fragile. A little broken.

Exactly what always stirred his Sir Galahad impulse.

Reality check, bonehead. She was richer than God and could hire all the pampering and ego-stroking she needed.

Speaking of pampering... Avery Lofton and all those packages came to mind. So this was who he was coming to see. JD wondered why. If she was so broken up over her marriage surely they weren't involved romantically. And he sure didn't want to think America's Sweetheart was involved in Lofton's sordid dealings. But even if she wasn't a part of the money laundering, how much did she know?

"Hey, you ready for some grub?" Zane asked.

"Always." JD dragged himself out of his musings.

"Me, I'm gonna sit with my lady." Zane nudged his side with an elbow. "Too bad you ticked off the birthday girl and blew your shot with the only other unattached woman here."

JD mock-punched his shoulder. "My heart belongs to Addie, anyway. I'll go sit with a female who appreciates me."

Zane snickered and waved over his shoulder as he walked off.

CHAPTER FOUR

EARLY THE NEXT MORNING Violet used the rope conveniently threaded through the hammock to send herself swaying again. So peaceful…she opened her eyes and watched the live oak branches above her, breathing in the serenity for which the hotel was aptly named. This morning was especially quiet since she'd urged Sophie to sleep in. Sophie had reluctantly agreed, but only after loading Violet down with enough muffins and fruit for a week.

Violet had had a wonderful time last night with the Montalvo/MacAllister clan. The party had reminded her forcibly of just how much she missed people. She'd slept more than any human should, read until her eyes blurred. This place was gorgeous, but she was close to begging Sophie to put her to work. Idleness had never been her cup of tea.

It was time to go out. Live in the world again. She'd always faced her fears in the past, and she wasn't going to give in to them now. She threw her legs over the side of the hammock and rose, glancing down at her attire. In plain black yoga pants and a hoodie, hair scraped back in a ponytail, surely she looked nondescript enough to avoid notice. She'd put a ball cap on her head and was wearing sunglasses to hide the eyes too much of the world would recognize.

There was a coffee shop a couple of blocks away, Jenna had mentioned last night.

She wanted desperately to go running, but she'd use this quick jaunt to reconnoiter the area, then make better plans for later.

At the notion of venturing out, her spirits lifted. She hurried to her quarters, grabbing cash and the key card Sophie had told her would, along with her personal code, get her in and out of the innocent-looking but highly secure walking gate beside the remote-control entrance used for vehicles.

Then she was on the other side of the gate, and for a moment the freedom was almost frightening. She had to remind herself that it was she who'd immured herself inside the fortress, that she was not a prisoner escaping. But she also felt naked and exposed, as she did whenever she left her compound in L.A. on foot.

Though, in reality, she could hardly remember the last time she'd done so in L.A. Too much of her life was spent being whisked from one safe vehicle to another, from one carefully chosen venue to the next.

When she was a kid, she'd ridden her bicycle everywhere, spent untold hours exploring with her brothers or friends. Ventured fearlessly and joyously into the unknown.

Had she realized, when she'd set her sights on acting, on being the best, what the price would be? The freedom she'd be sacrificing?

She had not. And yet, Violet grinned, ruthlessly honest with herself...she wouldn't have listened even if anyone had warned her.

But she wasn't going to waste this beautiful morning pondering the road not taken. She was going to remember what it was to be bold and fearless, and she would relish every second of this outing. She increased her steps to a good, strong stride, letting her muscles warm as she drank in her surroundings.

Soon she reached South Congress Avenue, for which this SoCo district was named, according to Sophie. She hadn't asked Jenna for directions last night, not envisioning that she'd leave the hotel this soon, so she glanced up and down the wide street, then spotted the sign for the coffee shop on her left, across the street and a block or so up.

She waited for the light then crossed, unable to resist smiling widely because no cars skidded to the side, no photographers jumped out.

No one noticed her. *No. One.*

"I love Austin." She laughed and barely resisted shouting, throwing her arms out wide to embrace this place. "Oh, yeah, Violet, that would be just genius. Draw attention to yourself." Still, she did a quick little dance step then forced herself to stop grinning like a fool.

She couldn't take it all in fast enough as she passed the old motor court all shined up, the mix of funky shops she was dying to prowl. Somewhere up here was a huge costume shop Avery had mentioned to her.

When she reached the coffee shop, she noted that it was more of a stand than a restaurant—all the seating was outside, some under an extended roof and some under the trees. She spotted a table and thought how lovely it would be to simply sit there unobserved.

Though it was early, there were still a number of customers, and she waited in line behind two. The street sloped ever upward, she noted, and then realized that of course it would because the land would drain into the lake she had glimpsed from her aerie. She turned her head to the right to get a different view.

And gasped. Lowered her sunglasses to see it better. There was the lake, a big slice of it, and beyond that downtown, all framing a building she thought must be the state capitol.

"Nice view, huh?" said the woman in front of her.

"Gorgeous," Violet responded. "Your first visit?"

"It is. I like the city."

The woman's head tilted slightly, her eyes narrowing in a questioning expression Violet knew all too well. Quickly she jammed her sunglasses in place. Mentally held her breath.

The woman shrugged. "Too many people do. It used to be a simple college town, and we preferred it that way."

A guy in front of her snorted, glancing back over the woman's head at Violet. "You'll get used to opinions like that. Around this part of town you find all sorts of folks who live in the past. Go across the river, and you'll find the future. People who aren't clinging to the Sixties and Armadillo World Headquarters."

The woman frowned slightly. "I'm not—"

He laughed and nudged at her. "You are. Give it up, Clarice. You came here from somewhere else, too. Most of us did. Austin's unique, and we all love it." He glanced at Violet again. "Welcome. You'll fall in love here, too. Even with curmudgeons like Clarice."

"I am not."

"You know you are."

The two paid for their drinks, still cheerfully quarreling as they walked away.

Violet stepped forward to place her order and felt a gaze on her. Out of the corner of her eye she could see that one of the baristas was staring. As quickly as she turned her head in his direction, he looked away.

But the glow of the morning dimmed a little. She nearly didn't order.

No. I am not running away.

She ordered and paid. Resolved not to duck her head and hide as she waited, feeling too exposed. The barista leaned toward another employee, and as he spoke, she felt the other barista's eyes dart in her direction, then shift away.

When her drink was ready, she hesitated. Suddenly she felt not free but alone. Vulnerable. Her phone was in her pocket. She could call Avery, but it would take him forever to get here. Sophie would come, but Violet had promised her a lazy morning, and Sophie more than deserved it.

No one. She had no one. She was in a place she didn't know, had no idea where to go to be safe if—

Stop it. No one is whipping out a camera. No one is approaching. No mob is forming.

But any of that could happen. More than one head was turning curiously in her direction now. But no one got up and came toward her with pen and paper. Not exactly a crowd gathering, but—

It could start with just one person. Her head whipped around, but she could spot nowhere that would be hidden, no seat where she could be tucked away to watch but not be watched herself.

Heart pounding, Violet nearly tossed her coffee in the trash and ran, but she refused to let herself.

The teenage boy brought her fears to life as he walked right up to her. "My sister and I are wondering. Are you Violet James?"

Hearing her name spoken out loud, seeing heads whipping her way...

You asked for this life. And you love your fans. Do not let one terrible experience turn you into a cynic and a coward, not after you've managed to remain human this long. "I am," she said, her voice only shaking a little as she watched for the cell phones to come out, the tweets to begin. "Isn't it a beautiful morning?"

"Not half as beautiful as you." Then he blushed.

Violet loosened her grip on her coffee. "You're very sweet to say so. I need to go, but would you like an autograph first?"

"Um, could I get a picture with you?"

Violet fought back the sickness in her belly, knowing that she'd destroyed her own haven. News of where she was would spread and the paparazzi would swarm her.

"Of course. Want to invite your sister?"

JD STOOD SIPPING COFFEE on the back porch of the South Austin two-story he'd bought a year ago and was slowly bringing back to life. He was late getting up this morning after a restless night of dreams peopled with terrified women crying out for his help.

Violet James had been polite last night, but she was clearly more at ease with the others. She hadn't stayed much longer at Jenna's party, so all he really learned was that she was the mysterious guest Avery Lofton visited daily. He certainly hadn't made a connection with her that gave him a good excuse to talk to her again.

His cell phone rang. "JD?"

"Yes?"

"It's Sophie. How are you?"

His forehead wrinkled. She'd only seen him maybe twelve hours ago, and she'd never called him before. "Okay," he replied cautiously. "Everything all right there?"

"Oh, yes. Of course it is," she said hastily.

"Cade's okay? Nothing's wrong with his family?"

"No… I mean, yes, he's fine. They're all right, too." She hesitated.

"Can I help you with something?"

Big sigh. "I need a favor, JD. It's going to sound weird."

He didn't know Sophie nearly as well as he did the rest of the family, but he knew enough to understand that asking for help was something Sophie did only rarely. She'd have killed herself trying to renovate and finish the hotel on her own, for instance. Cade and Jenna had brought all their family and friends— including him—to help Sophie finish the landscaping so that she could open in time, but her struggle to accept the help was clear to all of them. Life had not handed Sophie any breaks, yet she'd rebounded from tragedy not once but twice and had excelled in spite of it. She'd made herself a success. So for her to ask a favor now, she must not see any other option.

"I'm okay with weird," he said.

Faint laughter. "Well, that's good." Another hesitation, then a rushed breath. "Okay, here's the thing. It's not me who needs the help. It's Violet."

"Violet James?" His mind was racing. "What could she possibly need from me?"

"I need you to take her out," Sophie said in a rush.

"You need me…to take her out," he echoed slowly. His mind went temporarily blank. The request was a little like Santa Claus showing up on Christmas, New

Year's Day, Valentine's Day and Easter. But he didn't kid himself, the appeal wasn't only because of his current case. Violet James played a part in the dream lives of most American males. The woman could have any man she wanted. "What's the catch?"

"I'm not doing a very good job of this," she said. "Okay, let's start over. Has anyone ever broken your heart, JD?"

He tried to remember.

"Never mind." She laughed. "I forget who I'm talking to, Romeo."

He winced. "Aw, Sophie, don't…" He exhaled in a gust. "I can't help it that I get along well with women."

"You've never had your heart broken?"

"There was this girl…."

"Girl? How old were you?"

"Fourteen?"

"Amazing."

Somehow he didn't think she really meant that as a compliment.

"Then you may not understand Violet's situation," she said. "But maybe, since you're such a lady-killer, you'll understand what it's like to be put in uncomfortable situations because of your looks."

"Come on, Sophie. Cut me some slack. I'm not shallow."

"But you sure haven't put your heart out there for anyone to stomp on, have you?"

Wow. He'd have to think about that.

"I'm sorry, JD. I'm not really eliciting your sympathy, am I?"

That so wasn't his problem. He was too busy thanking his lucky stars. But he probably shouldn't appear too eager. "I've sure had better sales jobs." He chuckled. "Want to try again?"

"I think I'd better." She paused. "Hello, JD. This is Sophie. May I ask you a favor?"

He couldn't help laughing. "Why, sure, Sophie. Anything. Whatever you need—strong back, someone to play with Skeeter, a date for the hottest star in the known universe? Just say the word."

He heard the smile in her voice when she answered. "About that hottest star...funny you should ask..." Then her voice turned serious. "Here's the thing, JD. It goes against all of my principles to ask this without her permission, but I'm concerned about Violet."

JD's every sense went on alert. "Why?"

Sophie took a deep breath. "I've been very happy to provide a refuge for her here, and I would gladly continue, but...she's lonely. She has one friend who comes to visit her, but she hasn't left these grounds since she arrived, at least until this morning." Her tone was grim. "She walked down to Jo's for cup of coffee before Cade and I got up. She dressed not to be noticed, but someone still recognized her, actually a lot of someones. People were nice, she said, but there were all sorts of cell phones taking pictures and no doubt posting them to Twitter and Facebook. So now she's lost her refuge—I mean, still no one can get inside here, but the word is out—and, well, you know how it is for Zane...."

Yeah. All of them knew how crazy things could be for Zane. "Doesn't she have a bodyguard?"

"We promised her it would be different here in Austin. We promised her a chance to live like a real person."

Sophie's intent was beginning to come clear. "You're not saying…"

"I just thought… Maybe it was a foolish idea." She sounded so disappointed. "She would be safe with you, JD, I mean, you have all that training."

"You want me to be her bodyguard? I have a job, Sophie."

"I know." She sighed. "Cade would do it, but he has to leave on another assignment."

"Cade's a photographer, not a cop."

"But he's a man, and he's big. And everyone else in the family is married."

"You were going to pimp Cade out to Violet James?" he teased.

"No!" Then she huffed. "Do not be deliberately obtuse. I'm only asking if you would take Violet out a time or two. Give her a chance to have some fun, and still be safe. Take her somewhere where she doesn't attract attention."

"I practically knocked her down," he pointed out.

"She wasn't mad—oh, never mind," she said. "I don't even know that Violet would go for the idea, anyway."

Okay, he'd been cautious enough. Now he was going to jump all over this golden opportunity to spend time with the woman one of their prime suspects was coming to visit every day. She probably knew he was a cop since the family would have no reason to hide that fact, and this was the only innocuous means by which he'd have an excuse to snoop around and see what he could learn about Avery Lofton.

"Maybe she's the forgiving type," he said to Sophie. "And she'll consider me almost flattening her a novel introduction."

Sophie chuckled.

It wasn't without effort that he pretended nonchalance. "Okay, I guess. Feel free to try, then let me know what she thinks of your idea."

"Oh, thank you, JD. I owe you. Of course, I already owe you for all your backbreaking labor on my landscaping."

Oh, you really, really don't, he thought. Not if she could get him in the catbird seat on his investigation. But to Sophie he only said, "What are friends for? Anyway, better not celebrate yet. She might be a tough sell."

"I don't think so—I hope not. I mean, you do have a way with women, JD. She's such a nice person. I like her a lot, not only as a guest, but as a person. She's very fragile right now, and I really want to help her."

"You have a good heart, Sophie. Call me and let me know how the sales job goes."

"I will—and thank you so much."

Oh, no, thank you. You're the one who's dropping this right in my lap. "Bye, Sophie."

Doc would be ecstatic if it came through.

He wished he could explain to Sophie that he would be careful with Violet, that if she wasn't involved in this crime, she would be fine.

But he couldn't tell Sophie anything. He reminded himself that he worked undercover all the time, that the deception was necessary, that he was doing it for the right reasons, to save lives. To keep innocent young women who weren't famous safe from those who would brutalize and kill them.

VIOLET DIDN'T TELL AVERY about her ill-fated outing, though she wasn't sure why. She shouldn't have told

Sophie, but Sophie had been outside on the grounds looking worried when she returned. What an oaf she'd been, not thinking to leave Sophie a note. When she stayed in a hotel she never considered accounting for her whereabouts, but even though she was a paying guest here, somehow this was different. Sophie had gone so far out of her way for Violet, and Violet had rewarded her solicitous care by vanishing and leaving Sophie to worry.

So somehow all the details had come spilling out. Sophie felt terrible, not that any of it was her fault, but that was just who Sophie was. Violet had assured her she was fine, that the incident hadn't soured her on Austin, that she was fine staying inside the grounds and would be returning to L.A. soon anyway.

That only served to make Sophie feel worse.

Avery had arrived before they could finish the conversation and, as always, her hostess disappeared and left her to visit with Avery in private. That visit hadn't gone much better than the morning's outing. He'd been preoccupied and even a little irritable, so she'd sent him on his way quickly, pleading that she was tired— and frankly, he hadn't seemed to mind all that much.

She was not a duty call. She wasn't going to be an obligation or a worry. She didn't want to be anyone's burden, she just wanted—

She had no idea what she wanted. Except what she couldn't seem to have. How had she come to this point in her life? No man, no children, no one she really trusted except Avery…and their friendship wasn't holding up terribly well right now, either.

That was unfair. He was a busy man, yet he made time for her every day, he brought her countless gifts, trying to cheer her up.

But she wanted someone who couldn't wait to be with her. Someone whose day she made brighter, someone she could love as much as she wanted with this heart of hers that was starving to death. Someone whose motives she could trust completely, who saw her as she was, the East Tennessee girl, not the Hollywood star.

As the hammock she was trying to relax in slowed, a cold nose attached to a big furry head plopped over the side and stilled her. Violet smiled. "Hi, Skeeter." The Irish setter's tail thumped the ground, and his tongue swiped her arm.

"Skeeter! Oh, Violet, I'm so sorry. Someone let him out of the house." Sophie rushed to retrieve her dog. "I'm very sorry he woke you."

Violet stroked his head and smiled into the soft brown eyes, then looked up at Skeeter's mistress. "I wasn't asleep, and, anyway, I've slept for a year already. Besides, I grew up with big dogs. I'd have one if I didn't travel so much. Nothing better than a big old sloppy dog kiss, isn't that right, baby?" she crooned. "Much better than a yappy little thing."

Skeeter's tail wagged his agreement.

"He's supposed to be in his run when guests are on the grounds."

"Well, since you've been kind enough to make me your only guest, I think he should get a reprieve."

"Not so kind. You're paying a premium for the privilege." Sophie was relentlessly honest, cautious to her core and ruthless in her expectations of herself and her staff.

"I should. You sacrificed bookings to afford me the privacy of being the only guest."

Sophie waved off her concerns. "I'd do anything for

Cade's family. And once I met you, well, I'm happy if I can help someone I like so much."

"They're really nice, aren't they? I'd only met Zane until last night."

"They are. They treat me just like family."

Violet heard the wistfulness in her voice and decided to pry a little further. "From what I heard last night, Cade would make that legal in a heartbeat."

In a rare display of distress, Sophie was practically wringing her hands. "I know, but…" Abruptly she faced Violet. "I've been married before."

"Oh." Didn't she know only too well how much the past could mark you? "I apologize. I—"

Sophie pressed on as though Violet hadn't spoken. "I…we had a child." Her voice went very quiet. "My husband and baby, they…died."

Now Violet really felt terrible. She rose and laid her hand on the taller woman's arm. "I understand. I'm very sorry for your loss."

Sophie began to walk, and after a brief hesitation, Violet fell into step beside her. "I'm over it—at least, as much as you ever get over losing your family in an instant." She faced Violet. "I was in hiding, and Cade made me come out. Taught me that I could love again…but I'm scared." She flung her hands wide. "And I don't know why I'm talking about this."

"I won't tell a soul, Sophie, I swear. It stays between us."

"You are such a nice person. It's not just an image—you really are America's Sweetheart."

"Please." Violet shuddered. "Not here. I'm just me. And that's a gift you've given me, Sophie, the space to just…be. To not have to keep up appearances or worry about what I say or how I look or—"

"You're always beautiful. You'd be easy to hate if you weren't so lovable."

Violet rolled her eyes. "Yeah, yeah, blah, blah… let's get back to you."

"Actually, I came to talk about you."

"Me? Is this about this morning? Sophie, please don't worry about what happened. I'll be fine."

Sophie twisted her fingers together, an unusual sign of tension in someone normally so serene. "I—I arranged something for you."

Now it was Violet who tensed. "What?"

"You need to get out," Sophie said. "And I have a solution. JD is coming to pick you up this afternoon."

"JD?" Violet echoed. "From last night?"

"He's a good guy," Sophie said quickly. "And he's embarrassed about nearly knocking you down. That's very unlike him. He's usually great company, a lot of fun. Women love him."

"That's not exactly a selling point for me, you know." Violet smiled wryly. "I've had it up to here with pretty boys. My life is full of them in L.A."

"But he's not like that," Sophie responded. "And this isn't…he didn't ask for it. I was the one who asked him. He's got reservations, too."

Violet's eyebrows rose. "Really."

"What I mean is that he would never impose. You know he's a cop, right? So I thought that he could be good company but also watch over you and keep you safe. I mean, you could hire a bodyguard, but—"

Violet shook her head. "I'd rather not. I just wanted to be able to go and play tourist without being followed."

"Exactly," Sophie said. "Which is why I thought of

JD. He's not like a real bodyguard and he's really a lot of fun. Everyone in the family loves him."

Violet's instinct was to say no, but she recognized that Sophie was simply trying in a different way to give her a chance to get out and enjoy herself.

"Never mind," Sophie said when Violet didn't speak. "I'll come with you. I can be fierce when I need to," Sophie said. "Cade won't mind sparing me for a while."

Cade definitely would mind, Violet would bet. He'd been gone for three weeks, she'd learned during her stay here. He'd barely been back forty-eight hours and he was due to leave again in a few days. Plus, the two of them were so crazy in love with each other that Violet would be the biggest jerk to take Sophie away now.

She shouldn't hold it against JD that he was gorgeous. He might be perfectly nice. Hadn't she always been one to give others the benefit of the doubt? "No, I'm not taking you away from Cade," she said. "But JD is clear this isn't a date, right?"

"Of course," Sophie said. "He's only doing it as a favor to me." Then her eyes widened. "Um, I mean… Good grief, you'd never know I have a reputation for being cool under fire."

Violet grinned. "I don't think I've ever had a pity date," she said. "Much less a pity non-date."

"I should probably stop right now, shouldn't I?"

Sophie looked so distressed and embarrassed that Violet couldn't tease her anymore. "You did fine. Anyway, it's not your fault that I've made a real hash of my life."

The other woman's eyebrows rose. "You're famous and beautiful and you make millions." Then her eyes warmed. "But I guess I do understand. I wasn't around when Zane and Roan met, but I've heard the family stories. Even when he was on top of the world in everyone's eyes, his life wasn't nearly as perfect as it seemed."

"I hear that," Violet said. "I made one of my dreams happen, but I never understood back then that it wouldn't be enough." She reached out and clasped Sophie's hands. "You have a wonderful man who loves you. You stay here and play with him. I'll go with JD."

"You'll have fun, Violet. I promise."

It would be nice to get out, and it was the least she could do for the woman standing in front of her with worried eyes. Besides, she'd always been an optimist, and she wanted to be that Violet again.

She squeezed Sophie's hands. "I'm looking forward to it."

Sophie's delight was reward enough to balance Violet's misgivings. *Fake it 'til you make it, right, Mom?*

CHAPTER FIVE

GOOD WORK, DOC HAD SAID when JD called him to report their windfall. *Don't screw it up.*

There was a lot at stake here, not the least of which was that they weren't sure whether Violet James was involved in the human-trafficking ring. It didn't seem likely, but his years in law enforcement had taught JD that motivations were not always obvious, that the most innocent-looking parties could still be guilty as hell.

Why a woman as on top of the world as Violet would be involved in crime, especially one that hurt women and children more than anyone, he couldn't imagine. But Avery Lofton was definitely involved, and she was close to Lofton. Just how close was something he'd be paying rapt attention to. Even if she wasn't part of this horrifying scheme, she could know something. He took nothing for granted at this point.

He wasn't a trained bodyguard, either, and that could screw things up, too. Yes, he had formidable self-defense skills and he kept them honed. He didn't just run daily, he lifted weights and he'd studied various forms of self-defense. But with luck, none of that would be needed. As far as he was aware, she had no stalkers, no crazed fans lurking in bushes. Doc had tagged an old FBI buddy stationed in L.A. to check that out. Violet James was much loved, but her reputation for sweetness shielded her from the worst of the crazies.

Beyond all of that…he also couldn't think of how to entertain one of the world's most famous and beautiful women.

He pulled into Sophie's and used the code Sophie had given him when they'd spoken earlier. After the gate opened, he drove inside, still debating his options.

Could he actually be nervous? He didn't remember the last time he'd been nervous on a date—not that this was a date, but he really didn't know what the devil to call it.

He emerged from his truck, dressed in his usual attire of jeans, a T-shirt and boots, with a ball cap on his head from his beloved Texas Longhorns. Austin was a casual place, and Ms. Bigshot Star would just have to deal with it if she was expecting some guy in a silk shirt.

He started for the front door of the hotel, thinking he'd seek out Sophie first, but just before he made it to the steps, he heard Skeeter bark, followed by feminine laughter. He backed up several steps and peered across the grounds, seeing the woman he was here to pick up kneeling and rubbing Skeeter enthusiastically.

She looked about seventeen, her hair caught up in a ponytail, curls escaping all around her face. She, too, had jeans on, though he imagined hers probably cost much, much more than his. Whatever the cost, though, they were worth it. America's Sweetheart had one very fine derriere and impressively long legs for someone barely medium height. She looked amazing.

Whoa, boy. She's a case, not a woman. Certainly not a woman you'll ever find in your bed. Still, he changed course and crossed the grounds with long strides. Skeeter saw him first, barking a greeting, then racing his way.

When the dog reached JD, he leapt to his hind legs and planted his forelegs on JD's chest.

"Still not doing so hot at the obedience lessons, huh, boy?" JD grinned and scratched behind Skeeter's ears, then darted sideways, exciting the dog. They began to roughhouse.

Violet approached. "He's a great dog."

He was staring, he knew it, but couldn't seem to do anything about it.

The woman was just too beautiful to believe.

Her head tilted curiously, then disappointment crossed her expression and she looked away.

"I'm not thinking about how beautiful you are. I'm picturing you with a big wart on your nose."

Her head whipped back. "What did you say?"

"You don't like hearing that you're beautiful. Picturing you with a big wart will keep me from being just one more person saying that."

A sideways glance. "You're not into warts?" There was a tiny curve to her lips.

"Well, now don't get me wrong, with the right woman a wart could be just fine."

This smile was genuine.

"I'm much more evolved than that," he went on. "I couldn't care less what a woman looks like. I'm blind to all but inner beauty."

At that she laughed. "I think I'll try that wart image myself. I suspect you already have enough women falling all over you."

He grimaced. "Please, not you, too."

"But here's the thing: handsome men are a dime a dozen where I live. I'm immune."

He stared at her. "That's good…I think." His forehead wrinkled.

"I'm just saying…"

"Consider me forewarned." Well, now, this was… different. He saluted her then cleared his throat elaborately. "So, what's your pleasure, ma'am? Where would you like to go?"

"Surprise me," she said.

He considered her for a moment. "So are you a risk taker?"

"I dropped out of college and left for Hollywood against my family's wishes and with the sum total of three hundred dollars in my pocket, which I proceeded to lose the first week I lived in L.A."

"That only says you're not too bright."

She laughed instead of taking offense, and that impressed him.

"So how about now? Are you still adventurous, Ms. James?"

Her smile dimmed. "I'm trying to be. It's harder these days. Too many eyes watching. Too many people hoping I'll screw up. I brought it on myself, though. If I hadn't been ambitious, none of this would've happened."

"So where would you be now, if you hadn't been ambitious?"

She got this faraway look on her face. "Maybe back in Tennessee, maybe married to one of the boys I grew up with, a house full of kids…"

He considered and rejected any number of responses. There was an element of wistfulness about her when she talked about a home, kids, as if she would trade being queen of the universe, arguably the most famous woman in America, for that life. But would she really trade her life for what many would consider mundane?

Before he could decide, she straightened and tossed her head, sending that ponytail swinging. "So, what's the plan, Mr. Bodyguard?"

He winced. "Sure you don't want to just hire a real bodyguard?" Immediately he cursed silently. Why had he even asked her? Ten minutes in, and he was letting emotion and a beautiful face make him forget why he was here.

"Sophie said I'd be safe with you. Was she wrong? Aren't you a cop? Protect and serve, and all that?"

Here's where it got dicey. He couldn't hide his profession, but he had to walk a fine line. He'd already decided to give himself a different career path. "I teach at the Academy." It wasn't a total fabrication; he did teach a class now and again on undercover tactics. And the amount of time he spent undercover meant he was adept at lying, anyway.

But somehow he didn't like lying to her.

No other choice, son. Doc's voice rang in his head. No one knew who she was to Avery Lofton or how much she was aware of Lofton's illegal activities. JD had to keep his eye on the prize.

She scanned his body. "You're pretty fit for a teacher," she said.

He couldn't help reacting. *Down boy.* It was hard to ignore the impact of a beautiful woman letting her eyes walk a lazy trail over your flesh.

"I like to run," he said.

Her expression brightened. "Me, too. Every day?"

He nodded. "Five miles, rain or shine."

She sighed. "I miss it. It's probably part of why I'm going stir-crazy. I haven't left this place in two and a half weeks—until this morning, that is."

"Well, then, there's your answer. You got your shoes here?"

She glanced down at his boots. "Yes, but you don't."

He grinned. "Au contraire, darlin'. I keep my gym bag in my truck. You game?"

Caution crept in. "But where?"

"Oh, honey. Austin is full of places to go run. You get changed while I grab my bag and go say hi to Sophie. How far do you normally run?"

"Three miles," she said. "But only three times a week."

"Don't worry. I'll go easy on you."

Competition sparked in her eyes. "Don't you dare." She turned to go.

"Tennessee girl, huh?"

She glanced back. "Yeah."

"So you probably think pork is real barbecue."

"It's the only barbecue," she responded.

He walked backwards, still talking. "So you haven't been completely ruined by the land of fruits and nuts? I don't have to produce macrobiotic organic vegan food for you? I mean, I can, you know. Austin's nearly as weird as California."

Her smile spread. "Barbecue will be just fine, even if it's only beef."

"Oh, sugar, you are so going to eat your words." He spun and headed for his truck, smiling as he heard her laugh behind him.

VIOLET RACED THROUGH changing clothes. While the re-spite from her demanding trainer had been pretty nice up until now, she was antsy to stretch herself, to push hard, to feel the heat of well-used muscles.

So he was a runner, was he? He must lift weights, too. You didn't get those broad shoulders and ripped arms simply from running.

He was friendly, but he was also smart. He was still too charming by half, but he didn't kowtow to her, and that was worth a lot.

Anyway, she wasn't obligated to anything. She would gamble today and go on this adventure. At worst, she'd get some badly needed exercise and the chance to be free on the other side of these grounds. She hoped very much he'd take her someplace where she didn't have to be so guarded, where it could be just her and the outdoors, the sun, the breeze, the rhythm of the run.

She'd hurried so she could beat him outside, but instead he was throwing a ball for Skeeter and visiting with Sophie and Cade. There was an ease among them that she envied. Her time with the MacAllister family the night before had reminded her so much of what it was like to go home. Or, actually, what it had been like before she became famous. Now she brought trouble along with her everywhere she went.

But when she was with her family, it was so wonderful to just relax and be herself. She'd watched Zane doing the same thing, being teased by his brothers and giving as good as he got. Playing with his children, dragging his wife onto his lap and kissing the socks off her. He made everything seem so normal, but she knew very well how difficult achieving "normal" was.

How had he managed it? she wanted to know. A devoted mate, three beautiful children, roles he only accepted when the time and place worked out for all of them.

Zane had gotten it all right. She should take lessons.

Unless there was no point in teaching her. Maybe she was simply doomed from the beginning because there was something innately unlovable about her.

She danced away from that line of thought.

As she approached, she studied JD more closely. His shoes were clearly not brand-new, and he wore an ancient cops vs. firemen baseball game T-shirt with the sleeves ripped out and a pair of running shorts ratty enough to indicate that these were his real work-out clothes. It was the attire of the man who wasn't out to impress anyone.

And she'd been right about those arms, now that she saw them bare. In street clothing, he looked deceptively lean, but there was definite power in that frame.

He was indeed handsome, but not in a pampered way, not someone who had facials or manicures or a spray-on tan. This was a real man, the kind she'd almost forgotten existed.

At that moment Sophie caught sight of her and welcomed her with a smile.

Violet was grateful for the distraction. *No unwholesome thoughts about the bodyguard, Violet. Remember that.*

"Hi, there," Sophie said.

Cade turned in her direction, then JD did, as well. She was more than a little gratified to see his eyes widen at the sight of her. She hadn't gone to any special trouble; she wore her oldest running shorts and a sleeveless form-fitting T-shirt. For an instant pride ambushed her. She wanted him to see that she, too, knew what she was about, that she was no dilettante about her exercise.

"Did you bring sunscreen?" JD asked. "'Cause you're going to need it. This sun is brutal."

"I live in the land of sunshine," she reminded him.

"Texas sun isn't sissy sun like California. You'll need more. I have some in the truck." Then he turned back to Sophie. "Thanks for the loan of the extra water bottle. I only had mine with me." He glanced at Violet. "There are points along the trail where we can refill our bottles, if we have to. Gotta stay hydrated in this heat."

He wasn't kidding. She was used to sun and to protecting herself from it, but it had been a while since she'd had to deal with the deadly combination of heat and humidity. Tennessee could be the same, but she hadn't lived there in a very long time.

"Thanks, Sophie. Hi, Cade," she said.

"If Pretty Boy here doesn't take good care of you, he'll answer to me," Cade said.

Violet saw JD's shoulders stiffen. "Stop playing big brother. She'll be fine with me."

"Cade…" Sophie touched his arm. "I don't understand why men have to talk trash to each other."

JD grinned down at her. "If you had brothers you'd understand."

"Or if you're the only girl with two brothers," Violet added. "Let's just say it's a matter of survival to toughen up."

Cade nodded. "Jenna would completely agree with you, though I have no idea why."

JD chuckled. "Yeah, 'cause all of you treat her with such kid gloves." He glanced at Violet. "You have brothers?"

"Sadly, yes," she answered. "Both of whom think they need to tell me how to run my life."

"What else are older brothers for?" Cade asked.

"Mine seem to agree."

They shared a smile.

"You ready?" JD asked her.

"Absolutely."

"See you two later," JD said.

"When will you—" Sophie stopped abruptly.

"I won't keep her out late, Mom."

"I'll keep her too busy to notice curfew," Cade promised.

"THIS PLACE IS BEAUTIFUL," Violet said. They were two miles into the run, and he was impressed to see that her breathing remained steady.

"It's a dedicated wilderness area, but it's nice because it's still in the city and easy to access. We're lucky, though, that it's not jammed with people today." He glanced over. "The heat bothering you? Please speak up if it is."

"I'm fine. I like hot weather."

"That's good. You're lucky it's only May. It gets worse…way worse. August is a special kind of hell."

"How about some interval work?" she asked.

"Yeah?" He was delighted. And impressed again.

She checked her monitor. "I don't know how you usually do it, but how about twenty-second bursts every two minutes?"

"I'm game, except—" He looked her over dubiously.

"You don't think I can keep up with you?"

She'd surprised him so far. Her endurance was good. "No, but my stride is longer. I don't want to get ahead." He'd been pacing himself thus far, but the shorter strides didn't come naturally.

"I don't mind if you get ahead."

"Uh-uh. I'm your bodyguard, remember?"

"You said you're not a real bodyguard."

"If you think I'm facing Sophie after something happens to you…"

She grinned in response.

"I know. I'll run backward."

"Please. Don't be insulting."

"Okay, how about I run around you during the burst? That'll keep my heart rate up but keep me nearby."

"So you can tell your buddies you ran rings around me?"

He laughed. "Yeah. I kinda like the sound of that." He winked. "Seriously, though, no insult intended. You can't help it that you're smaller."

She watched him carefully, suspicion in her gaze.

He crossed an X over his heart. "I promise I won't talk out of school about you, to anyone." That wasn't a stretch, not exactly. He didn't owe the task force personal details. They were only interested in her for her access to Lofton…unless she was somehow involved.

But he'd already decided she wasn't. Undercover work meant you listened to your gut, and his was telling him she was clean.

Not that he wouldn't remain vigilant. He didn't want to think a beautiful face could sway him or that he was too starstruck to see her clearly. There was much he still had to learn about the woman beside him, and he would pay attention.

But he wouldn't be spilling secrets no one needed to know.

She was watching her monitor. "No circles. I'll keep up. Ready?"

He had to appreciate her resolve. "You bet."

She kicked it into gear, and he did the same. After they'd completed two intervals during which he'd shortened his stride, he decided he wanted to see her smile again. On the next one, he kicked his pace higher again and went past her, then circled around in tiny steps, chanting, "I can run circles around Violet James, uh-huh, oh, yeah."

She laughed as he closed on her and kept pace. "Nobody warned me you were a brat."

He chuckled, and they kept running.

CHAPTER SIX

"I AM STUFFED TIGHT AS A TICK," Violet said, patting her belly.

"Told you beef barbecue was better," he said.

"You are asking me to betray generations of my ancestors, you realize," she drawled. Good grief, her Southern accent was sneaking back in. Not that she was ashamed of where she'd come from, not one iota, it was only that to play a full range of parts, she'd had to work hard to rid herself of the extreme Tennessee drawl she'd grown up with.

"If they'd eaten at the County Line, they'd be in full agreement," he argued. "You have to admit that."

"Anything else for y'all?" the waitress asked. "More hot washcloths? These have cooled off."

"Naw," JD answered. "She's doing fine licking her fingers."

Oh, good gravy, he was right. She'd gotten so relaxed with him she hadn't realized she was doing exactly that. "Um, a couple more would be great." She wanted to look up and smile at the woman, but she'd kept her cap on and pulled down over her forehead.

"Right away."

"Oh!" She'd nearly forgotten. "Could you bag up those bones, please?" The waitress nodded, and Violet turned to JD. "Surely Sophie will let Skeeter have some, don't you think?"

"I don't know…she treats that dog like her baby, so she might not." He grinned. "But you can bet the farm Cade will."

The waitress came back with their check, more cloths and a bag with the bones. JD reached for his wallet.

"No, please, let me buy dinner," Violet said.

He shook his head. "I've got this."

"It's not a date, JD, and you won't let me pay you for your time."

His face screwed up in disapproval. "I'm doing a favor for a friend."

"You've given me hours of your day, you've provided transportation." Men were so touchy. For heaven's sake, she was a wealthy woman, and he lived on a cop's salary. She sighed. The eternal conundrum of her situation.

"You got cash? 'Cause they're going to see your name on the credit card."

She smiled. "This ain't my first rodeo, cowboy. The card has my production company name on it."

"Smart girl. You don't even sign with your name?" He paused. "Is Violet James your real name?"

"It is. But for the card, I use my middle name…and I scribble." She placed her hand on his. The immediate zing made her realize—yet again—just how real he was, how alive and how seriously sexy. *No way,* she thought. *Don't go there.* Quickly she removed her hand. "Please, JD. This day has been such a gift. It's the very least I can do. Please." She waited for the reactions she was more accustomed to, either the happy acquiescence of a man who was attracted to her for her money and fame, or the injured pride of a man who knew she was richer than him and resented it.

But JD only smiled. "You won't try to pay every time, right?"

She stilled. "We aren't doing this again."

"Of course we are. We've barely scratched the surface of the glories of Austin, and anyway, you need a running partner. Can't have you getting soft. It was nearly too late already." Mischief shone in his grin.

She smiled in response, then narrowed her eyes. "I'll be running rings around you before you know it."

He laughed. "You talk mighty big, sugar. I think I can see how you came to be so successful." He glanced at his watch. "Oh, man, we gotta hurry."

"I'm sorry. I didn't mean to keep you out so long. Do cabs come all the way out here? I could catch one and you could go on."

He studied her. "I said *we,* Violet. There's one more thing we need to do, though you've probably already seen it."

"What?"

"The bats. But you might have already watched them from your room."

"Bats?"

"There's a bat colony that lives under the Congress Avenue bridge, about a million and a half of them. They swarm out at sunset, and it's quite the sight. I'm surprised Sophie didn't mention it." He smiled. "Maybe she thinks you're too sophisticated for that."

She liked that he didn't. "If you don't argue and let me pay, we can be out of here sooner."

"Go for it," he said easily. "But we have a deal, right? My turn next time. Oh, but first you have to tell me your middle name."

"I don't know you well enough."

His eyebrows rose. "A mystery. I love a good puzzler."

"You'll have to work for this one." She placed her card on the bill and signaled the server, still keeping her head down. This dim corner booth had been a blessing because few people could see her, but she wasn't going to push her luck. These last couple of hours had been just what she'd needed.

When the receipt lay on the table, she signed quickly, using her other hand to hide the name on it from him, the way she had in school to keep someone from copying from her. This was too crazy. JD made her feel like a teenager again.

She jumped up and waited for him to rise from the booth. As they walked out, she kept her head turned toward him, and he drew her closer, one hand on her hip.

His touch was a warmth she couldn't ignore, caused an awareness she didn't want. *Just a bodyguard,* she reminded herself. *He's doing a favor for a friend, that's all.*

But she'd had more fun today than she'd had in months. Only now, contrasting JD's warmth to Barry's cool distance, did she realize what a desert her marriage had been. How she'd deluded herself because she'd needed to believe that she could find a real love that lasted.

"Almost there," JD murmured as they approached his truck. He hit the key fob to unlock the doors, but as he'd done before, instead of going around to his door, he opened hers.

"You don't have to do that."

"Are you kidding? My mom would tan my hide if I didn't hold a door for a lady."

Southern manners. She'd missed them. "Well, we wouldn't want to upset your mom, now would we?"

"You got that right." He smiled. "Come on, Robin. Let's head for the Bat Cave."

She chuckled and climbed in.

Thirty minutes later, they were on the north shore of Lady Bird Lake, tucked in a relatively secluded spot away from the crowds gathered on boats and on both shores flanking the bridge, yet still with a view that should give her a good look at the bat flight.

Violet's eyes went wide and she bounced on her toes at the sight of the boiling cloud swarming out of the roost, her childlike pleasure getting to him in a way he couldn't afford to let it.

"That's amazing!" She swiveled toward him, her gaze alight with wonder. "I can't believe this has been happening every evening, and I've missed it. Thank you so much!"

Her delight warmed him, and he realized with a start that her outrageous beauty no longer gobsmacked him because her personality was even more magnetic.

Whoa, boy. Don't go liking her so much you forget why you're here. She's a means to an end, a key to your case. But that felt wrong in a way he'd never experienced on the job.

Then Violet turned to him again, joy beaming, and their eyes locked. Held.

When she finally looked away, he wanted to stop her, to stop time, to have the luxury of simply enjoying being with her. She was nothing like he'd expected. She might be a fantasy for millions, an idol, a dream lover…but he wondered how many people knew the real Violet.

And why in the hell any man would even notice other women existed if Violet belonged to him. Bastard.

No. Oh, no. This was *not* personal, could not ever be. He had a job to do, and he couldn't allow himself to get distracted from his goal—bringing down the trafficking ring and saving lives. To keep himself from making a big mistake, he dredged up mental images of the bodies he'd seen only a few nights before, the young, innocent victims who were the reason he was here at all.

While his fingers itched to draw Violet close, instead, he made himself back away, put a step between them.

A job. She's just a job.

Violet noticed the distance and looked back. "You okay?"

Face grim, he nodded. "I have to go."

The light went out of her. "Oh. Of course. I've taken up enough of your day." She put additional space between them and started toward where they'd parked.

"I'm sorry," he said. "I—I have an appointment I can't miss." *Very smooth, JD.*

"I understand. You've been terribly kind to give me so much of your time."

He could sense the hurt his abrupt excuse had caused. Damn it. This was an intolerable position to be in, and he hadn't even probed for information on Lofton yet. "I had a great time, Violet." That much was true, though he had no business having fun.

She angled her head partway toward him. "I did, too. I appreciate your going to so much trouble, even if it was only for Sophie's sake."

Man, he'd made a hash of this. He gripped her elbow and turned her to face him. "I might have said yes because Sophie asked, but Sophie's not here now. I meant what I said. I like you."

A smile of scant mirth. "And that surprises you."

"It shouldn't. I know how much more complex Zane is than his reputation, and he's as famous as you."

"But?"

He shrugged. "No buts." He wished he could separate business from pleasure with her. That might be the strongest reason to get to the bottom of her relationship with Avery Lofton, so that he didn't have to keep walking this line that made him feel like a fraud.

Hell, he was a fraud, who was he kidding? He never got confused about his role undercover, ever.

But this time was different somehow. Because this woman was different, unique.

Not because she was famous or beautiful—though God knew looking at her was no hardship—or probably rich enough to buy and sell him many times over, but simply because something in her spoke to something in him at a level he hadn't experienced before.

It scared the crap out of him. He couldn't do his job if he felt something for her, if she became important.

He needed to back off nearly as badly as he wanted to draw her close; he needed to be near her nearly as much as he wanted to run away.

The job. Focus on the job. Save wondering about the rest for later.

He didn't have the information he was here to obtain, it was that simple.

That complicated.

"Is your dance card full tomorrow?" he asked with a lightness of tone he didn't remotely feel.

She studied him for a long moment. "No, but I'll be fine. You have a job and a life. I appreciate the day, but you've discharged your duty to Sophie, and I'll tell her that."

Neither the cop nor the man wanted to hear that. "So if I called you tomorrow, you wouldn't even consider another adventure?"

She appeared torn. "Why would you want to?" When he didn't answer immediately, she went on, "I mean, yes, I'm Violet James—" here she made air quotes with her fingers "—but I'd hoped we were beyond that. Are we?"

He felt her slipping away. "I thought we were, and I'm sorry as hell if you can't see beyond your position as queen of the universe."

Her jaw dropped. "Excuse me?"

"Oh, hell." He rubbed his forehead. He was so damn tired. "I didn't mean that. Most people think of me as easygoing and that's generally true, but that doesn't mean I don't have a temper. My family would tell you that it doesn't make an appearance often, but when it does, it's evil. I'm really sorry about that."

She subsided. "It's okay. I know I sound paranoid and probably whiny when I have no right to complain, given all my blessings, but…" She sighed. "It's just…I try to believe the best of people, to remember where I'm from and the world view I was brought up with. But sometimes I get fooled by those I let in, like the assistant who took some of my lingerie and sold it on the internet."

He couldn't help a bark of laughter.

Her expression was rueful. "I know. It sounds absurd, doesn't it? But would she have done that to a friend? She never even thought of me as a real person who could be embarrassed. It hurts when I think people like me because I'm a celebrity, not because

I'm me. And boy, doesn't that just make you want to puke, hearing me complain when many have it so much worse in life?"

"You had every right to feel embarrassed and hurt."

She sighed. "I try really hard not to get out of touch, to remember what's real, but…" She lifted her gaze to his. "I'm the one who needs to say I'm sorry. Let's try this again."

She took a deep breath. "I had a lovely day, and I'm grateful you would take time out of what is no doubt a busy schedule to squire me around, especially after how I behaved last night. If, after you leave and have a chance to think about it, you decide you're up for more punishment—" here she smiled wryly "—at the hands of a woman who clearly has issues." She shook her head and gave a self-conscious laugh. "Then, yes, please call me tomorrow, should you find yourself with more time to spare. But don't do it for Sophie, okay? I'll make sure she takes you off the hook. And I will absolutely understand if you aren't available." Then she flashed a genuine grin that made him like her even more. "Or interested, for that matter. I do get that I'm not without my negatives."

Damn it. He couldn't afford to fall for her.

But what man could turn down a woman like that?

"It's a deal. Any particular time better for me to call than another?"

"Not really. I mean, I have an old friend who comes by in the mornings occasionally, but I can still take your call. Make it convenient for yourself."

An old friend who comes by in the mornings. Holly Patterson would know Lofton's pattern already, but having this discussion with Violet would help him steer clear of any chance of crossing paths with Lofton and getting on his radar before JD was ready.

"Will do. Now, madam, much as parting is sweet sorrow…"

"You're not the one on vacation. Got it."

He proffered an elbow. "Your chariot awaits, my queen."

"Why, thank you, kindly knight." She took his arm with a quick curtsy.

Oh, damn. He really did not want to like her this much.

CHAPTER SEVEN

VIOLET AWOKE EARLY but didn't remain in bed long. Unlike too many of the mornings since she'd arrived, she was no longer drained by an exhaustion that seemed to go bone-deep. Instead, she was energized and ready to greet the day. This was more like her normal state. She'd never become blasé over the fame and success that had come her way. It was her basic nature to be energetic and enthusiastic about life, she'd certainly been raised that way.

The morning held new promise, and she knew who to thank.

One very hot not-bodyguard.

Easy, girl. But she grinned widely at the thought of JD Cameron, all gorgeous six feet of him. Yes, as she'd told him, she was surrounded by handsome men so often that she dismissed them, and, yes, he was as good-looking as any of them—but to her delight, she'd learned that he was not simply playing the charm game…he was the real deal.

Mostly because he was so much fun.

Sure, he was smooth and clever, but prolonged exposure to him the day before had taught her that she'd gotten him all wrong at the party. His smooth ways were genuine; he was thoughtful and kind. And full of mischief. Quick to smile and intelligent, to boot. She couldn't recall when she'd last had a more fun day.

He'd given her an extraordinary gift by simply being himself and allowing her to do the same. He didn't curry her favor, and he was secure enough to argue with her over the bill for dinner but also to accept her need to pay it.

They may have had an awkward moment or two, especially there at the end, but that was more her fault than his. She could trust him. Even if Sophie hadn't recommended him and the lovely MacAllister clan hadn't taken him to its bosom so heartily, she just had this strong sense of who he was.

Her family would like him. He would fit right in.

Whoa, whoa, whoa. None of that is-he-the-one thinking.

There was nothing wrong, though, with getting involved with an interesting and—oh, yeah, baby— sexy man. He liked her, too, and that certainly soothed some of the ragged edges of her heart. Maybe her dream wasn't dead, if such a decent and honorable man found her appealing when she wasn't in star mode. She'd been herself yesterday, the Violet James who'd grown up in Tennessee.

She rolled out her yoga mat on the lovely balcony that faced the lake where, until last night, she'd had no idea a whole colony of bats lived. She could have been watching them every evening instead of sleeping her life away or burying her nose in a book or having a pity party.

But in truth, she wouldn't have traded anything for experiencing them for the first time, up close and personal.

And, okay...with JD.

She hoped he'd call. Which made her smile at herself because in that moment she could hear herself as a girl, sighing over some jock. It was the modern age, and *she* could call *him* if she wanted him, or she could have any number of men available to squire her around.

But she wanted the one with the wheat-gold hair and the long-lashed eyes that could be sparkling silver or storm-cloud gray.

Oh, girlfriend, you have the beginnings of what sounds suspiciously like a crush.

So what? A good crush got your blood pumping. Violet smiled and began her stretches to greet this glorious day.

JD WAS LATE TO THE TASK-FORCE meeting Monday morning. When he entered the conference room, Doc nodded at him with one arched eyebrow as JD took his seat, but he never stopped the briefing.

JD didn't make a habit of being late—no one did. Doc commanded too much respect for that. But after he'd left Violet and then spent hours combing the area in and around Danger Zone looking for the mysterious Candy—to no avail—the accumulated miles on his feet should have made him tired enough to fall into bed and crash for the night.

No such luck. He'd tossed and turned until two hours before the alarm was set to go off. Candy and her warning about women about to be moved God knows where were partially responsible.

But so was Violet James.

"JD?"

He jerked to attention. "Huh?" His colleagues all had turned toward him with expectant looks on their faces.

"Anything to report?" Doc asked with barely concealed irritation.

He scrubbed one hand over his face. *Pay attention, dumbass.* "Yeah. I do." He glanced around. "I know who Lofton's been visiting." He shot a look at Vince. "Did you already tell them?"

Vince shook his head. "You made the contact." His eyes gleamed with humor at the literal interpretation of "making contact" at the party. "Thought I'd leave that for you."

"Who is it?" Holly Patterson asked.

"Violet James."

Silence, then an explosion.

"Violet James?"

"*The* Violet James?"

"America's Sweetheart is in Austin?"

He nodded. "Vince and I both met her at a party."

"Yeah," Vince drawled. "But JD made a much bigger impression."

"Bite me," JD snapped.

"Romeo and America's Sweetheart," Bob mused. "It figures. You have the devil's own luck with women."

Vince snickered. "You gonna tell them or shall I?"

JD shot him a glare.

"Clock's ticking, people," Doc reminded.

"Okay, we were there for Jenna MacAllister's birthday party, and I ran into Violet. Literally," JD said.

Some wide eyes and chuckles.

"I know," JD sighed. "Not my best work. Had to grab her to keep her from falling to the ground."

Two whistles. One catcall. "Go, Romeo!"

JD shrugged it off. When you dealt with the darkness so often, humor was to be savored wherever you found it. "Yeah, yeah, yeah. She was nice about it, but she also left the party not long after."

"Lover Boy strikes out. Never thought I'd see the day," said Bob.

"What's she doing in Austin?" Trini queried.

"What's she doing with Avery Lofton, is the question?" interjected Doc. "Guess that wholesome reputation is unwarranted."

JD raced to her defense. "I disagree."

Doc lifted an eyebrow.

JD looked at Vince. "Everyone there really liked her."

"They did," Vince answered. "She wasn't a prima donna at all. She played horseshoes with Hal MacAllister, sat on the ground and rolled a ball with one of the babies. She was very normal." He tipped his head. "Unbelievably beautiful, of course, but she seemed genuine."

"So why is Lofton visiting her?" Doc asked. "What's the connection?"

"Zane said they knew each other in L.A.," Vince commented. "Lofton invited her to visit."

"Why?"

JD spoke up. "She's had a rough time out there with the breakup of her marriage. The press has been brutal. So she came here to hide out."

"How do you know all that? I thought you ran her off," noted Bob.

"I got a second chance."

Now even Vince snapped to attention. "Meaning?"

"I'm still not sure how Sophie talked me into it, or how she convinced Violet to go along with the idea, but you're looking at Violet James's new bodyguard."

Mack Lawrence whistled through his teeth.

"You go, Romeo," said Trini.

"You lucky son of a bitch," remarked Bob. "Your streak is intact."

JD squirmed mentally. "It's not like that. She just had a scare when she finally emerged and went out on her own. She has security in L.A., but she'd been promised she wouldn't run into problems in Austin, and she'd rather not have a shadow. I told her I'm not a trained bodyguard, but she doesn't really want that, anyway. I just run interference, pick places where she won't be noticed, that sort of thing. I'm mostly acting as a companion so she can safely get out and see the sights." If only he could keep reminding himself of that and forget the charged atmosphere building between them.

"So what's the connection with Lofton?"

"Not sure yet. I can't rush it."

"She know you're a cop?"

"Yeah. The family had no reason to hide that fact, and Sophie surely explained why she thought I'd be qualified to help. I told her I only teach at the Academy, though, so if she mentions me to Lofton, it would sound like I'm no threat."

"We need to know about him, JD. ASAP."

"I understand, Doc, but this woman has been through a lot."

"Not compared to our vics."

JD rubbed the bridge of his nose. "I know that, too." He glanced up. "After I left Violet last night, I cruised the area, looking for Candy, but not a trace of her. Anybody hearing talk about that shipment she mentioned?"

"Not talk," Mack said, "but some movement at a

warehouse owned under a dummy corporation. Lofton's a partner in it."

"One of our guys in Houston got word of a new shipment coming in, too," offered Holly. "Likely within days."

"I need something to get a warrant for a wiretap on Lofton," Doc said, his look at JD pointed.

"I really don't think she's involved, Doc."

"And what's your evidence?"

They all had to trust their instincts, but instinct didn't get warrants or impress the DA. "I have an opening I can exploit to see her today," JD said.

"Good. First, you meet with APD's sketch artist and get us a face for the Turkish girl. Then you keep your focus on Ms. James, and we'll have other eyes on the area around Danger Zone. Holly, what do you have to report on the surveillance of Lofton?"

Around the table Doc went, and minutes later they were all dismissed.

JD rose to go.

"JD, a minute, please," Doc said.

JD halted. Turned. "What's up?"

Doc studied him for a minute. "You look like hell. You're pushing yourself too hard."

"I thought you wanted me pushing harder on Violet."

"I'm not talking about her. I'm speaking in general terms. You've been on VICTAF longer than anyone but Bob and me. Too long, maybe? I wonder."

JD stiffened. "If you don't think I can do my job…"

"Son, if I thought that, you'd already be gone," Doc said gently. "You've done one hell of a job here, but I'm realizing I've asked a lot of you. No one has spent more time undercover than you, and we all know too much of that is a soul-draining experience. You're damn good at it, but everyone has a limit."

"You going to pull me, Doc? I'm okay, I promise." He had to pursue these bastards and take them down. Had to find justice for the victims who robbed him of sleep.

"JD, I've been in law enforcement as long as you've been alive. I know what burnout looks like, and I'm looking at it."

"Those women and children who died an ugly death last week don't care much about my tender feelings."

"Unfortunately, there will always be victims, and there will always be bad guys."

Didn't he know it? The world seemed to hold an endless supply.

"We can't fix everything, JD, much as that motivates all of us here. But we can't fix *anything* if we burn the candle at both ends. So, I want you to focus on Violet James and stop venturing out on your own surveillance. You will get three square meals a day and a full night's sleep every night you possibly can. Things are coming to a head, and you can't run on adrenaline forever."

"I'm not—"

"Son, don't try to con me. I've been there. We can't lock all the bad guys away and we can't keep all the victims safe, but we damn sure increase our odds if we're in peak shape ourselves. Youth will cover a multitude of abuses to the body, but even you, Mr. Fitness, are not invulnerable. So don't give me any crap, just say, yes, sir, and do it." There was a fond smile in Doc's eyes.

JD sighed. "Yes, sir."

"Good. Now get the hell out of my hair, what I have left of it."

"Don't take me off VICTAF, Doc." JD couldn't leave the room without that being settled. He couldn't go back on patrol or return to the detective squad. What the hell would he do with himself?

"No one else has ever stayed this long, JD. The strength of the concept lies in rotation." He shook his head. "But don't worry about that right now. We'll figure it all out once we've punched a hole in this trafficking pipeline."

JD wanted to stay and argue his case, but he knew Doc too well to believe that would make any difference…never mind that he'd been wondering lately himself about how much longer he wanted to do this work.

But he wasn't suited to anything else. VICTAF fit him like a glove. It was only that he was tired right now, Doc was right about that.

Since there was nothing he could do at the moment to resolve the situation, he focused on what he *could* impact. He'd call Violet and make plans for later, then head to APD and the sketch artist.

"You look different this morning," Avery said. "Sleep well?"

"I did," Violet responded. That wasn't the real reason she was lighter of heart, of course, but she wasn't ready to tell Avery about JD. He'd only worry about her and insist on meeting JD so he could be all big brother about it. He'd earned the right to do it, though, after years of watching out for her and being the most real person in her life, the one she trusted most after her family.

But he'd also feel bad that he wasn't the one introducing her to Austin and standing guard over her. He was under enough strain without her making things worse. He was faithful about visiting, busy or not, and searching for treats to brighten her day took even more time she sensed he couldn't spare.

So she turned the tables. "You, on the other hand, look terrible. Is there anything I can do?"

His expression clouded, but almost instantly he smoothed it over with a fond smile. "Just some... unexpected difficulties to iron out, and only I can solve them. But that's life, eh? Success comes with a price tag...but you know how that is."

"Aren't you the person who kept urging me to hire people to help? And not to micromanage but let them do their jobs? Are you heeding your own advice?"

"Well, listen to you. Want to be my management consultant?" He shook his head and sighed. "I'm sorry I've neglected you so badly. When I persuaded you to come to Austin, I thought I'd have more time to spend entertaining you."

"Avery," she chided. "We're long past that. You're my best friend. You have a life. You've made time for me every day since I got here, and even when we're half a country apart, you're always there for me. It goes both ways. I'm not company. We're practically family."

For a moment he looked unutterably sad, and she found herself wanting to hug him and make whatever was bothering him all better.

But their relationship had always been strictly hands-off, though she wasn't sure why. He was an attractive, intelligent man who, in many ways, should have been perfect for her.

But he was far too crucial to her as a friend. If that door to more had ever been open, it was long ago, and she had the sense that neither of them wanted to risk messing up what they had.

"I just…" He rested his head against the high back of the willow chair under the pergola. "I thought it would be like the old days, where we could hang out, have some laughs. Be young again."

"You're thirty-nine, Avery, hardly rest-home material."

He smiled, but even that was weary. "I know, Vee, it's just—" His cell rang again, and he swore vividly before answering. "Lofton." Whatever he heard had his brows snapping together. "Jesus Christ, can't it wait? What does he want?" He sat up straight as he listened, a muscle flexing in his jaw. "Where is Sage?" If anything, his jaw went tighter. "Get a hold of her and tell her to come in— No, I don't care if she doesn't usually get up this early." A deep sigh. "It's not your fault." His voice softened. "If he calls again, tell him to keep his shirt on. One of us will get back to him." He finished the call and stared off into the distance.

"I can walk around while you make your call," she offered.

"Huh?" His head whipped around as he struggled back from wherever he was mentally. "Oh. No, but thank you. It'll take more than just a phone call." He slapped his palms on his legs then rose. "I'm sorry, damned sorry this keeps happening. I'll make it up to you, I swear." He gave her the quick one-two L.A. air kiss and stepped away, clearly preoccupied. "I just can't tell you when."

"Don't worry about it. I'm doing fine, I swear." She traced an X over her heart. "Thanks for dropping by."

But he was already heading off, shoulders rounded. She'd never seen him like this before. Oh, Avery wasn't playful like JD—he'd always tended more toward the serious, but then, he'd had to be. His father had abandoned Avery and his mother when Avery was only twelve, and he'd had to grow up fast. If his mother hadn't died when he was in high school, Violet doubted he would have ever pursued his acting dream because he'd have stayed back in Colorado to be the man of the family.

Now Violet was his only family. He'd taken her on to protect, just as she'd tried to care for him by getting him roles.

She didn't know this world he was involved in now, hadn't met or spoken to anyone at his club but him. In fact, he'd always made certain she had his personal cell number and always called her back promptly. So she had no idea how to help him or give him relief from his burdens except to stay out of his way and accept whatever time he could give her.

But that didn't stop her from worrying over him or wishing she had the power to smooth those frown lines away.

After a moment of staring off in the direction he'd departed, Violet shook herself and looked around the grounds, trying to figure out how to occupy herself until she might have the opportunity to hear from JD. She decided to walk over to the main building and see if she could tempt Sophie into putting her to work so she wouldn't feel so restless.

Instead, about ten paces into her journey, as if she'd conjured him up, her phone rang, and it was JD. With a smile, she answered.

"Hello?"

"Mornin', Glory."

"That's what my daddy calls me," she said.

"I have to confess you don't make me feel particularly paternal." His baritone voice got a little husky. He cleared his throat. "Hope that doesn't bother you."

Her heart gave a foolish little flutter. "I think it would bother me a lot more if I did have that effect."

She heard him exhale. "You make it difficult for a man to think clearly."

"Yeah?"

"Don't sound so proud of yourself."

She chuckled. "So how was class today?"

A slight hesitation. "I don't teach every day. I sometimes get called in on other stuff."

"Like what?" She chewed her lip. "Dangerous work?"

"Naw. Mostly just lending another set of experienced eyes to put the pieces together. I was on the streets, then I worked Vice for a while."

"Sort of a cop consultant, is that it? You could make big money in L.A., consulting on scripts."

He snorted. "From what I see on film and TV, I don't think the script writers are listening to their experts. Either that, or their experts really aren't experts."

"Oh, really? Not real enough for you, Mr. Policeman?"

"Do I hear insult in your voice, Hollywood?"

"Not really, just…I always do a lot of research for my parts."

"You ever played a cop?"

"Only in a romantic comedy."

"There you go."

"Excuse me, but comedy is difficult to pull off,

much harder than drama, I'll have you know. If you ever tried it, you'd see what I mean."

"Whoa, now. I also wasn't insulting what you do. You happen to be very good at it."

"But it's all anyone wants to see me do. I'm tired of being typecast."

"That last film sure broke the mold. You got nominated all over the place for it, didn't you?"

"But I didn't win the Golden Screen Award."

"Well, that's because the voters were blind. And jealous."

Stated so simply, as though there was no question, his response warmed her. "I was really disappointed," she confided. She'd said that to no one else, not even Avery.

"But you know you gave an excellent performance, right?"

She nodded, though he couldn't see her. "I did. I gave it my all."

"That's the real reward, isn't it? Knowing that you put everything you had into it? You don't control the rest, but with what you could control, you hit the ball out of the park."

Listening to him was like having a thorn removed from tender skin. "Thank you."

"For what?"

"For bringing me back to common sense. You're absolutely right—I was focusing on the wrong thing. Usually, I'm fine knowing I did the best job I could, though of course I have to be careful about which roles I choose because the films have to make money. That's all most of Hollywood worries about, not critical acclaim. I mean, acclaim is nice, but the money guys only care about that if it increases box office. As an artist, though, you don't perform for the money. You do it because it satisfies something in you that needs to create. Performing on stage is actually much more rewarding—you get immediate feedback from your audience. In film, you shoot it out of order and in pieces, and the only feedback you get is from the cast and crew, but all of them have their agendas. At least until you see it with a test audience, and then—" She halted. "Sorry. Talking too much about things you can't possibly be interested in."

"You don't know me well enough to be familiar with what I'm interested in."

A dose of reality. "That's true."

"So you shouldn't be worrying about whether I'm bored or not. Tell you what—I'll be sure to snore real loud if you put me to sleep, that a deal?"

He made her smile. "Deal. But anyway, I'm done nattering on."

"Not nattering, but we can save it until I see you. Did I give you time to visit with your friend?"

"You did."

"So your dance card is freed up?"

"It is. How about yours?"

"I decided to take some vacation days. I've got too many stacked up."

"Oh, JD, I don't want to—"

"They were so happy to see me go, they practically carried me out the door. The rest of today, I'm all yours—that is, if you don't get sick of me."

That span of time loomed bright on the horizon. "Well, I'll snore really loud if I get bored," she echoed.

He laughed. "A clever woman is worth her weight in gold, my dad always says. 'Course that's because my mom is scary intelligent and would bean him with a skillet if he said otherwise."

Violet grinned widely. "I would love to meet your family. Maybe to commiserate."

"Well, ouch."

"Do they live nearby?"

"Nope. They're way out in Lubbock, where I grew up."

"Your brothers there, too?"

"One is. He farms cotton with my dad. The oldest one. The good son."

"And what are you?"

"The baby boy."

"You have my condolences. I'm the baby girl."

"I knew I liked you. So do your brothers think you don't have the brains God gave a flea, and your mom still calls you her baby? And everybody believes they need to tell you how to do every last thing?"

"It's a little scary how well you know my family."

"Amen. When I have kids, I'm letting the little one boss everybody around and making the big kids take orders."

She giggled. "You want kids?"

"Oh, yeah. I mean, I wasn't in any hurry and I'm still not, well, not exactly, but…things I see in my line of work remind me often that you don't know how much time you have. I guess I'm finally about tired of fooling around. Might even have to grow up, sad as that is to have to say."

"So is Mrs. Cameron all picked out?"

"Uh…no. Not even on the horizon. I did say *about* tired of fooling around. How about you?" He hissed as he remembered. "Sorry. Forgot. Honest, Violet, I said that without thinking."

"It's okay."

"It's really not."

"You don't have to tiptoe around me. Yes, that's a painful subject, but mostly because I'm the only divorced person in my family in anyone's memory, and here I am, a two-time loser."

"There's not one ounce of loser in you."

She hesitated, then confessed her fear, "Maybe there's something in me, some ingrained failing."

"That's ridiculous. Neither man deserved you."

She sighed. "Even if that's true, how come I have such poor judgment?"

"'Cause you're a romantic, just like your movies."

She did a mental double take. "Wow. I never looked at it that way."

"There's no shame in it, Violet. The world needs more romantics. Where would we be if no one believed in love?"

Her heart squeezed. "I do want children, but I can't seem to figure out how to find their father first."

"You could be a modern woman and have them without a man."

"No. No, I couldn't. Or at least, I won't. I know it's terribly old-fashioned, but I believe in the traditional family. I don't pass judgment on others, but I really hope I can manage to follow in my parents' footsteps. I know a lot of single mothers who do an excellent job raising their children, but it's a hard life for them, and it's lonely. There's enough of a romantic in me to keep hoping I'll find that one man who loves me for myself and who wants to build a home and a family together." She sighed. "But in my business, that's not easy. Zane is one of the few who's managed it."

"He's a good dad. All the men in that family are."

"They remind me of my father and brothers that way."

"Mine, too."

They fell silent for a moment.

"Well!" he said brightly. "Now that I've got you all bummed out, I'm sure you'd like nothing better than to spend the rest of the day with me."

"I'm not bummed out. It's kinda nice to be able to talk to someone who understands the world I came from."

"Someone disgustingly normal?"

"Normal squared."

They shared a chuckle.

"Okay, so since I'm on a roll, let me ask you just how much you like the outdoors."

"I told you yesterday that I love it."

"Up for a little hike?"

"Absolutely. Where are we going?"

"Well, I was trying to think of where we could go that you'd encounter the fewest people, and there's a place about a half hour's drive called Hamilton Pool. It's a nature preserve with a waterfall where Hamilton Creek spills into a pool with a grotto."

"Sounds gorgeous."

"It is, and the best part is that school isn't out for the summer yet, plus it's a weekday, so it shouldn't be crowded. But it's a dusty trail, and there are rocks to climb over to get into the heart of the grotto. You have clothes for that?"

"I'll figure out something."

"We could swim, too, if you wanted to."

"Maybe."

"You don't like to swim?"

"Love to, just…" She only had a bikini with her, and suddenly that seemed intimate.

"Well, bring your suit if you want to, and if you feel like swimming when we're there, fine. If not, fine, too. The water will probably feel good on a day like today. But whatever you decide, I'll throw some towels in the truck, and I'll pack us some snacks."

"Oh, JD, don't go to all that trouble. Couldn't we stop at Whole Foods and pick something up? Isn't it close to here?"

"Yeah, if you like healthy stuff. Girly food."

She laughed. "Girly food. Whereas you'd pack, what, some white bread and bologna?"

"Hey, what's wrong with good old bologna?"

She shook her head. "You are too much. Okay, here's the deal. I happen to have access to an amazing kitchen just across the grounds. Let me see if I can wrangle something for us from Sophie, since you're arranging all the rest. Or if she doesn't have anything, since she's only feeding me right now, with my—gasp—girly tastes, then we'll stop somewhere and grab something on the way."

"At Whole Foods?" He sounded slightly sick at the prospect.

"You didn't get that physique from only eating barbecue."

"You noticed my physique? Score!"

"Oh, get out of here. Bring your bologna if you just have to have it, you plowboy, but I'll arrange my own. We'll see who winds up eating whose food. Now I'm going to get ready."

"That's harsh, Hollywood. I think you hurt my feelings."

"I'll be ready in thirty minutes, plowboy."

"Me and my white bread will be waiting."

She hung up, laughing.

As he drove back to the club, Avery Lofton's phone rang.

"What's going on? Why did you have Leslie wake me up?" Sage demanded.

"Are you alone?"

"Yeah, but I didn't get to sleep until nearly five." She yawned. He could easily imagine her there, tawny hair tousled by sex, long, supple she-cat body naked in the satin sheets she preferred.

They'd had a go at each other, several torrid months, until his head had cleared enough to realize that they could be lovers or partners but not both.

Sage Holland was greedy and venal and ambitious. Also smart as hell. And damn good at making money.

But lately her vices were causing him concerns.

"Not my fault you insist on picking up hotties at the club."

"Not my fault you're living like a monk lately. It's making you surly."

Enough dithering. "What's making me surly is cleaning up your messes."

"What the hell does that mean?"

"Bately called the club this morning. Thank God he didn't say anything specific to Leslie, but he insisted he needed to speak with me when she told him you weren't available."

"What did he want?"

"I haven't talked to him yet. I've been tied up."

"Another of your mysterious morning errands? Where do you keep disappearing to, Avery?"

"You get to have a life outside the club but I don't?"

A charged moment of silence. "You're the one who thinks we should keep things strictly business between us." Her voice turned to a purr. "I miss you in my bed, Avery. Nobody does it for me like you."

If he let himself, he could fall right back into her quicksand. Sex with Sage was explosive and dangerous and…unforgettable. But you could never be sure if you'd escape without parts missing.

One of those parts that had gotten lost had been, too often, his brain. Hence his current situation. "Sage…"

"Screw you." Then she laughed, but it was brittle. "You're no fun anymore, anyway."

That was another concern, Sage's mercurial moods. Sometimes they were drug-induced, but there was an instability to her, a counterbalance to her brilliance, that threatened to explode even when she was stone sober.

Dealing with Sage was like juggling lit sticks of dynamite.

But he was in too deep to do anything but keep juggling. Their fates were inextricably intertwined.

"Bately probably wants to beg for more time," she sneered. "Or lower payments. He's a pain in the ass, a constant whiner."

"Should've thought of that before you decided we needed to get into the blackmail game."

"Don't give me that. We couldn't run enough money through here to stay in Lima's good graces. He was going to cut us out, you know that as well as I do. We needed options."

"Well, you sure found them, didn't you?" Avery gripped the steering wheel with white knuckles. "I can't talk about this right now. I'm at the club."

Spending time with Violet and then reentering his

own world was like breaking open a scab and watching the blood well. Being with her reminded him too much of the young dreamer he'd been.

And how far he'd drifted from the man she'd known.

"I'll call Bately," Sage said.

"Let me know if there's a real problem."

"I can handle him." Her voice was icy as she disconnected without saying goodbye.

You'd damn well better, Avery thought. *We can't have anyone get out of our control, not now. It could cost us our very lives....*

CHAPTER EIGHT

"So we're west of Austin now, right?" Violet rode in the passenger seat of his pickup, scanning the scenery.

"We are, indeed, out in what's called the Hill Country. This used to be strictly ranch territory."

"Cattle?"

"More often goats. This land is so rocky, it's hard to grow good crops, and you'd go bankrupt bringing in hay for cattle. Goats can fend for themselves. They'll even eat trees, if they have to. If you have goats, you don't need a lawn mower."

"Goats are cute."

"See them much in LaLaLand?"

She looked at him askance. "Have you ever actually been to California?"

"Nope. Don't need to." He said it just to get a rise out of her.

It worked. "Excuse me? You can't just say something like that."

"Sure I can. I know everything about the place already. Land of fruits and nuts. Granola country. The Left Coast—home of every crackpot in America."

"Seriously? You can't spout such drivel—" Her head whipped toward his, and he could just imagine the sparks in those turquoise eyes currently concealed by sunglasses. Then she shook her head. "Of course you're not serious. What was I thinking?"

"I can be serious," he protested. She had no idea.

"Uh-huh." She tipped down the darkened lenses, her luscious cherry-red lips curving at the corners. "Be sure to alert me when that happens. I wouldn't want to miss it."

"Deal. But let's just remember who bought hummus and fruit and junk."

"How does a plowboy know about hummus?"

"Hey, I read." He grimaced. "Looks nasty, though." Actually, he liked all kinds of food, including hummus—but he wasn't about to tell her so.

"If you're nice, I'll share a taste, and then you'll be hogging the container."

"Nope. Got my bologna sandwich, so I'm good." She hadn't actually seen what he'd packed.

"If you honestly eat as badly as it seems, it's a miracle you don't weigh three hundred pounds. My trainer would expire from fright."

"You have a trainer?"

"It's Hollywood, JD. The script girl has a trainer."

"I guess it's sort of your job to stay in shape."

"You have no idea. Fortunately, I like exercise—well, until Randy gets too brutal. It's the not eating that kills me. I do love food." She glanced over. "Ergo the healthy *junk,* as you call it. I've eaten much too well since I got here and had far too little exercise, mostly only my yoga."

He looked her over. "You seem pretty prime to me. Not to be a chauvinist, of course."

"The camera adds ten pounds."

He sensed a strange undercurrent of insecurity in her words. "Do all those women really think having a teenage boy's figure with boobs is attractive? Me, I think the fashion world is run by gay guys, and their idea of beauty is a woman who looks just like them."

"That's terrible," she spluttered. But her shoulders were shaking with laughter.

"Am I right? You bet I am. A woman looks like a woman, and people tell her she's fat. Then folks wonder why teenage girls are bulimic and such. Well, excuse me, but a man wants his woman to have curves. Hips he can put his hands on. Softness, not a body that feels like his own." He glanced over. "Sorry. Didn't mean to rant, but if your trainer is selling you that hard body crap, you need to ditch him. Real men don't want stick figures with fake boobs."

Her head was cocked as she studied him. "I guess you can be serious."

"Don't get me started. In my line of work, I see what happens when people treat others as if they're not human. There's too damn much 'me, me, me' attitude these days, folks being so callous about others, and it sure seems as though your business is one of the worst for that. Everything's about what's hot right this second, and good people like you are chewed up and spit out as though they don't have feelings, as though they aren't people. Am I right?"

She removed her sunglasses. Blinked.

"Sorry. It gets me wound up. I just… I just think it's a crime, all this emphasis on the superficial. That whole attitude of use them and discard them, that sense of survival of the fittest and dog-eat-dog competition…I've seen the hell that results when people are reduced to commodities. When they are loaded in trailers with no food or water and some of them—"

He exhaled. "I'm sorry. Not sure where that came from."

Except he did know.

But he couldn't afford to let down his guard like that. Especially not with her.

"Don't apologize. I can't imagine how you do what you do— I mean, back when you were on active duty." She shook her head. "You witness the worst of mankind, don't you?"

Yeah, and you never forget it. He shrugged. "You just…you handle it." Or you burn out.

"I never thought about how that creed of cynicism and depersonalization spins out from the world I operate in to become something evil, but you're right. I live in the most artificial atmosphere imaginable, yet most people have bought into it. Even me, to some degree. It's all about the surface and almost nothing is about the person you are inside." She stared ahead, elbow on the window frame, head resting on her fist. "That's part of why I ran away to Texas. Things seem so important in Hollywood that really aren't." She glanced at him. "Especially compared to what you've seen. I feel foolish, ever worrying for a second about crazed fans or tabloid rumors."

"Don't. In your world, they can be just as dangerous."

"My small and incestuous world."

"What you do has a positive impact, though, never doubt it. You reach a lot of people."

"Even with my little comedies?"

He snorted. "Not so little." Man, he'd sure derailed their easy mood. "Okay, I'll just say one more thing, then enough with philosophizing. My point is that there's nothing wrong with a real woman's body and a real woman's face, like yours. Never let them make you feel otherwise. There's more to you than your appearance, and age won't change that. My grandmother is more beautiful than ever, and she's eighty-five. Her beauty comes from who she is."

Her brows rose, and her smile was brilliant. "I wish you called the shots out there. Professionally, I will pay a price for it soon, but for your information, no one's coming near me with a knife or a needle. That very well may mean the end of my career, especially in the genre where I've been pigeon-holed. Once I'm not pretty and young, I'll still be able to do comedies, but I'll be reduced to supporting roles and slapstick, to being a caricature. Still, I hope that when that day comes, I'll retain at least a little scrap of my upbringing, enough to prevent me from stooping to cosmetic surgery."

"You're smart and talented—you can be whatever you want. Haven't you already proven that to yourself?"

She bit her lip. "I don't think you understand the essential insecurity that's at the core of every actor. If we were happy being ourselves, we wouldn't need to escape into a character." Her smile at him was fond. "If you could bottle your confidence, you'd make a killing in my world. Of course, then there would be no movies because we'd all be too steady and secure and real."

She laughed, and he tried to laugh with her. Would she be laughing if she knew who he really was?

"Nearly there." He pointed at a sign and turned off into the parking area. "Cool. No one here but us." He parked his truck and cut off the engine. "Ready?"

She nodded. "Ready."

JD HAD WAVED HER ONTO THE PATH in front of him, but she'd demurred, preferring to follow him since she was in unfamiliar territory. The preserve they'd run in yesterday had seemed remote and peaceful compared to her life in L.A., but this…the wind seemed exceedingly loud until she realized that was simply because nothing else competed with it.

Though she'd already spent two weeks unwinding, she could feel her muscles unknotting, her mind clearing…opening to new possibilities and unfamiliar sensations.

And to his credit, other than glancing back now and again to be sure she was with him, JD didn't try to fill the silence.

She'd been astonishingly wrong about her first impressions of him. He was charming and handsome, yes, but he kept surprising her with depths and sensitivities she didn't expect.

He was funny and kind. He was confident enough to be generous—he didn't need to build himself up by bringing anyone else down. His silence now was another aspect of that confidence. Secure in himself, he didn't have to draw attention.

And he was wiser than she would ever have imagined. His vehemence over how girls and women were brainwashed to view their bodies…none of that was feigned. How would any woman hear him speak of his grandmother's beauty and not be moved?

Plus, she liked that he acknowledged her own looks as simple fact without being smarmy or manipulative, without making her feel either hunted or begrimed. *It's nice that you're beautiful,* he seemed to say, *but tell me who you are.*

She could be in real trouble with this one, oh, yes, she could. He had all the earmarks of The One.

Don't get ahead of yourself.

He halted, and she'd been so lost in her thoughts she nearly ran into him. He stepped aside to show her the view.

"Oh," she said reverently. "Oh, my."

"Yeah," was all he said.

The trail wended its way into an honest-to-goodness grotto. The azure pool lay before them, fed by a waterfall spilling from the land above. Behind the waterfall, a shallow cave, cool and shady. Moss and greenery draped over limestone, the air still and cool in the summery day. Across from the waterfall, a jumble of huge rocks formed a platform perfect for sunning or diving into the cool water below.

JD remained still at her side, allowing her space and time to absorb it all. To simply be.

At last she blinked and resurfaced. "I would almost say we could go now. I feel restored already."

He gave a quick slash of even white teeth. "There's more where that came from."

She inhaled, a deeper breath than she'd taken in forever. "I am so there."

"I hear you. I found this place when I first moved to the area, and it still helps me clear my head. I've never brought anyone here before." He extended a hand. "Come with me."

She placed her hand in his. The warmth of his palm, the firm yet gentle clasp of his bigger hand around hers made something inside her feel cosseted. Safe.

Somehow understanding what she needed, he led the way behind the waterfall, coming to a stop half in and half out of the sunshine, where both shade and sun were accessible.

Giving her options. Being thoughtful. Very much like his basic nature, she was beginning to grasp. That he was sharing his refuge with her touched her.

"This look okay?" he asked.

"It's amazing." She closed her eyes and breathed deep. "What a great idea."

"Even with bologna on white bread?" he teased.

"You remind me of my brothers."

"You could have talked all day without saying that." She grinned. "You know what I mean."

"Yeah." He spread the blanket he'd brought along. "Milady…" He gestured with a sweep of his hand. "Your banquet awaits."

She settled on the blanket. "I'm not really hungry yet, but you go ahead."

He sank down beside her. "I'm fine, too." He stretched out his long, muscled legs, his cargo shorts revealing golden skin dusted with hair a few shades darker than on his head. "Water looks inviting."

"Is swimming allowed?"

"Most of the time, except after heavy rains. They put up a sign, or there's a ranger to keep people out. Why? You tempted?" He waggled his eyebrows. "You bring your swimsuit, Hollywood?"

"Wouldn't you like to know?"

His eyes went hot. "That's wicked cruel. My guess is that you're wearing it, and—" He slapped one hand dramatically to his chest. "That is not an image to make a man rest easy. Have mercy, darlin'."

She rolled her eyes. He might be a better man than she'd originally given him credit for, but he hadn't forgotten how to be a flirt. "What about you? I don't see swim trunks anywhere."

"I'll show you mine if you'll show me yours." He mimed a villainous twist of an imaginary mustache, eyebrows raised.

She chuckled. "Maybe later."

They sat in companionable silence as the waterfall provided background music. After a few moments, Violet lay back and simply let the peace soak in. She must have dozed for a few minutes because she didn't realize he'd moved until she heard the splash.

She opened her eyes but didn't sit up.

Oh, my. She watched as JD swam quietly across the pool and lifted himself out on the opposite bank, muscles rippling across his back. Water sluiced off his broad shoulders, trailing down to lean hips. His soaking wet cargo shorts clung, outlining one very fine behind.

He turned and prepared to dive in again, flicking a glance in her direction. Quickly she squeezed her eyes shut, feeling as though she'd violated his privacy. She kept them closed as she heard him slice through the water on his return.

Still she didn't look. Not, at least, until he moved close enough to drip on her. When she felt the cold water on her heated skin, she popped her eyes open and squealed.

"Faker." He roared with laughter. "And here I thought you were an accomplished actress." Before she could dodge, he'd scooped her up in his arms and wheeled toward the pool.

"Oh, no, you don't—"

"Come on, Hollywood, live a little." He climbed up

on the rock, carrying her as easily as if she weighed nothing.

"JD…"

"Water feels great." He stepped forward then hesitated. "You don't have your phone in your pocket or anything, right?"

"What if I do?"

He studied her for a second, then that beautiful mouth curved. "Don't gamble with a gambler, sugar."

And he leaped.

She didn't have time to scream before they went under. She tightened her arms around his neck as, with a powerful kick, he brought them back to the surface.

And grinned unrepentantly.

They began to sink, but she wasn't worried about drowning because she'd already seen that he was a strong swimmer.

So was she.

With another strong kick, he lifted them both to the surface and swam with her to the rock ledge. His flesh was warm against the cool silk of the water. She didn't break away, instead letting herself revel in the feel of his body against hers.

Time rocked to a halt. The moment spun out. She had a sense of a threshold reached, a choice to be made. She could pull away, reduce the moment to harmless flirtation. Avoid any possible risk of choosing the wrong man again.

Or she could see what happened next. Right here before her was not only a very sexy man, but one she was increasingly sure had a good heart. If she never took another chance on a relationship, however brief, she would never know if her past problems were due to her choices in men…or some fatal flaw in herself, something that rendered her unlovable and doomed to never make her dream happen.

She hadn't gotten to this point in her career by running away from risk.

Keeping her eyes locked to his, she slid her arms up his chest. Their legs tangled together. The water was cool, but not enough to chill his body's powerful response. Before she lost her nerve, she pressed her mouth to his, sliding her tongue slowly over the seam of his lips.

A small shudder ran through him.

With a rush, he gathered her in, seizing her in a torrid kiss, the taste of him bold and spicy and dizzying.

She tossed any remnant of caution to the wind, grazing her mouth across his jaw and down, nipping at his throat.

"Sweet Mother MacCree—" His voice dropped to a near-growl, and he proceeded to deal out his own torture. One hand slid beneath her shirt, fingers skating over her belly in teasing circles.

She arched to bring him closer. Her legs parted and wrapped around his waist.

"Violet…" His voice was a harsh whisper as she rubbed against him with painful slowness, tormenting herself as much as him.

Then they heard voices.

"Oh, hell." JD lifted his head and swore colorfully.

"Amen." Her sigh was heartfelt. She looked over his shoulder. "I don't see anyone yet."

"It won't be long." He rested his forehead against hers and echoed her sigh. "Come on, sweet lips. I need to get you out of here before somebody recognizes you." He pressed one last, quick kiss to her mouth then lifted her onto the bank, following her with a powerful thrust of his muscled arms.

They began gathering their things.

"I still don't know if you have a swimsuit on under there," he whispered, as the voices got nearer.

She grinned and faked a leer. "Find us another picnic spot, and maybe I'll show you." She was surprised to feel mischievous, not terrified of exposure.

"Stop tormenting me, woman. I don't know if I can stand up straight as it is." He slid the tote bag with their food over his shoulder, then balled up the blanket and held it against him, walking in an exaggerated hunch.

Violet laughed. "Whine, whine, whine." She smacked him on the behind and went around him.

He chuckled. "Don't think you won't pay for that."

She flashed a smile over her shoulder. "You have to catch me first." She ran, barely stifling a foolish, girly squeal as she heard him catching up.

He tossed the blanket at her so fast she automatically grabbed it, then he scooped her up in his arms before she could blink.

"JD!"

"Hide your face in my shoulder. Someone's coming."

She squealed again, and he threw part of the blanket over her head. She felt his chest vibrate with his laughter.

Until, that is, she began to nibble her way up his chest.

Then all she heard was a barely suppressed groan.

Along with a few muttered promises about what would happen when they were again alone.

CHAPTER NINE

AVERY WENT UP THE STAIRS to his office, right next door
to Sage's. They shared a connecting door, though each
had an entrance from the hallway. Both offices were
heavily soundproofed because they overlooked the
dance floors. Though he liked most of the music the
club played, hearing it night after night could get a bit
much. As it was, the heavy bass beat still made their
office floors vibrate, but that was part of the deal. A
low, thumping base was an intimate part of the sexual
dance that was the reason places like Danger Zone
existed.

It was all about sex, the forbidden undertow of the
carnal, the appeal of danger and risk that kept the club
bouncing seven nights a week. He was so tired of it.

He glanced out the one-way smoked glass of his
office, automatically checking to be sure the cleaning was well underway, the liquor deliveries were on
time. Sage wouldn't be here yet; though she lived in a
sky-high condo only blocks away, Sage never rushed
her toilette. All the pots and potions that resulted in
her sex-bomb-meets-Amazonian-goddess allure took
time to apply.

Even he, who'd been as close to her once as she ever
allowed anyone to be, had never witnessed the process. Sage let no one beneath her formidable armor,

not even him. She was a black-widow spider, deadly and irresistible all at once.

He'd seen her body naked countless times, but never her face. Her makeup, whatever it consisted of, wasn't heavy or thick, and he wondered just how much she needed it to be beautiful.

She didn't, he suspected.

But what she did need was its protection. He'd asked, but she'd never told him why. Threatened to throw him out of her bed if he ever asked again. In thrall to her potent allure at the time, he'd complied. And now they weren't close enough. If they ever had been.

He glanced at his watch, but only ten minutes had passed. He cursed and thought about calling Bately himself.

Just then, he heard footsteps he recognized. He started toward his hallway door to greet her, but she went on past and into her office without pausing. She had to know he was here—his Jag was parked in his usual spot.

Never mind. He needed her focused. For a second, he glanced at their common door but decided against cracking it open. She'd arrived surprisingly quickly; she must be as concerned as he was. Let her keep her attention where they needed it—on Bately. He'd hear the results soon enough.

He sat at his desk, the sleek black console in keeping with the décor that carried out the theme of the club below—thick, sensual cushions, subdued mood lighting shimmering off metal and leather and glitter... techno meets power meets sex. He tried to concentrate on the schedule of acts over the next six months, but one ear was always cocked for the sound of the connecting door and the verdict.

Alan Bately owned key warehouse properties in Houston and San Antonio—one was a port city and the other was on Interstate 35 which ran from Mexico to Canada—both were crucial to a step he wanted to take.

Why be only a money man for Jorge Lima when he could supplant Lima altogether? In fact, he'd already begun the process.

Sage didn't know—she thought they'd chosen Bately to ingratiate themselves with Lima for a bigger piece of the money-laundering pie. It was true that Bately gave them additional capacity for laundering money, since many tenants paid in cash. Avery had originally thought that way himself, but then he'd realized he'd set his sights too low. He could *be* Lima, not work for him, if he played his cards right.

The connecting door's knob clicked as Sage turned it. He spun around in his palatial leather chair. "Well?"

"He wants out. He's lost his nerve."

"And then you discussed how his family and friends will react when the video of him with a fourteen-year-old girl winds up on the internet?"

"I did. He says he's going to confess to his wife."

Avery arched an eyebrow. "That ought to go over well. You believe him?"

"I don't know. He says he'll go to the cops after that. He says he's talked to a lawyer buddy of his who claims we'll be in more trouble than he is. Says we have until midnight."

"Or what?"

"He's probably bluffing." Sage seemed unusually

shaken. "But we can't take that chance. We have to stop him. He's a danger to us now."

"No shit. We won't have to worry about the cops. Lima will kill us first if Bately talks."

"I know someone. I'll make a call."

"To do what?" But he knew. Somehow it wasn't hard to believe that even murder wasn't beyond Sage. "Not yet. I'll go down there, talk to him in person."

"I don't think it will help."

"I never signed on for murder, Sage."

"I'm not going to jail."

"Just let me see what I can accomplish. I'll leave now." He'd have to cancel with Violet, probably tomorrow, too. Damn it.

But he couldn't worry about Violet right now.

"Do not do anything until I get back in touch with you."

She waved him off. "I'm calling my guy. I'll put him on hold, but I want him ready."

"Sage, chill. Do not screw this up."

"Bately's the one endangering us all. I'm giving you until ten, then my guy goes in."

Avery clenched his hands into fists and glared at her, but Sage's chin jutted in defiance.

That unpredictable mood of hers was a problem. *She* was a problem.

One that might need solving, too.

He left without another word.

DAMN. VIOLET WAS NOT ONLY beautiful but nice, intelligent, sexy…and surprisingly down-to-earth for a woman so many put on a pedestal.

Plus, she was fun.

JD had been in a lot of difficult situations on the

job—his life on the line, beat all to hell, excruciatingly bored on stakeouts, sickened by man's cruelty to his fellow beings…

But his current dilemma was misery of a sort he'd never encountered. He was an undercover cop; part of his job was to deceive people for the greater good. He'd told more lies than he could count, feigned innumerable identities, used his skill with words to portray situations however he needed them to appear—but always in the name of justice. Of course there had been unavoidable collateral damage sometimes. He'd never welcomed it, but he'd known it was necessary to take down the bad guys, to keep good people safe.

But deceiving Violet…

He never had trouble maintaining a cover while still keeping sight of who he was at his core and why he was there.

Today, however…for long moments he'd skated dangerously close to forgetting his case, his goals, the fact that she was—had to be—a means to an end. A very important, very crucial end.

Close, hell—when they'd been in the water, he'd forgotten everything but her and how very, very much he wanted her. And worse, how easily he could fall for her.

And wouldn't that just be a kick in the ass? He could picture Doc now: *so let me get this straight. You learned absolutely nothing about Avery Lofton, who likely is laundering millions for a cartel that has enslaved countless women and children, has murdered more than a few of them…because you couldn't keep it in your pants?*

It's not like that, Doc. Is that how he'd explain? *She's… much more than that. I like her. I could even fall—*

Oh, no. No, no, no. *Do not even think the L word. Because that is so not going to happen.* He had a job to do, and that was all that could matter.

"JD?" she said as she used a towel to squeeze the water from her hair while he drove.

He didn't even know where he was going.

"Are you all right?"

"Me?" He forced himself to look at her, to dredge up a smile. "Hell, yeah." *Gotta do better than that, dummy. Get a grip.* He tried to unscramble his brains, back up from that cliff. "I mean, for a guy with clammy, wet shorts, that is."

"I hear you. So where are we off to now?"

To hell in a handbasket, his grandpa would say. "I'm thinking about that. You want me to drop you at Sophie's so you can change?" *And then I can get the hell out of there,* he thought, even as his mind was stuck back in that pool, still craving her. *Think.*

"The way things were going back there, I thought maybe…"

Her cell phone rang. Her glance darted at him, then away. She opened the glove compartment and removed it. "Hello?"

Her face brightened. "Oh, hi, Avery. What's up? Did you get free, after all?"

JD could only hear the man's tone faintly.

"Oh."

But he could hear her disappointment. Vividly.

"That's all right. Don't worry, really. Things come up. When will you be back?"

Where could Lofton be going? Shit. He had to let Doc know. What if he was taking a powder? Could he be feeling the heat already? Had something happened that JD wasn't aware of?

"One night. Big deal. I'll be fine, really."

JD wondered if Lofton could hear her lack of conviction.

"Of course. Makes sense that you'd be coming in late. Two days without your smiling face won't kill me. It's not like we don't usually go months without a visit. And I can always call you if I— Oh." Her voice fell. "Sure, that's fine. Cell coverage isn't good everywhere. No one gets that better than me. Reception on location is always dicey, so I understand. Just call me when you get back and have time. I can take a cab to your place, you know." She listened again.

"My bodyguard?" She cast JD a sideways glance he couldn't decipher. "Well, I can see if he's available to bring me to you so you don't have to...oh. Okay, sure. I understand. Sophie's isn't that far from your club."

Even a blind man could see her disappointment that Lofton wasn't welcoming her to his place. What the hell was he hiding there? If only JD could learn enough to justify a warrant....

"We'll work it out, Avery. You don't have to take care of me. I'm a big girl." Then she chuckled. "Okay, so you've been taking care of me for years, but what's your point?" This smile was more genuine. Fond. "You have a safe trip, hear?" She disconnected the call and held the phone close to her chest, staring out the windshield.

"Problem?"

"What? Oh. No. Just my friend Avery, the one who invited me to Austin to visit. He's designated himself my one-person entertainment committee, and he's been religious about coming by every day to cheer me up. Now he has to make a quick business trip to look at a possible second location, and he just wanted me to know why he wouldn't be coming by tomorrow. Not that I asked him to come every day, but…it has been nice."

"Second location? Must be doing well. What kind of business?"

"He owns two businesses, actually, Scarlett's, the restaurant, and a club called Danger Zone. I haven't been there yet. Do you know it?"

"Sure do. It's a hot spot. No wonder he's looking to expand." If that's what he was really doing. "He say where?"

"Houston, he said."

Ah. Houston. A port city. Where he could meet a shipment? Maybe this guy was more involved than they thought.

He had to get in touch with Doc. But he also had to find a reason to get away long enough to do that.

Meanwhile, Violet was watching him. He scrambled to fill the gap. "Well, hey, that sounds like a good thing for him. You've known him a long time?"

"Nearly half my life. He was my Sir Galahad when I moved to L.A., fresh off the turnip truck." Her smile was both sad and fond.

"Sounds like a story."

"He's the best friend I ever had. He showed me the ropes and kept me from starving. When neither of us had two pennies to rub together, we shared what we had. He had faith in me when no one else did."

Oh, man. So Lofton was truly important to her. How far would she go to exorcise her sense of indebtedness?

"He must be proud of you for all you've accomplished."

A line formed between her brows. "Mostly. It's been

hard for him, though. He was an actor, too, but…he never got the breaks I did."

"Maybe he didn't have your talent."

He could practically see her back arch. "Avery was talented—is, I mean. And I tried to return the favor. Once I had the leverage, I made sure he got a part in every production."

"Ouch."

Her head whipped around. "What does that mean?"

"Nothing. Sorry. None of my business."

She sighed and slouched against the seat. "No…I know what you're saying. He's a proud man, and it didn't take him long to realize I was behind the offers." A faint smile. "We had quite a shouting match over that." She was silent for a minute. "I meant well, but I think I broke his heart. Working on my films and getting no other offers was a nasty wake-up call. He left to come to Austin not long after. I try to tell myself he's better off."

"Isn't he? I mean, it sounds like he's a success."

"He is, no question. It's just…" She shook her head. "Everything's different now. He's so stressed out, and even though he's the one who invited me here to visit, he didn't ask me to stay with him. I shouldn't be hurt—his hours are hideous—but…" She blew out a breath. "And this can't possibly be interesting to you, even if my reactions weren't so…girly."

"But you are a girl," he pointed out. Then, to cheer her up, he waggled his eyebrows. "As I can readily attest." It was his turn for a gusty sigh. "At least, sort of, I can. Damn tourists."

That elicited a faint grin. "I'm a tourist, if you'll recall."

"Naw. You're an international star. That means you waltz right in anywhere and fit in." He glanced over. "Don't be bustin' my bubble now. You won't, will you?"

His foolishness seemed to lift her spirits—at least, enough for her to roll her eyes. "Right. I just show up and—poof! Everybody loves me."

"Exactly my thoughts. It's sort of a superpower." When she giggled like a girl, something new inside him unfurled.

No. He could not get his heart involved. Period.

And he still needed to call Doc. Pronto. "Okay, let's test your mettle."

She lifted one eyebrow.

"I'm going to run you back to Sophie's so you can get out of those wet clothes. After you've changed, we can go to my place so I can do the same—but you have to wait on the porch long enough for me to shove laundry under the bed, throw out pizza boxes, get the place presentable. Shouldn't take more than, oh, an hour or two."

"That bad, huh? Bachelor pad?"

"Worse. See, I got this idea—okay, my mom had been hammering on me, and Vince was just as bad, but then Jenna started in on me, and—hell, I still don't know how it happened, but I bought a house. *Do you know how much money you're throwing away on rent, sweetheart?*" he said in a falsetto. "My mom is ruthless."

"So now you have more room to make a mess of?"

"Well, not exactly. I got a great deal because Vince found this fixer-upper. No surprise—the whole clan is completely unbalanced over the do-it-yourself deal.

Vince was remodeling his house when he met Chloe, who had done much of the work on hers. Jesse and Diego have a sick level of talent at anything creative, and Jenna heads this nonprofit that helps the disadvantaged become homeowners, sort of like Habitat for Humanity. So everyone's all *'JD, there's nothing to it. Here's a hammer and some nails and a paintbrush, now get to it.'* And, yeah, I was raised on a farm, and we learned to do just about everything for ourselves, but—"

She was outright laughing now. "So how bad is it?"

"One room is almost finished."

"I'm afraid I have to see this."

"Oh, you should be afraid, all right. Be very afraid." They exchanged grins.

"Sounds perfect. I'm in," she said.

"In over your head, Hollywood, I'm warning you."

But not any more over her head than he was.

He turned into the drive at Sophie's and punched in the combination for the gate. "Oh—I just remembered that I need coffee. And, okay, toilet paper. I'll go grab some and be right back here before you finish changing."

She was shaking her head and grinning as she emerged from his truck. She waved goodbye, and he waved back.

But he noticed as he left that she was still standing there, watching.

And when she finally turned, she seemed so fragile and small, so vulnerable.

JD rubbed one hand over his heart. *What in the hell have you done, dumbass?*

He couldn't begin to formulate an answer.

Instead, he pulled out his cell and called Doc.

VIOLET WAS DOUBLY GLAD right now that her quarters were separate so she didn't have to drag herself through any public areas looking like a drowned rat.

Though at the moment, she wasn't sure how much she cared. Her body was still buzzing from that interlude in the water, and she wasn't at all sorry they'd have a chance to be alone later at his place. Yes, she was a paying guest here and shouldn't be concerned over what anyone thought of her choice of guests or whether anyone slept over in her quarters, but Sophie's was so much more than a hotel to her already—and she did care what Sophie thought.

The MacAllister clan was a close-knit bunch, and they included friends in their definition of family. She was the interloper, and JD was well loved. Sophie and Cade would feel protective of him. JD had been asked to provide security for her as a favor to them, and they might see her as preying upon a relationship that should have been only business.

But there was absolutely nothing businesslike about the way JD made her feel. That man could kiss…oh, lordy, he could kiss. Then there was that strong, gorgeous body, those changeable, magnetic gray eyes, the sharp intellect, the humor that sent all her defensive walls tumbling…

This trip to Austin to recuperate had suddenly taken on a whole new shine, and that was pretty amazing, considering she had intended to swear off men after Barry's betrayal. She'd come to Austin wanting only to feel safe, to find time to heal out of the public eye. Never once had she even considered meeting a man, much less getting involved with one.

But this man…JD might be called a lady-killer, but there was much more to him. He felt like someone from home, someone of the same background and values. He could be much more than a fling.

Hold on now. Half a country separated them, and they had incompatible careers, she reminded herself. And she was still raw from betrayal.

Violet unlocked the door to her suite and entered, then leaned back against the door. JD made her forget all about her real life when she was with him. Taking her to his special spot, creating a bubble around her, a lovely little time out of mind…it was easy to spin out fantasies of what could be.

And L.A. did have a police academy, plus Violet knew the mayor personally, so she could—

Wow. So tempting to blot out the fact that any relationship between them would have to survive the harsh glare of her celebrity, the spotlight that would be turned on him, too. He'd brought a ray of hope and joy into the last two days, but how fair would it be to subject him to the nastiness of Hollywood, the gossip, the constant pressure to play a role?

He was strong and secure in himself, but what would he think of her milieu? Could he possibly understand the pressure for her to pretend constantly, to have so few places where she could be herself and not have to worry about letting anyone down?

But he did have all the makings of the man of her dreams, and his reactions to her healed a lot of the damage Barry's infidelity had inflicted. JD gave her hope that maybe she wasn't fatally flawed. Maybe some man could come to truly care for *her*…maybe even this one.

Good grief. Avery had often teased her that she should have been a writer because she was so good at spinning out fantasies from a simple statement, a faint impression.

And he was right. Here she was, worrying about JD and a future when they'd only shared a couple of hot kisses. JD wasn't pledging his undying love or begging her to stay—he was hot for her, yes, as she was more than a little ready to take things further with him, but the most he'd offered was today and tomorrow.

Violet shoved away from the door and headed for the bedroom, stripping as she walked, rolling her eyes and laughing softly at herself.

The universe had aligned to grant her good fortune: two days with a fascinating man while Avery would not even be around to ask questions. She would leave a message for Sophie, should events proceed as her sizzling nerve endings wished, keeping her away for the night. Maybe Sophie would understand and maybe not, but Violet had to get over her too-sharp need for the approval of others.

JD was a big boy. Violet hummed deep in her throat, remembering how that applied in more than one sense. She grinned at herself in the bathroom mirror— *oh, you bad girl*—then stepped into the shower, singing.

JD TEXTED DOC. Lofton leaving for Houston ASAP.

His phone rang before he'd even parked at the grocery.

"Hey, Doc."

"Leaving as in running away?" Doc asked.

"Not that I can tell. He told Violet he'd be back late tomorrow."

"What else?"

"Only that she's not part of it, Doc. I'd stake my life on it."

"I guess that's nice to know."

"Yeah. Though it doesn't much help our case." But he was relieved to know his sense of her hadn't been off. Or that he was this attracted to a monster hiding behind a beautiful facade. He realized Doc had said something. "What?"

"I asked what your plans are now."

"I told her I was off today and tomorrow." Though he was more reluctant than he ought to be if he really had his mind on his job, he made the offer to Doc, anyway. "She's expecting me back any minute. Need me to…damn. That's the problem with saying I teach at the Academy. Tough to manufacture an emergency."

"No, we're covered. You stay close. Even if she's not a part of it, he checks in with her. That gives us another way to keep an eye on him."

"Yeah, but I could be doing something more important. Like nosing around Danger Zone or helping to follow leads on the waitress." Or on Candy. He still hadn't been able to track her down.

"The others can handle that. You've got access no one else has. What's their relationship, her and Lofton?"

"Long roots. Deep ties. Calls him her best friend. But complicated, too. They were both starving young actors, but she made it. He didn't."

"Anything we can learn about him or his movements is information we need. You stay with her as much as you can. If I have to pull you, I will, but for now, you're on vacation through tomorrow. I'll get the word to Houston, and we'll be watching that warehouse. Lofton say where he was when he called her?"

"Not that I could tell. He said he'd be back late to-morrow and would come see her the next day. He usually comes in the mornings, but from what she's said, he just drops in. I hadn't thought it a good idea to be around when he was, but want me to change that?"

"No. If you're there when he shows up, we'll deal with it, but otherwise, I agree with your take. Don't give him a reason to become cautious."

"Got it." Should he tell Doc he might be spending the night with her? "Doc…things with Violet are…a little heated."

"Romeo strikes again, huh?"

It's not like that, he wanted to protest.

"Whatever it takes, JD," Doc continued before he could respond.

But there was a sly amusement in Doc's voice that JD couldn't just slough off as he usually did. "She's a good person, Doc. She's not…it isn't…" But he had to stop because he honestly didn't know what this was. He just knew it wasn't simply a job.

"Whatever keeps you close." The humor was gone, and somehow he felt even worse. "That's your assignment right now. Stay close. If she trusts you, Lofton might, too. That kind of access is everything. I gotta go now. Be safe."

"Yeah. Always." JD disconnected and walked inside the store, but it took him a minute to remember why he was here.

If she trusts you…

She was already starting to.

And he'd never felt more tainted by the life he led.

CHAPTER TEN

VIOLET HAD, AS PROMISED, showered and changed quickly. Her stomach was jumpy in a way she hadn't experienced in a long time. She glanced out the window and spotted Sophie and Skeeter.

Good. She'd go down and visit until JD returned.

As she descended the stairs, Skeeter saw her and dashed over, leaping up, tail wagging.

"Skeeter, no!" Sophie reprimanded. "Clearly, we still have work to do."

Violet laughed and bent to him, ruffling his fur then clasping his jaws. "Oh, but who cares? You are the most handsome boy," she crooned.

"It's a wonder he can get his head through a door. I tell him the same thing all the time." Sophie approached, smiling. "Cade says I spoil him terribly."

Violet grinned. "Like I haven't seen him sneaking Skeeter treats."

Sophie shared a smile. "Too true."

"Has Cade already left?"

Sophie nodded and sighed softly. "I always miss him so much, but his work is important to him, and he's so good at what he does."

"He's extremely talented, that's for sure. But it's not hard to see that he's reluctant to leave you."

"He doesn't actively court danger anymore, thank heavens, but neither of us counted on him needing to travel so much when I couldn't go with him. His new book about his best friend Jaime has hit big." Her smile was fond. "I couldn't be happier for Cade. Jaime's death haunts him still, but the book's proceeds go to a fund for Jaime's family, and the strength of reader response helps with the guilt he still feels because he survived when Jaime didn't. Knowing he's taking care of Jaime's family eases his mind."

"That has to be hard for him. If I weren't here, could you go along on this trip?"

"Oh, heavens, no." Sophie's response was instant. "We went into this knowing our lives wouldn't be like others', that we'd have to forge a different path to accommodate our diverse careers. One of these days, I'll feel more able to leave the hotel in other hands for a time, and once he's done with the publicity for this book, Cade hopes to be able to stay around more, but…" She shrugged. "It's not like we met when we were young and unformed and could build our life together from scratch. We have to be inventive. Flexible. But love will find a way, right?"

"I'm not really the best person to ask that."

"Oh, Violet, how thoughtless of me. I'm so sorry."

"Don't be. I'm honestly glad for both of you. I still believe in true love, however much I've bungled my own relationships."

"You're hardly the one who bungled them." Sophie's indignation was heartwarming.

"That's a matter of opinion."

"Well, anyone who disagrees is just wrong. You're a good person, Violet. You deserve a happy ending."

"Let's not get ahead of ourselves," Violet responded drily. "I think I'll leave that to you, at least for now. You're clearly better at it."

Abruptly Sophie teared up.

"What's wrong? Did I say something—"

Sophie waved off her concern. "No, it's not you, it's—I'm sorry. I don't know what to do. I love Cade so much."

Violet touched her arm. "But Cade's crazy about you, too."

"I know. It's just that…I suspect I might be pregnant."

"Oh." A little tendril of envy. Sophie had a man, a wonderful man, who loved her…and now that man's baby. "So…" she began cautiously, "you don't want it?"

"No! Oh, no." Sophie spread her fingers over her belly. "I love her already—or him. I don't care, it's just that…"

"From what I can tell, the MacAllisters are big on family. Are you worried that Cade will be unhappy?"

"Not really…or at least, he'd never say so, but…it's too soon. And I don't want us to get married only because we're having a baby. I haven't done a test yet, but I remember how this feels. I just couldn't tell him before he left. Not until I'm sure. And I'm—" Sophie's slender fingers pressed to her lips.

Scared. Suddenly Violet heard the words Sophie hadn't said. She'd lost her family once before. Violet touched Sophie's shoulder gently. "Tragedies like yours don't happen twice, Sophie."

Sophie turned, gripped her hand. "I realize it's not logical, but I'm just so happy and…"

"Can you talk to your family about this?"

"I don't have any family. I lost my parents when I was a child."

Good heavens, no wonder Sophie was spooked. Tragedy had indeed struck twice. Violet tried to imagine a world in which she had no one who loved her, no one to turn to. "I'm sorry. And I'm an idiot. I'd be scared half to death, too." Violet was renowned for her clever wit, her ready repartee, but right now she had no idea what was the proper thing to say.

Sophie grinned. "Thank you."

Violet stared. "Thank you?"

"It helps to hear someone say it out loud. To know I'm not crazy or paranoid or…" She smiled at Violet, and her eyes shone. "Cade'll likely be thrilled, as will his whole family…I just…this love was so unexpected. I thought I was done with love, that I was better off without all that you risk, given all that can go wrong…" In an uncharacteristic move for her, Sophie clasped Violet in a quick hug. "It's terrifying to be so happy, you know?"

Violet understood intimately the risks of letting yourself revel in that emotional abandon. Sophie had suffered enough in her life. Violet hoped with all her heart that this woman she'd come to like so much would never have to come down from her cloud.

She'd like to think that she'd be on that cloud again herself—only with a man who truly loved her. Ruthlessly banishing a little tug of envy, she smiled back. "What plans could you possibly have that are better than having a good man love you and the two of you cherishing the child who's the result of that love?"

Sophie teared up again. "Oh, look at me. I never cry. Never." She hugged Violet again. "Thank you." For a moment she clung.

Then she straightened. "There's JD."

"Oh." On the heels of Sophie's revelation and all the longings it stirred up in her, Violet wasn't sure how she felt about seeing JD now.

"Violet? Is JD…he's treating you right, isn't he?"

"He absolutely is." She glanced over her shoulder to see him coming through the gate. Oh, but that grin of his… She couldn't help a little sigh.

Sophie smiled. "Yeah. A nice hunk of man candy, isn't he?"

Violet spurted out a laugh.

"You're blushing. Not that I blame you. Go for it, girl. He's not only gorgeous, he's a good man. I trust him completely."

Before Violet could respond, JD was right in front of her, a look in his eyes making her glad she'd chosen the halter-top flowered sundress instead of jeans. "Hey, Sophie," he greeted without ever taking his eyes off Violet.

"Hi, JD. How are you?"

I want to get you naked, his expression clearly said.

Violet felt her body react. She arched an eyebrow, meeting his challenge with her own.

He rewarded her with a quick, devilish grin before he tore his attention away. "Uh, did you ask me something?" he said to Sophie.

Sophie shook her head. "You two kids go have some fun. You have plans?"

"He's taking me to see his house."

Sophie's eyebrows rose. "Really?"

"You haven't seen it, Soph. You don't know how it really looks."

"Stories abound."

"Jenna and her big mouth," he complained. "I'm making progress, honest."

"I hear we need a work day," she teased. "Like you all did with me here."

"Not that I wouldn't appreciate taking you folks up on it, but my manhood's been challenged. I have to do the work myself or I'll never hear the end of it from Vince, for starters."

Sophie glanced at Violet, shook her head. "Men. They're so predictable."

"Hey, now," JD began.

"So it's in worse shape than he warned me?" Violet asked her.

Sophie opened her mouth, but JD spoke over her. "She hasn't been there. She doesn't know. Repeat, she does…not…know. Not for sure, anyway."

Violet looked at Sophie. "It's a test of my courage. I have to do this."

"I guess so, but don't say you weren't warned. And call me if you start feeling faint."

"Yeah, yeah, yeah. Very funny, you two." JD took her hand. "I won't let anything scary get her, Sophie. Cross my heart." He demonstrated.

"I'll sic Jenna on you if you don't."

"Now that's just mean. Ready, Violet?" He glanced down at her, eyes more serious than his words.

To be with a kind, generous, extremely sexy man? Was she ever.

"Yes." She turned and hugged Sophie, whispering in her ear. "Don't wait up."

"I won't," Sophie whispered back. "Have fun. And, Violet…?"

Violet mimed zipping her lips. *Our secret,* she mouthed as JD towed her off.

"Look, we really don't have to go to my place," JD said as they drove. "I could take you back to Sophie's and come get you after I shower and change or…"

"What? You're reneging on me? Wild horses couldn't keep me away."

Oh, man. Her cheer and mischief only made him feel worse. "I'm not sure if it's better to tell you that the place isn't so bad and hope that predisposes you to believe it when you see it…or tell you it's one step up from a dump. Then you might feel so sorry for me you'd work hard to disguise your horror."

"Does it matter what I think?"

Their gazes locked. "I'm afraid it might." Then he pulled his eyes away to concentrate on his driving.

Keep it light. Don't think about all the lies under-pinning everything.

Easier said than done. He grasped for the first topic that hit him. "Skeeter's great, isn't he? I've been con-sidering getting a dog, except—" Crap. He'd been about to say that his work hours were so unpredict-able. "It wouldn't be fair to have a pet in a war zone."

"Now I really cannot wait to see this place."

"Well, you're about to get your wish." He rounded the corner and onto his shady street. Halfway down, he pulled into what could laughingly be called a driveway—two parallel, broken tracks of concrete about forty years past useful. He glanced at the two-story structure that could be the setting for a haunted-house movie, its weathered paint—what there was left of it—a contrast with the brand-new roof that he'd just paid for with money that could've bought him a Harley instead of merely keeping him dry.

"As bad as you thought?" He tried not to wince as he waited.

She didn't say anything as she emerged from his truck and turned a slow circle to take in the houses around him, a jumble of beautifully-restored Victorians side by side with teetering bungalows and single-family-turned-boardinghouses for students.

Get back in the truck, he wanted to order the longer she went without speaking. *I know it's a dump, but—*

"The trees are amazing," she said first.

He didn't give a damn about the trees. Though he did, of course—they were a compelling reason to buy here. But—

"This feels like a neighborhood, a real one. Like you could make a home here." Her eyes were wide with wonder as she looked at him.

His tension eased a little. "Sort of. I mean, people are trying." He gestured around. "But there are hold-outs, landlords who don't give a damn about the neighborhood or its character—such as that one." He pointed to a bungalow across the street and down, dirt lawn and junker cars lining the driveway and in front.

"But look at that one," she said, gesturing to the house to his right. "They've really made it shine." She focused on his then. "Your house has good bones, doesn't it?"

It did, but he was surprised that she saw that. "You know construction?"

"Um, does it count that I love to watch HGTV?"

He enjoyed the relief of laughing. "You're ahead of where I was when I started looking. I got the MacAllister clan full-court press on what to search for. My real-estate agent was ready to kill me because I had to have every house vetted. According to the family, my life would have been worth nothing if I'd screwed this up." He nodded toward his house. "So I can verify that, yes, it does have good bones. The structure is sound, and I can make something of it if I really want to." He glanced over. "That's a direct quote from my mom, by the way."

They shared a quick grin. "So do I get to see the inside?"

"You do recall the whole shoving laundry, throwing away pizza boxes thing, right?"

"It can't be that bad. I have brothers. I've been in their bachelor pads, and I survived." She shuddered dramatically. "If only barely."

"Consider yourself warned—again." With great trepidation, he unlocked the door and gestured for her to proceed ahead of him.

She stepped into the wide entry, gazed at the staircase that curved upward to the bedrooms. "Oh, that's beautiful."

Beautiful? The scarred banister, the treads that dipped in the center?

"Don't you love it?" She turned to him, eyes wide. "Can't you just picture a woman descending this a hundred years ago, her long skirts trailing behind her as her hand glides down the banister?"

He blinked. Took another look. "I'll be damned."

But she was moving ahead of him to the right, going for the heavy sliding doors that sealed off what had once been a parlor. She tugged at the doors, but couldn't make them budge.

He put his muscle into the task. "These rooms are closed off for now."

When the door opened, she made her way to the center of the room, taking in the peeling wallpaper, the high windows and their dirty glass. "Oh, look at this old wavy glass. You can't find these windows anymore."

"You're telling me," he muttered. He'd priced replacements, and these windows would be waving for the foreseeable future, no matter how much wind whistled through the panes.

She ran her hands over one sill. "The woodwork is beautiful." Then she glanced down and gasped. "And random-width pine floors!" She gazed up at him, eyes glowing, noticing his staring. "What?"

"Don't tell me—the MacAllisters recruited you to their unholy alliance. Either that or you're blind and can't see all the stains and scarring on this floor."

A white smile sparkled as she flicked away his negative comments. "Nothing a little elbow grease can't fix."

He made an elaborate show of perusing his elbows. "The grease done dried up, Miz Scarlett."

Violet laughed. "Okay, so there's a lot of work here, but still… JD, this will be a showstopper when you're done. Aren't you proud of yourself for how you've rescued this lovely lady?"

Wow. All he saw, most of the time, was what was still in desperate need of repair. "Thank you." He studied her for longer than he should have, then caught himself. "Okay, one room down. Don't assume you've seen the worst. You're in for it now. No stopping until we're done. You'll just have to buck up." He proffered an arm. "Madame, shall we continue the tour?"

"Oh, please, kind sir." She dropped into a playful

curtsy then slipped her small hand into the crook of his elbow.

The dining room, straight across the hall behind another set of sliding doors, sent her into another swoon. He had to admit that under the influence of her admiration, even he regarded the place differently.

"A buffet here, against this wall, and a big oak table centered on an area rug…" Violet had deserted him and entered the room, tapping one finger on that lush lower lip that he wanted another taste of. "A big mirror over the buffet would give you another view of the— what?"

"I think I'm jealous of my house."

One delicate eyebrow arched. A slow smile curved her lips. "You could show me your bedroom."

It was all he could do not to growl like some caveman and grab her.

But she hesitated, as though she felt awkward. Violet James, famous movie star, awkward?

He didn't know what the hell to do. No way was he pushing her into anything, yet she'd already expressed enough self-doubt that he knew he could hurt her by rejecting her.

Apparently she decided, though, as she sauntered toward him. "We do have some unfinished business, don't we?" Her fingers walked up his chest, and she rose to her tiptoes against him, her body soft and sweet, enough to make a man lose his mind.

"You are killing me," he said.

"I really, really don't want to do that." When her hands slid into his hair and her mouth brushed over his, he was most of the way to gone.

He fought his way back to the surface. "Violet, um, are you sure…"

She hesitated again. Lifted uncertain blue eyes to his. "You're not?"

"No, that's not it. I just—"

"If you don't want…" Hurt crept in, trapping him between a rock and a hard place.

"Oh, honey, I very much want." Though his soul was surely damned. He gathered her in and returned the kiss.

Doc's words echoed in his head: *if she trusts you, Lofton might, too. That kind of access is everything.*

Damn it, Doc, how the hell am I supposed to do this?

"JD, stop worrying. We're both adults."

"But you're—"

"If you say I'm Violet James, I won't be responsible for my actions." She smiled up at him then sobered. "And if you're worried about my bruised heart, well, that's really nice and just tells me you're as good a man as I thought." She trailed her forefinger down his chest. "You also have this very hot body. I'm told there are those who think the same of me."

He raised his hand as though he was voting.

She chuckled. "I like you, and back at the pool, I thought we were both very interested in each other. Was I wrong?"

It was so much more complicated than that, but there was no possible way for him to explain, so he went with the simplest, most basic answer. "Absolutely not."

"So maybe we could just spend a little time enjoying ourselves and not thinking?" Her sideways glance was full of mischief.

"Thinking is overrated." Which was God's honest truth.

She smiled and tightened her arms around his neck. Then kissed his socks off.

He scooped her up in his arms and headed for the stairs. She focused on driving him out of his mind.

When he stumbled crossing the entryway, he leaned his head away from the temptation she presented, even though his libido whimpered for him to give in. "You have to stop that," he ordered as she nibbled her way over his jaw. "I'm only going to give you another hour of my time. Or two." He tried to focus on negotiating the stairs.

Then she slicked her tongue down his neck. "Okay, okay, a week, but that's my final offer." She chuckled softly, blowing warm air across his skin.

Sweet heaven above, his eyes all but rolled back in his head.

With grim determination and more than a few missteps that had his heart doing double-time in fear they'd wind up in a heap at the bottom of the stairs, he somehow made it up both flights. Why in the hell had the master bedroom been put all the way at the back?

Violet's hand slid inside the collar of his shirt and her fingers walked their way across his bare skin.

The upstairs hallway took an hour to cross, he would swear.

When he finally got them inside his bedroom, she lifted her head and began to look around.

"No." He tossed her on the mattress. "Don't start talking to me about woodwork."

She giggled. Glanced upward. "But the ceiling is—"

He planted his arms on either side of her head, his body hovering over hers. "No ceiling. No floors. No glass."

A smile danced over those lips before she licked them, slow and sultry. "That's okay. I like what I'm looking at better." She began to unbutton his shirt, spreading the panels wide. "Much…much…better." She began a provocative survey of his chest, stroking his pecs, drifting down his belly, tracing a lazy line along the waist of his jeans….

"Mercy," he murmured.

"No mercy here." She challenged him with knowing eyes.

He leaned back on his knees and grabbed her hands. "Uh-uh. My turn." He spread her arms wide and took his time looking. "Your beauty staggers me."

"Thanks." Her tone said she'd heard that a million times.

"But I'm more intrigued by what's beneath this gorgeous exterior. I want to know the real you."

To his astonishment, the light in her dimmed.

What had he said? Shouldn't she be pleased that he wasn't focused on her as a star?

Maybe there's something in me, some ingrained failing.

She actually thought her husband's adultery was her fault? That it was due to some flaw in her? For a stunned second he said nothing. Could she possibly believe she was unlovable?

Would anyone ever imagine that America's Sweetheart, adored by millions, didn't understand that the pure, amazing person she really was shone from her like a beacon? Was the reason everyone worshiped her?

As his silence mounted, she yanked her arms down and began to roll to the edge of the bed.

He stirred from his reverie and caught her. Tucked

her into his arms and cradled her. "Hey...talk to me."
He went with his gut and hoped to hell he wouldn't
make things worse, however astounding it was to think
that he could. "Is this about you believing you have
some fatal flaw?" When she didn't speak, he settled
back against the footboard, holding her on his lap.
"Because that's just crazy."

She shoved away his arms. Scooted all the way
across the bed and pressed herself against the head-
board, arms wrapped tightly around her middle. Her
eyes blazed. "It's not your concern. I don't need any
coddling." She uncoiled and made her way to the edge
of the mattress. "And I sure don't need your pity. I
am sick to death of people feeling sorry for me." She
jumped to her feet and prepared to leave.

He lunged and caught her, turned her around not at
all gently. "You honestly believe I see you as pathetic?
Were you not listening when I told you that I think
you're amazing? You're funny and kind and damned
normal for someone in your situation." His voice vibrated with barely contained fury, though it was di-
rected squarely at himself, at the situation.

"So why are you angry?"

"I'm not."

One imperious eyebrow arched. "You are." She
paused. "Perhaps I should go."

He hated this. Despised knowing that he couldn't
have an honest conversation about how he felt about
her, that he had no choice but to continue to deceive
her until VICTAF could get what it needed on Avery
Lofton and be sure exactly how involved he was.

And if she ever found out, his betrayal would make
a lie of every reassurance he'd just uttered. Would
make her only more convinced that so-called flaw

was real, that no one could love her simply for who she was.

This case could not be over soon enough.

He had little control over the situation he was in, but there were a few things he could do. One was to quit focusing on what he couldn't change—and do something about what he could.

He could salvage this day. At least he hoped he could.

"The anger is for me. I'm supposed to be showing you a good time, and I'm blowing it." He extended a hand. "If you're willing to give me a second chance, may I show you the rest of the house?"

After what seemed like a year, she put her hand in his. Met his gaze. "I'm the one who should apologize. I'm trying to put the past behind me, but I'm not there yet. And I've made things awkward when all you were trying to do was be nice."

God, could he feel any worse?

"I think you're managing a lousy situation with a lot of grace. Does anyone in your life understand the true cost of your success?"

She cast him a grateful glance, if a cautious one. "It's not exactly a hardship to make a lot of money doing something you love."

"Maybe not." A predicament he'd likely never experience. "But it's not that simple, either, is it?"

"Nobody held a gun to my head and forced me to become famous. I asked for this."

"But nobody prepared you for it, either, did they?" She shook her head sadly.

"I'd like to be your friend, Violet." He hoped she could tell he meant it. "Not the actress but Violet from Nowhere, Tennessee."

"Elizabethton, I beg your pardon." Her lips curved a little. "I'd like that, too."

He breathed an inner sigh of relief as the atmosphere between them lightened. He drew her through the doorway out of the bedroom. Humor had eased her before; maybe it would again. "So if I let you ogle my claw-foot tub, what are my chances of getting you naked later?"

Violet snickered as she preceded him down the hallway.

But he was pretty sure he heard her say *not bad.*

CHAPTER ELEVEN

THE CLAW-FOOT TUB WAS INDEED gorgeous, especially in a room with bead board on the walls—however many coats of paint covered it—and a lovely stained-glass window. With a crack, yes, but the deep purple, golden-throated irises and the white dove set a scene she could easily imagine sighing over as she stretched out in that tub. As she felt knotted muscles untangle inch by inch while steamy water soothed her skin and lapped at the curve of her breasts...as JD slowly trailed his fingers up her legs and—

"Does that smile mean you like it?"

Violet whirled too quickly and overset herself.

As he had been so many times before, JD was there to steady her. Tenderly he stroked a lock of hair back from her face, tucking it behind her ear. His eyes were a smoky seduction, all by themselves. Idly she noticed a bump on the bridge of his nose and reached up to caress it. "How did you break it?"

"Brothers tend to fight." His gaze was zeroed in on her, too, though he held himself still. Letting her choose what would happen next.

She traced the line of his nose, the plane of one chiseled cheekbone. Curved a trail back over his jaw then, fingertip by fingertip, her hand walked toward his chin. She brushed the pads of three fingers over his skin, then stroked downward, skimming his Adam's apple to land in the hollow of his throat.

And this big, strong man...shivered.

She returned her gaze to his for a long, somber moment. Words died, but her nerve endings thrummed to life with his nearness, with the desire that was a throbbing presence between them.

Violet lifted herself to her toes, but even as she brought her lips to that dip above his collarbone where she could see his pulse bump up, she wondered if JD realized that what attracted her far more than his beautiful exterior was his goodness.

He played at boyish charm, at devil-may-care insouciance...but within this man, she thought, was someone who took his word seriously. Who would never cause harm if he could help it, who would think of others first.

A protector. A champion. A hero, however he might protest.

His looks would change over time. Age would have its way. But the man he was at his core...that was rock solid.

She'd settled on her heels, but now she rose again to slip her fingers into the rich pelt of his hair. She pressed her body to his body and wondered if the uneven thudding she felt was his heart...or hers.

Might be both.

"I was going to show you the downstairs," he murmured.

"Later."

"Violet, maybe we should—"

She nipped at his ear and felt his whole body quiver. "Don't you want me, JD?" she murmured. "Have I ruined it?"

"Of course I want you, but—"

She slid her tongue into the heat of his mouth.

And JD's iron control broke. He gathered her closer and slanted his mouth to take more of her. Without ever lifting his lips from hers, he bent and scooped her up, then walked out the door. "Should we go somewhere else?" he asked as they neared his bedroom.

A clean slate? she suspected he was suggesting.

"Uh-uh," she said against his mouth. "It's a good bed. A big bed." In fact it was a massive, gorgeous four-poster in some golden wood that looked like it could sleep six people.

He smiled but didn't stop kissing her. "Room to roll around." He revolved and fell back on the mattress, still holding her. Then he proceeded to do just that— logroll them to the opposite corner, then back again.

She was breathless with laughter by the time they stopped.

Could he possibly understand the allure of his willingness to be foolish? In her world, appearance was everything, followed closely by an outsized sense of dignity, by the need to be taken seriously, to be respected…or, at a minimum, to be feared. Glamour might seem to be the game in Hollywood, but power was the real aphrodisiac, the gold standard by which everyone judged or was judged.

Lying on his back, JD spread his hands across her pelvis and lifted her into the air the way her father had done when she was a child. She held her body in a plank, astonished at his strength.

Then he lowered her, inch by inch, her hair hanging down between them, a tangled black curtain sealing them off from the world…until her body was lined up on his, belly to belly, breast to chest…loins to loins.

She didn't even try to stem the urge to bring her softest spot against his hardest one.

"Unh…" His was a heartfelt groan.

It was all she could manage not to echo him. Instead, she planted her arms on either side of his chest and straddled him, her skirt shifting upward, baring her thighs as she rubbed herself over him and wished for more.

"Violet…" His plea was a harsh whisper, an urgent demand.

"We're attracted to each other, JD. You make me happy, and you want me. I want you. Let's not make it more complicated than that." She lifted her arms and caught up her hair as her body reveled in the feel of him. She lowered over him, undulating against his groin and ratcheting up the torment, teasing them both to a nearly unbearable degree. Through her lashes she watched him, watched the hunger drawing his skin tight over his cheekbones. His fingers flexed at his sides, grasping thin air as though he longed to be grasping her flesh.

But still he held back. Was strong enough, kind enough to let her set the pace.

She let the moment spin out until within her desire wound tighter and tighter, nearing the breaking point—

At last she released her hair and let it spill out in all its glory. Slid her hands beneath his shirt, her nails dragging over his chest until his belly was bared, revealing golden muscles lightly dusted with hair.

When her lips touched his skin and her tongue dipped into his navel—

JD gasped. Grabbed her. Flipped her over.

Rising above her, he tore off his shirt and quickly untied her halter top, then drew it down slowly, teasing her already-peaked nipples. He fanned the fever, swirling his tongue over one crest, humming a low laugh as she squirmed beneath him. His big hands grazed her thighs, driving the skirt higher and higher until his fingers found her panties. Slid beneath the silk.

Made her back arch. Made her moan.

Then his mouth replaced his fingers, and she cried out.

Desperation had her pleading. "Don't go slow, JD. Not now."

His chuckle was low and throaty. "The claw-foot tub might not work its magic next time. I'm not wasting this one." His words were a tease, but his voice was rough. His eyes dark as pitch.

She laughed softly. "If I promise?"

He was doing unspeakably carnal things to her flesh, so many sensations at once that her brain gave up trying to sort them out. Pleasure rolled through her in swells, dragging her into the undertow where she couldn't think, couldn't see....

All she could do was fly. Shatter.

"JD..." she sighed sometime later, pliant as candle wax.

"I'm here." He rose to her, kissed her again. She tasted herself on his lips. Then his big, warm body was covering her, shielding her...

But she felt the tension in his body, the steely, wire-tight draw of a man holding back a savage hunger.

She lifted slumberous eyelids to meet his gaze, hot as the fires of hell and dancing on the edge of control. "I want you."

His smile was strained. "In a minute. Hold on, honey." It was all she could do not to shriek in protest as he rose from her and leaned across to fish in a drawer for protection, but she was grateful for his care. The shift proved just enough to bring her back from that bliss-filled languor of repletion, to recover her wits the tiniest bit. As he returned to her, she smiled, slow and wicked. "Oh, please...let me." She took the condom from his hand and nudged him onto his back. Then she bent to him and proceeded to apply it with her mouth.

"Sweet mother of—" His swift intake of air was quickly drowned by a groan as she cupped the family jewels in her hand and slicked around them with her tongue.

"Okay, that's it." In one quick blur of strength, he had her on her back again. And thrust inside in one powerful stroke.

She sighed. He groaned.

They both smiled, a smile Violet felt to her toes.

"Hold on, sugar. This ride is gonna be intense," he warned. And made good on his word.

It was all heat and speed and need after that, but no matter how Violet tried every wile she'd ever learned to make him break, JD would not let go first. Her second climax took her by storm, one minute dancing just beyond her reach, the next sweeping over her like a fireball.

Barely, only barely, he waited until she started up the next peak, hovering on the edge of a scream—

Then, at long last, he cut the reins of his control and followed her, pitching her back over the edge one more heart-stopping, soul-restoring, unbelievably beautiful time.

"I CAN'T FEEL MY FINGERS," he murmured into her breasts, where his head lay pillowed.

She picked up his hand and sucked the index finger into her mouth.

"Okay, that's one. One finger is enough for most activities, right?"

Her abdomen bounced with her chuckle. She exchanged that finger for the next one.

"Two. Even better." He didn't know why he kept up a patter at a time like this.

Except he did. He'd just had the most astonishing orgasm of his life, and oh, hell, yeah, every straight guy on earth would kill to trade places with him. Of course they would. She was not only phenomenal to look at, but making love with her was off the chain.

But that wasn't his problem. That wasn't what had his brain running around like shell-shocked hamsters, had him feeling the urge to leap up—assuming he could actually move—and run as far and fast as he could away from her.

Oh, no. What had him spooked, had him core-deep petrified, was something different altogether.

He'd been with Violet the movie star, yes, but he could deal with who she was to the world by ignoring it. That was manageable as long as she was here in Austin, hiding out where almost no one knew where to find her. Where she could be herself.

But herself…that woman was the real problem, the Violet who was a Southern girl, a funny, bright and normal woman, country-born and raised. A woman a man could imagine in his home, his bed. Rocking his babies. Nestling in his arms, content and happy spending her life with him.

That Violet he already liked far too much. Was way

too attracted to what was inside her, the gutsy, tart-tongued creature he'd swum with, run with, teased and played with.

But even if he didn't feel like crap having to lie both to her and to his friends about why he was with her... even if he didn't have to keep deceiving her for God knows how much longer because it was his job and people were dying out there...

If she ever found out why they'd come together in the first place, any chance they might have for a future would vanish. He could not stand the thought of hurting this remarkable woman he—

Oh, no. God, no. I can't love her. No way would he let himself.

That Violet, the one he truly wanted, might only come out when she was away from her real life. And how often would that happen? Already she was making noises about going back.

Talk about opening Pandora's box...

You just couldn't let it be, could you? Couldn't step back, keep your distance, keep your hands to yourself, however much hers were on you. Oh, no—and now look what you've done.

You deserve the pain headed your way, sucker.

Just then he noticed that her body had gone tense beneath his, probably in response to his own unease. If he rose from the bed now, what would she see on his face?

He might be one hell of a professional liar, but he wasn't good enough to hide what was surely written all over his features.

"JD?" Her fingers tightened on his hand, her voice uncertain.

Do right by her. She's the innocent in all this.

He pressed a kiss between her breasts to buy himself time. "Hmm?"

Then her stomach growled, and he seized the distraction. He could feed her, that's what he could do next. While he was figuring his way out of this mess he'd made.

"You lucked out. If I hadn't needed to buy coffee and toilet paper, there would only be frozen pizza in this house. But I bought a few other things while I was out."

"What, chips and beer?"

She smiled and he wanted to open his mouth and confess everything. But what good would that do? He might feel better, but she'd feel one hell of a lot worse.

And there were lives at stake. They were innocent, too.

Pretending a light heart took all he had. "I'll have you know I went to Whole Foods. Even got you hummus and—" he gave an elaborate shudder "—quiche. I'm telling you right now, though, you have to take any leftovers back with you. No way am I letting anybody find it in my refrigerator later."

A cloud drifted through her gaze. "Because, of course, there will be a later, won't there? Only not for us."

JD blinked. Did that mean she would mind? "Are you leaving already?"

"I should. I ought to get back to L.A. I have scripts piling up, and I have to start rehearsals next month, but..." Her conflict showed.

That would be best for both of them. Only pain lay down this road. *Oh, Doc. Free me from this. She doesn't know anything about Lofton's crimes.*

Once again, he resorted to humor to disguise his

misery over his role. "On second thought, the quiche stays here, and you can't leave until it's all gone."

A tiny smile pushed some of the clouds away. "I'd like that."

"I should have bought a bigger one. Even though my manhood would definitely be compromised."

She twirled a lock of his hair. "Your manhood seems quite healthy to me." A challenging arch of her eyebrows.

"I thought you were hungry."

"I am." She wiggled out from beneath him. Shoved at his shoulder and rose over him, then nipped lightly at his throat. "Ravenous."

"Well, I can't let a guest starve." He crushed her to him, buried his face in her hair to hide the bleak look in his eyes.

Then he forced all that despair away and rolled her again, determined to apologize to her in the only way he could right now. The only way he could be honest. "Let's see what we can do about that." He bent to his task with every weapon at his disposal as regret pummeled him. She would hate him in the end, and he would take the punishment—which he would deserve—along with the loneliness headed his way. Life would never be the same once she was gone.

Whatever has to happen to me, so be it.

Just, please...let her be okay.

VIOLET SAT CROSS-LEGGED on his kitchen counter, clad only in JD's shirt while he ranged the kitchen in a pair of jeans and nothing else. "Why did you finish the kitchen first?"

"Why wouldn't I?"

"I don't know...I guess because most guys wouldn't."

"Most guys don't have my mom."

"Don't tell me. She made you do it. You poor thing." She snorted. "Not. I bet your mother is sweet and kind and worships the ground you walk on."

"Well, of course she does. Who wouldn't?" He paused a beat. "That doesn't mean she won't kick my ass from here to Dallas if she thinks I need it."

"Does that happen often? How tall is she?"

"It's not the size you bring to the fight, Hollywood. It's the size of the fight you bring."

She grinned. "I wish I could meet her."

His brows rose nearly to his hairline. "Now that's just scary. Next thing I know, you two would be swapping stories. Can't have that."

"Because I'd find out you're stretching the truth just a tad?"

He looked away, then back. "She'd like you." All mirth had fled his voice.

"I bet I'd like her, too."

He looked so sad then, and she felt it, too, the distance between this little fantasy island they were on and the real world each of them lived in. The tug on her heart at the thought of leaving him was nearly unbearable, but it was worse to see his light dimmed.

She seized on a distraction. "A pity someone with a kitchen this beautiful can't cook."

"You think I can't cook?"

"Well…"

He snorted. "Sexist."

"It's not sexist if it's true." Then she reconsidered. "But now that I think about it, I never noticed any pizza boxes." She cocked her head, trying to recall the bedroom floor, then had to shrug. "I have no idea if there was laundry on your floor. All I can remember is the bed."

Their eyes met. Held. "Mmm…." She licked her lips and smiled. "Guess I'll have to go back and check."

"If you get near my bed, we won't be leaving it any-time soon."

"Is that supposed to scare me?"

"I don't believe there's much that scares you, Holly-wood. I sure as hell don't want to." But he looked trou-bled.

He didn't scare her…except with how much he could make her want him. "Come here." She held out her arms.

He hesitated. Just as she was about to retract the invitation, he crossed the floor in two strides and wrapped her in an embrace she was terribly afraid she needed too much. She snuggled in, anyway, sa-voring the feel of safe harbor. Of course it was mostly illusion—not that he wasn't a born protector. But this was a time out of mind, a flight of fancy, nothing more.

"Violet…"

"Hmm?"

"I wish…" He didn't finish, only went very still for an endless moment.

Then he squeezed her so tightly she could barely breathe.

And stepped back. "I haven't run today. I need to. Want to get your gear from Sophie's and come with me or would you rather just stay there?"

He was distancing himself, and she should be glad. She had to regain some objectivity herself. "Maybe I should go back. You must have plenty else on your plate." The seesaw was excruciating, the drop from sheer glory to near despair too fast. Too painful.

"I'm not asking you to go. I just…" He looked away, his brow furrowed. "I need to run."

His outlook was always so positive that he made life seem effortless. She had to remember that this situation might be difficult for him, too.

What was the fair thing to do, to stay or to go? What was best for him?

He tossed her a lifeline. "We could go have Mexican food after."

Her relief was boundless. She didn't have to say goodbye yet. "We'd better run twice as far, then. My trainer is definitely going to kill me."

His expression lightened. "If you had a good body-guard, he'd protect you."

"My body's never been cared for half so well." She turned away before her heartache got the better of her. "I'll get dressed."

Mercifully, he stayed downstairs while she made her way up.

JD WAITED UNTIL SHE WAS OUT of hearing then punched in Doc's number.

"Romero."

He hesitated. He couldn't ask to be relieved unless he wanted to explain why. Because his heart was getting involved wouldn't be reason enough. He had a job to do. "I just have a second. Any news?"

"Lofton went to the warehouse in Houston."

"And?"

"He was inside about two minutes then hightailed it out. He's on the road again and should be headed back. You need to stick close to her."

"Why?"

"He left a body at the scene."

"What? Whose?"

"His partner in the warehouse. Too soon to know for sure, but the coroner doesn't think Lofton did it. Neither does our tail. He came back out looking the same as he went in. No blood spatter, no weapon left at the scene and none on him, best the tail could see."

"Gonna pick him up?"

"No. Don't want to spook him into running. There's too much we can't put together yet, and he's our best lead. Stay with her in case he calls. Don't let her out of your sight…or your hearing, either."

"Wish I could help back there."

"I don't. You're with the best asset we've got right now. Hang tight."

"I will." He'd hang very tight now. Maybe Lofton wasn't the killer, maybe he was—but the rats were turning on each other, and that's when things got really dangerous. He was damn glad he had an excuse to be with Violet. She needed to be as far away from Lofton as possible until this was over.

No way he was letting her get hurt.

All ambiguity fled. He would be allowed to tell her the truth as soon as they pinned down Lofton's involvement in the latest killing. The news that her friend was a criminal would be painful for her, but he would be there for her until she had to return to L.A. Until then, he was exactly where he needed to be. No one else would guard her as he would.

When he went back upstairs to change, he made sure his clutch piece came with him. When he rejoined her downstairs, he smiled without his earlier reservations. "Come on, Hollywood. Let's stretch our legs."

When she smiled at him, he bent and kissed her. "And pack a bag while you're at the hotel. If you want to, that is." *And even if you don't, I'm staying with you.*

"Oh, I want to." She went through the door, looking over her shoulder with a cheeky smile. "I mean, there's all that quiche to work my way through."

He laughed and followed her.

CHAPTER TWELVE

"YOU HAVE NOT READ JANE AUSTEN," Violet spluttered into her margarita.

"I swear to you I have."

"Why? Never mind. Of course, there must be a woman involved in the story."

He looked indignant. "Maybe I just read it because I wanted to."

"Uh-huh…just like you're going to take that quiche to work with you." She studied him. "Recite me the first line of *Pride and Prejudice*."

"Some junk about a rich guy needing a wife." He crunched another tortilla chip.

She blinked. "Very badly put, but basically correct." She narrowed her eyes. "But that's one of the most famous lines in literature. You could have heard it somewhere."

"You call that stuff literature? No, babe. I'm sorry, but literature is, like, 'I hate rude behavior in a man. I won't tolerate it.'"

"What on earth is that?"

He clapped one hand to his chest. "Oh, man…now you've really got me worried. That's from *Lonesome Dove*, honey. Larry McMurtry. A true classic."

"It is, huh?"

"Please. Next thing you know, you'll tell me you don't read comic books."

"Sure I do."

"Don't toy with me, sugar. What comic books?"

She'd read her brothers' comic books a million years or so ago. What were they? "Um…Spider-Man?"

He snorted. "Bush league. I'm talking serious comics, like Avengers or X-Men. Peter Parker's for babies."

"Well, excuse me. I bow to your superior taste."

"Damn straight."

She broke up laughing. "You are incorrigible."

"So we've covered important literature." He went on over her splutter, grinning. "What kind of music do you like? You're a Tennessee girl, so country, right?"

"Riiiight. You don't typecast much, do you?"

"Wait—so you're saying you don't honor your roots?"

"Boy, you play rough." She was having a blast. "Okay, nothing wrong with country. Keith Urban rocks, and I adore Tim McGraw, but I also love Coldplay and Dave Matthews. Is country your thing?"

He shook his head. "Heavy metal all the way. Metallica, Poison, AC/DC…hair bands rule."

"Seriously?"

He grinned. "Gotcha. Nope, blues is my favorite, but my mom is still crazy over Motown—bet I could sing you every Temptations song ever made. And Toby Keith kicks butt." He leaned across the table. "Austin has every kind of music you can imagine. Want to catch some afterward?"

"Is Avery's club very far away?"

His jaw flexed. "Didn't you say he was out of town?"

"He's due back soon, but…" He hadn't offered to

see her. Just dropping by his club might not be the best idea. "Never mind. Surprise me."

His gaze warmed. "You got it."

THE MILES ROLLED PAST SOMEHOW. Avery didn't know where he was or how long he'd been driving aimlessly around until he realized he was nearing Galveston.

He was headed in the wrong goddamn direction.

He stabbed a finger at the GPS to zoom out. What the hell was the best way from here? He didn't want to go back through Houston. What was the fastest way around? He zoomed out too far, closed in too much—

Damn it! His fist slammed down onto the console. He swerved into the first convenience store he spotted. Jammed the car into park and shoved his head back into the headrest.

Damn it, Sage. Damn you.

For a second, he imagined not going back to Austin. Leaving this disaster in the hands that had created it.

He'd told her he'd take care of it. Bately would have listened to him. They had a deal; he could have worked something out.

But Sage hadn't trusted him to do that, oh, no. She always wanted to take the lead, to call the shots.

Or maybe she'd figured out that he had plans that didn't include her. Bately and he had been exploring a partnership of their own.

Now Bately was dead. Would anyone remember Avery being at the scene? Had he been spotted, coming or leaving? Had he left fingerprints? From the moment he'd picked up that sweet, metallic odor, his movements were a blur. Something deep in his animal brain had sensed that the smell was blood, but it had taken seeing the man lying on concrete, a gaping hole where his heart should have been, for Avery to flee without thinking.

He could have touched a dozen surfaces in that warehouse. He didn't know.

Sage, you bitch.

What he did know was that everything had suddenly turned very, very serious. He had a partner who was vicious and not quite sane. And they were in bed with men who made her look tame.

He eyed the road ahead of him. He could keep going until he crossed the border.

No. Lima would find him. Mexico was the cartel's turf.

He'd be dead in days.

Maybe he'd find his way to I-10 and just keep driving cross-country. He could light out for the West Coast and drive straight through. He'd be in California in twenty-four hours or so if he didn't stop to sleep.

He might never sleep again, anyway.

Bately's dead eyes wouldn't let him.

But the person who'd offer shelter to him in L.A. wasn't there—she was sitting back in Austin, innocently waiting for him to return. He couldn't leave town yet, but Violet needed to do so, immediately. She had to get as far away from the looming disaster as possible.

He fingered his phone. Started to punch in her number.

The hour was late. He would wake her. What would he say, anyway?

But he had to go back. Face down Sage and figure his way out of this mess. Fortunately, he'd had misgivings early on in this enterprise and had socked away money along with two passports, one his own and one that only looked like him.

A visceral sense of danger was kicking in, sharpening his wits. He would return, get the money and passports and keep them with him at all times. He'd call Violet in the morning and determine her plans for going home. She should be going back soon, anyway, but he'd nudge her gently.

Once that was accomplished, he'd face Sage with a cool head, playing the role of his life, the one where he wasn't scared senseless, where he studied his partner and figured out how to either get rid of her...

Or vanish himself.

JD TOOK HER TO ANTONE's and introduced her to the blues. Memphis was solid blues territory, but she'd grown up on the opposite end of the state and had never taken much notice of that genre.

"Those lyrics are downright dirty," she marveled. "And here I thought blues was all about social injustice."

"Oh, honey...blues is about life. Just in coded language." He drew her onto the dance floor and tugged her close. "With amazing vocals and world-class guitar playing. And every bit of it crawls right down where you live."

The floor wasn't overcrowded, but she couldn't find any reason on earth to move away from where their thighs brushed and their bodies entwined, responding to rhythms as primal as the act of love itself.

"This music is made for hot summer nights," she murmured in his ear.

"And sweet, slow lovin'," he agreed.

She didn't know how much time passed as they lost themselves in each other. Before she knew it, the band was playing last call. She and JD blinked at one another, climbing out of the spell of great music and all the ways in which dancing brought two people together.

"You're a really good dancer," she said to him.

"Easy to do when you've got an angel in your arms."

She tried to save herself before she went down for the third time. "You, sir, are an unregenerate flirt."

He brought their joined hands to his lips and brushed them over her fingers. "I'm not flirting, Violet. You're the one who's breaking my heart." For a moment, who he was at his core looked out from those usually playful eyes.

"I don't want to," she whispered. "I wish…"

He shook his head to stop her. "Sometimes we don't get our wishes, Hollywood. We just have to live in the moment and be grateful as hell we get that much. That's what I'm trying to focus on."

"I'll try, too." But, oh, it was hard. "Can we go home, JD?" There was an odd expression on his face. She corrected herself quickly. "I mean…to your place."

"It's yours for however long you can stay." He tucked her into his side, and they walked out. As they neared his truck, he bent to her. "We have tonight. Let's make it count."

She smiled up at him. And tried her best to forget anything beyond the next few hours.

They went back to the house that felt more like home than anywhere she'd lived since she'd left Tennessee. They made love through the night, desperate and beautiful, fevered and savage…ragged and sweet…

And exquisitely tender.

WHEN VIOLET AWOKE, SHE WAS ALONE. Soft pale light filtered through the window. She rolled over and opened
her arms wide, her whole body awash in a dizzying
sense of well-being.

She looked up at the ceiling she'd teased JD about
and smiled. So many images flickered through her
mind, all of them filled with him. Some were fun,
some were…delicious. Some were X-rated.

So where was he?

She rose and once again donned his shirt. Sniffed
the air and detected the scent of coffee, which lured
her downstairs. She padded through the kitchen,
searched out a mug and poured some for herself. She
leaned back against the counter and took the first, re-
viving sip.

The man made excellent coffee.

She'd like to tell him…if she could find him.

Just then, the sound of his voice filtered in from
the back. She crossed to one of the wavy windows and
made out his form as he crouched on the porch and
continued speaking.

Was he talking to himself? He didn't have a phone
to his ear.

Just then he rose, and she could see beyond him.

A kitten, scrawny and pathetic, lapped at a saucer
of milk.

"Oh." Unbidden, the sound came from her throat.

JD pivoted and spotted her. Helplessly shrugged
those bare, broad, yummy shoulders.

She grinned and pointed to herself. *Okay to come
out there?* she mouthed.

He nodded, but put a finger to his lips for quiet.
Carefully he backed away and opened the screen door
for Violet to come through and join him.

"Where did you get her? Or him," she whispered. "Boy or girl?"

"Haven't checked," he replied in a low voice. "I went out to get the paper, and it was outside yowling like crazy. I assumed it was just looking for its mother, so I watched for a few minutes, but no mother showed up. Then it spotted me, and came bounding over. I figure it belongs to somebody around here, but it's too early to be knocking on doors and the thing wouldn't stop crying, so…" He lifted both palms.

She smiled up at him. "So Sir Galahad rescues another lost soul."

"Not really, not—" He broke off when she laughed. "Cut it out. I'm no hero, I just…"

"Rescue damsels and kittens in your spare time."

His cheeks took on charming color. "Quit that." He grabbed her mug. "Gimme. I never got my coffee." He sipped then made a face. "Christ on a crutch, how can you drink it sweet like that?"

"Then give it back. You don't use sugar? I couldn't find any sweetener."

"Cop coffee is never sweetened."

"Wouldn't be macho enough?"

He grinned. "Nope. The stuff at the station is beyond redemption, anyway. No amount of sugar or milk can fix that diesel oil. And you don't always have the time. You just learn to be thankful for the caffeine and ignore the rest."

"Really." She smiled at him over the rim. "For someone who's apparently so used to the bad stuff, you make an amazing cup of coffee."

"Guests deserve better treatment…especially certain guests. You know, pampered movie stars, for instance."

Before she could argue, he dipped his head and kissed her. "Good morning."

"Good morning." Oh, lordy, those kisses were as lethal at dawn as in the depths of midnight.

"Want to sit in my porch swing with me, Hollywood? I'll get a cup and join you. You're on cat-watching duty until I get back."

She blinked. She'd already forgotten the kitten. Oh, man, he got to her in more ways than she could count.

Instead of sitting down, though, she set her mug on the porch railing and crouched near where the kitten was lapping milk, though not too close.

Then she couldn't resist. Just one little touch...she reached for the kitten, but it jumped and hissed.

Then it started batting at her finger.

She remembered this, the hours and hours she'd spent playing with her own kitten as a girl. She glanced around her for something to use as a toy and found a twig that had fallen from one of the trees shading this beautiful old porch. She brushed it along the floorboards while the kitten stared, mesmerized.

Then it pounced. Violet chuckled and kept dodging and darting the stick around, drawing the kitten closer and closer until finally she could drop the twig and stroke one finger down the spiny little backbone while the kitten attacked the vicious enemy.

A few more strokes, then the kitten stopped attacking and arched its back against her hand, purring like a tiny motor. She scooped it up and held it against her, the vibration of the purr making her smile. She lifted it up, and a quick glimpse answered their question. "Where's your mama, little girl?" she asked as she cuddled the small gray and white. The kitten let her cuddle and pet her for a couple of minutes, then Violet's hair swung too temptingly, and the kitten leaped. Her claws tightened and she clung for dear life, frantically trying to climb upward to something stable…in this case, Violet's scalp.

"Ow!" The yank on the roots of her hair made her eyes tear. She tried fruitlessly to untangle the kitten, who was getting ever more entrapped as she struggled.

Behind her, JD's laughter warmed her. "Want some help there?" He set his mug down and knelt beside her, using one hand to capture the kitten and still it while the other held onto Violet's hair before it could be yanked out by the roots. The kitten yelped, and JD nearly dropped her, setting up a further struggle. "Hang on," he said. "I've nearly got it free…ta da!" He held the kitten up in triumph, but a tiny screech had him instinctively bringing the cat to his chest.

Immediately the kitten rubbed her head against him and resumed purring.

Violet completely understood the reaction, surrounded by him as she was. One powerful thigh brushed her back, his other leg bracketing her where he crouched on one knee and held her within the vee of his legs.

She shivered. Never in her life had she felt the potent combination of being both protected by and so powerfully attracted to a man. JD made her feel safe… but in some thoroughly delicious ways, not safe at all.

"Are you all right?" His eyes were bright with both concern and suppressed humor. "I can't really blame the kitten for wanting to get lost in that beautiful hair. I've wanted to just roll around in it myself." Humor quickly slid into heat.

"Her," Violet said absently, lost in his eyes.

"Oh." JD's were locked on hers as his head lowered

until his lips brushed hers. "Did I say good morning?" His voice was husky.

"Yes, but don't let that stop you," she murmured, stretching upward into him like a daisy reaching for the sun.

A screech jerked them apart.

They shared a laugh, and Violet realized then just how seductive shared laughter could be.

JD set the kitten down by the dish of milk, and she returned to her eager lapping.

He didn't move away but stayed right where he was, surrounding Violet with a warmth that was both physical and an indelible part of his personality. He slid his fingers into Violet's hair, cradling the back of her head as he watched her solemnly. "Now," he said, his voice low and intense, "where were we?"

"A proper good morning," she said, staring at that mouth that had given her so much pleasure already.

"Right." He bent to her, cupping her cheek with his free hand and stroking her skin with his thumb. "Let me know when I get it right," he murmured.

She closed her eyes and sank into his kiss. Small sips at first, then faint, tantalizing tracing with his tongue until her nipples ached and her body trembled with need for him. "JD…" she said against his mouth. Then she rose to her knees and took the lead.

"God—" he gasped when they both came up for air. "You absolutely kill me, Violet." He clasped her head in his hands and restrained her. "You are so damn sweet. I wish…"

His eyes were dark and sad and a little haunted. She understood completely. Hadn't she started that same sentence? She was bewildered by how quickly this had accelerated, since she'd sworn never to fall hard and fast again.

But this was JD, and he was, she realized more every second they spent together…special. Absolutely unique.

She could trust him, surely. His background was like hers. He came from the same kind of people, the same moral code. He'd shown in the last couple of days that he was a Boy Scout, he was John Wayne, he was Sir Galahad.

"Violet…we have to talk. I—"

"No." She stopped his words with her fingers, replaced them with her lips. "You make me believe in dreams again." Another kiss, then she threw her arms around his neck and whispered in his ear, "Let's enjoy the magic."

He crushed her to him with a fervor that gave her hope. He pressed his face into her hair and held on so tightly she could barely breathe.

The very thought of saying goodbye to him sent an agonizing pain stabbing straight to her heart.

She used every last bit of strength she had to hold on and not beg.

Inside on the kitchen counter, his phone rang. She started to release him, but he only lifted his head and looked at her with an echoing pain in his own eyes. "I don't care who's calling."

Fiercely he kissed her, and they let their bodies speak, letting them drown out the words neither wanted to hear.

And when her cell chimed, ruthlessly she ignored it, as well.

CHAPTER THIRTEEN

AVERY STOOD IN HIS OFFICE and listened to Violet's phone ring then go to voice mail. *Damn it, Violet, pick up! Where the hell are you?*

He didn't want to leave a message, but he was afraid not to. "Violet, I know it's early, but I have to talk to you. It's important. Call me back the second you get this." He disconnected and stood at the one-way glass, staring out at the darkened club, trying to think his way through an alternate plan if it turned out that he had to go over to the hotel to talk to Violet in person.

The connecting door opened. Sage strolled in.

"Pretty early for you, isn't it?" he asked.

"I never left. Someone has to take care of things around here."

"Yeah, like you took care of Bately?"

"I don't know what you mean," she said coolly.

"The hell you don't." Rage swept over him. "What were you thinking? Aren't we in this deep enough, Sage? Now, thanks to you, we could have cops looking at us for murder?"

"Us?" She arched an eyebrow. "I wasn't at that warehouse. You own it. There's no connection to me."

Fear stabbed an icy finger in his gut. "What are you saying?"

"You didn't think I was smart enough to know you were cooking up a little side venture and leaving me out?" Her expression was withering contempt. "I'm the smart one, Avery. You're only the greedy one." She turned toward her office. "And I don't need you anymore."

The shock staggered him for a moment, then fury came to his rescue. "I'm all that's kept us from going down already. You're impetuous, and your impulses are going to get both of us killed. Lima listens to me, not you—"

"Are you so sure of that?" She examined her manicure. "The pieces on the board are changing." A smug lift of an eyebrow. "And you lack some essential assets Jorge likes very much."

"You—" He blinked. "You're screwing him? You whore." His hand made a fist.

"Touch me, and your little girlfriend is dead meat."

"What?" Horror made all his muscles go lax. "No."

"Did you think I wasn't having you followed when you conveniently disappeared every day? When I already knew you were double-crossing me?" Her smile was vicious. "Imagine that…Violet James…" She stared upward, her expression calculating. "I wonder what the gossip rags will say about her when they find out America's Sweetheart is connected to a sordid little murder in Houston. Poor thing, she doesn't choose men well at all, does she?"

"You leave Violet alone." He took a menacing step toward Sage. "She's got nothing to do with this. You'd better not harm one hair on her head. If I hear the slightest whisper about her…"

"You'll what? I could have her picked up—" She snapped her fingers. "Like that. I could make things much, much worse for her than simple rumors. At a minimum, won't she be distraught to find out her lover is a criminal?"

"We're not lovers," he snapped. "She's…" If he said she was his best friend, would that put her in even greater danger? His blood went cold with dread. Violet was the only good thing in his life.

He had to turn this confrontation way, way down, so he shrugged negligently. "She's only someone I knew in L.A. She did me some favors back there, and I owed her. But there's nothing between us."

"Then why the threats?" Her eyes narrowed.

Terror for Violet gripped him. He had to do more to soothe Sage. "Look, I'm sorry. It's—" he exhaled heavily "—been a long day. A long drive." Apologizing to her stuck in his craw, but the stakes of not appeasing her were too high. "Violet's a nice person, that's all." A quick smile of conspirators. "Something neither of us knows much about." He watched Sage carefully, and when her posture eased, he took his first real breath. "She's had some hard times lately. She needed to get away, and she asked me about Austin. So when she decided to come here, I couldn't just ignore her."

Sage shrugged then, but he knew she was still a viper poised to strike; he couldn't discount the threat she presented. "Poor little rich girl. Boo hoo."

"I feel a sense of debt to her—and, anyway, think about it, Sage. If I keep my connections with Violet, we could go out to L.A. sometime. I could introduce you. She'd give us access to all the best parties. You could meet anyone you wanted to." Appealing to Sage's vanity was never a bad move. *Take the bait, Sage. Leave her alone.*

"Maybe." But he could see her calculating the possible benefit.

He seized the moment to buy himself some time, too. "Look, you were right to do what you did, I get that now. Bately would have talked. And, yeah, he was trying to get me involved in a side deal, but I'd already told him you and I are partners and there was no way I was cutting you out. That's why I wanted to be the one to talk to him." He was spinning lies like crazy, hoping she'd buy it. Sage wasn't stupid, but she wasn't completely rational, either, and her immense ego could override her brain. "I had to work on Bately some more so he'd understand how important you were to making the deal work."

She stared at him, but her eyes were the flat, empty stare of a predator. "Don't you ever call me a whore, Avery. I simply have assets it would be foolish to disregard. Sex is no big deal, after all." Her shoulders relaxed a little, but he didn't let himself relax, not yet. Then she smiled. "You certainly enjoyed my…assets once."

The bait was out there, should he want to take it. Sage was thoroughly amoral, and she also had the sex drive of any five women.

It would be like having sex with a crocodile, though…any second, those jaws could snap you in half. He pulled out the stops on whatever bravado he could muster. "I've never found anyone to replace you." He summoned his own smile. "And God knows I've tried."

"I seldom revisit lovers."

A pause ripe with an invitation to flattery he'd better not discount.

"You sure?" He put just a tad of pleading into his voice and thanked every acting class he'd ever taken.

Her expression was a mingle of contempt and pity. "I break a lot of rules, but never that one."

It wasn't hard to sigh convincingly, even if the sigh owed more to the relief of a man seeing the specter of pardon when he was one step from the gallows.

Then he added the coup de grâce of humility. "I'm not absolutely sure what I touched in the warehouse. How bad is that going to be?"

"I'll send someone to clean it up." She turned to leave, then paused. "Don't doubt me again, Avery."

He swallowed his pride. "I won't."

"It's been a long night," she said. "I'm tired."

"You go on home and get some sleep. I'll handle things here."

"You sure? You haven't slept, either."

"I might go for a massage once the crew shows up," he said, thinking fast. "But for now, I'll catch a nap on my couch until Leslie and the crew get here."

"Maybe you can take the night off once I return."

"Sounds inviting, but you take your time." As if he was going to hang around after this. He'd wait until their manager, Leslie, arrived, then make some excuse to run an errand.

The errand would be getting everything lined up so that if things went south again, he could escape at the first opportunity.

WHEN JD'S PHONE RANG AGAIN, Violet went still in his arms, and he cursed under his breath. "I'm sorry."

"It's okay. I'm the one on vacation, not you, I know that." Her smile was both brave and sad. "Want me to fix you some breakfast while you shower? What time do you have class?"

Inwardly, he swore again. He wanted to come clean with her so bad. "I have to be there by nine. Unless—" He made a face. "That call was about work."

"Another consultation?" She rose and extended a hand to him.

The trusting gesture made him feel even more of a scum. "Something like that." As he followed her inside, in his mind he tried out and discarded every half explanation he could think of, searching for a means to both honor his duty to the job and still do right by a woman who had her delicate fingers wrapped firmly around his heart.

He picked up his cell where he'd left it on the counter and listened to the voice mail Doc had left. *Candy has turned up. She'll only talk to you. Need you ASAP.*

Crap. He'd never wanted more to toss his phone out the window and pretend he hadn't received the message. But Candy could break the entire case. "I'm sorry," he was saying as he turned toward Violet. "I have to—what is it?"

She was looking at her own cell. "It's Avery. He sounds frantic, and he wants me to call him immediately." She smiled past her worry. "I'm sorry. What did you say?"

"I can't hang around for breakfast. They need me there right away." *Another instructor is out sick,* he was going to say to explain, but the lie stuck in his throat.

"I understand. I should call Avery back, anyway. I'll just…you go ahead and shower, and I'll see what he wants. This is very early for him to be calling."

He didn't want to move out of hearing. And at the

same time he wished he could warn her, *Don't—don't call him back. He's a lying piece of shit.* He didn't want her anywhere near Avery Lofton. Maybe Doc was right, and Lofton hadn't killed the guy in Houston, but that didn't mean he wasn't a threat to Violet simply because of the company he kept.

Like it or not—and increasingly he didn't—his job was to learn what Lofton would tell her.

"Go ahead. I'll make a fresh pot of coffee. Least I can do before I take you back to Sophie's." Where, of course, there would be perfectly good coffee waiting for her.

But she didn't point that out, only nodded and punched a button to call Lofton. "Oh! The kitten—" As she waited, she pointed to the porch.

Hell. He'd completely forgotten the cat. He nodded and headed onto the porch, leaving the door between them cracked. He'd have to make arrangements with his neighbor next door about the cat. The kitten had probably just wandered off from a home nearby, but he didn't have time to canvass the neighborhood to find her owner. If his neighbor couldn't come right away, he could put the kitten in his utility room with food and water—the lack of a litter box wasn't ideal, but it wasn't like she could do that much damage before his neighbor could come get the cat with the key he'd given her a while back.

"Avery?" he heard Violet say. "What's up? Are you all right?"

He picked up the kitten and petted her while he stayed out of sight.

"I don't know exactly when I'm leaving Austin." Her tone held a tinge of hurt. "What, are you ready to get rid of me?" Her jocularity was forced. "I guess…

in a day or two, probably." She sighed. "My assistant is getting restless, as is my agent. Work is stacking up, and rehearsals begin sooner than I want to think about. I'd like to see you before you go, though. Let me buy you dinner to thank you for everything. Do you have a free hour or two?"

No. Stay away from him, Violet.

"That would be great. Call me back, and we'll set a time." Violet disconnected but remained still, staring off into space.

JD grabbed the kitten's dish and walked inside holding both. "Everything okay?"

She frowned. "I don't think so. He sounds almost… scared. Definitely worried. It's not like him to keep his concerns from me. We tell each other everything."

Not everything, sweetheart. "You said he seemed overworked. Maybe he just needs to get away."

"Maybe." She sounded doubtful. "But I'll find out when I see him."

"No!" He hadn't meant to bark it out like that, but the threat to her chilled him.

She frowned. "What do you mean, no?"

"Sorry." But he wasn't, really. He had to proceed carefully, however. "It's just that I'd prefer it if you'd wait until I could go with you."

She blinked. "Why on earth would you say such a thing?"

He made his decision. If Doc was upset, so be it, but no way could JD risk Violet putting herself in harm's way because she didn't know what was going on.

"Look…I'm not sure how to say this, but there are…rumors about Danger Zone."

"What do you mean?"

He exhaled and raked his fingers through his hair.

"I know he's your friend, but there have been reports of criminal activity in connection with the club."

"Avery would never be part of something criminal."

If you only knew…. But he wanted to go gentle on her. "Are you so sure?"

Her eyes flashed. "I know him as well as I know myself."

"I don't think you do."

"Tell me exactly what you're implying. There has to be some sort of misunderstanding. I'll ask him and he can explain everything."

"No. Absolutely not."

She bristled visibly, and he forced himself to speak calmly. This was surely a shock to her. "Violet, you can't say one word to him about this. There's an investigation—"

"An investigation?" she echoed. "Of my best friend? How long have you known this? Why didn't you say anything?" She reached for her phone. "You're wrong—he would be horrified that anyone could think he'd ever be a part of something illegal. He deserves a chance to defend himself."

"You can't." He snatched her phone out of her hand. "I shouldn't be revealing even this much to you. The only reason I said anything is that you're not safe around him. There are…things going on right now, serious things. People could get killed. You can't say a word to him."

She stared at him. "Does this mean…" Her expression was dawning horror. "Are you saying you're involved?"

He hesitated too long.

"No." Her face lost all color. "You are, aren't you?" She took a step back from him, her hand rising to her throat. "You— That's why you spent time with me? Why you…"

"No—that's not it. You have to believe me." He closed the gap between them.

"You're a cop." Never had those words sounded more like a curse to him. "But…you said you taught at the Academy."

"I do…occasionally."

"But that's not why you're with me. I was only a means…"

"That has nothing to do with why why we're here, you and me. I mean, yes, the task force was looking into Avery, so when Sophie asked me—"

Her beautiful eyes went dark with pain.

"Violet, it's not what you think. I didn't—you have to let me explain." He reached for her.

"No!" She yanked her arm from his grip. "Don't touch me!" She crossed her arms over her middle. "I…I trusted you. You knew what I'd been through. Knew how hard it was for me—" She doubled over.

"It wasn't a lie, Violet, what grew between us. I—I've never felt about a woman like I—"

"Stop!" Her face was white as parchment now. "Don't say another word. When I think of how we— And how I thought…" Tears rolled down her pinched white cheeks, and he wanted so badly to hold her, to protect her—

His goddamn phone rang again. "Shit!" There was no way he could avoid answering again. "Violet, please…just give me a second. Please…I have to ex- plain to you." He held his phone but didn't answer. He took a step toward her and nearly landed on the kitten, who screeched.

"Answer your phone," she said, in the coldest voice

he'd ever heard. "I have nothing to say to you. We're done." She bent and scooped up the kitten, then ran unsteadily up the stairs.

"Violet—" The phone started up again. "Goddamn it, what?" he barked into it.

"I don't care what the hell you're doing, you'd better be on your way here, JD," Doc said in a voice nearly as cold as Violet's. "Why haven't you been answering your phone?"

"Violet knows."

"What?" The quieter Doc's voice got, the more dangerous things were. "How the hell did that happen?"

"Look, call me on the carpet later. Right now, I have to keep her from calling Lofton."

Doc cursed vividly. "What are you going to do?"

"I'm going to finish the conversation you interrupted."

"Make it fast. I need you here to talk to Candy. She may be able to tell us where to find Hector. We can bring Violet to the station, if necessary."

"Oh, yeah. That'll go over great."

"If you can't control her, I will."

"Screw that. You leave her alone."

"Are you threatening me, JD?"

He didn't care that he was bordering on irrational. All he could see was the devastation on Violet's face. With great effort, he brought himself under control. "I just…she doesn't deserve how this hurts her, Doc."

"That can't be our priority right now. You know that."

"Yeah." But it didn't make his heart ache any less. "Can you keep Candy under wraps a little longer?"

"I guess I'll have to."

"You've got a tail on Lofton, right? I think he's getting shaky."

"Any more good news for me? You're going to explain to me at some point exactly how my best undercover agent got outed, right? And it better be more convincing than just sex fogged your brain."

"Don't talk about her like that," he snapped.

"Don't act like you've forgotten who you are. What your job is."

Violet was so much more than a job, but he couldn't begin to make Doc understand, not if he had hours. He didn't understand himself exactly how, in the space of a couple of days, he'd lost an edge that he'd spent years honing. But now wasn't the time.

Suddenly he felt old and weary. And what he'd lost…he couldn't think of it. He had to focus solely on keeping Violet safe.

"I want to hear back from you in an hour or less. Preferably less."

"I'll do my best." He looked up the stairs, wondering how in the hell he was going to convince Violet to trust him and not Lofton after what he'd seen on her face.

Then he remembered the kitten. Much as it grated to have to detour like this, he'd better make arrangements for the cat before he talked to Violet so that nothing got in the way, however this worked out. He made a quick call to his neighbor, then jammed his phone in his pocket and started climbing the stairs.

VIOLET DISCONNECTED HER PHONE after calling the taxi. An unnatural calm seized her, the calm of someone who can't bear to think about what she'd lost.

But she hadn't lost anything, really, had she? What

she'd thought was between her and JD had never actually existed.

What was wrong with her? Didn't she know better?

'Cause you're a romantic...the world needs more romantics.

Not anymore. She was done with that. Her heart was empty now, a dry, dusty chamber littered with the ashes of a faith and an optimism that once was second nature. She'd always believed—even after Barry, she realized—something in her had clung to a hope that out there in the world, love still waited for her.

But not now. She glanced at the bed, was immediately bombarded by memories of the fun, the sighs, the bliss—

No. She couldn't bear thinking of it. Only a few short days, but those days had burned so brightly. Succored her, sustained her...

Gone. All gone. The man she'd thought had genuinely cared for her, the real her, not the fantasy woman millions adored...he was a mirage, the cruelest of illusions. There *was* something wrong with her.

She'd wanted to believe she could have the dream, that true love could still be hers, that she'd found the man...

But not anymore.

Footsteps sounded on the stairs. No. She couldn't be with him in this room again. Swiftly she grabbed the bag she'd thrown her belongings into after dressing in haste. No makeup, hair scraped back in a ponytail—what did it matter what she looked like?

But suddenly she wanted her makeup. Longed for the safety of her protective coloring, the careful disguise her glamour gave her.

Patience. In a few minutes you'll be gone, and you'll never have to see him again.

She scooped up the kitten and fairly raced down the stairs.

He caught her halfway, but she thrust the kitten at him.

And ran.

"Violet!" He charged after her, grabbed her before she made it to the front door.

She quivered in his grasp, then, piece by piece, she rebuilt herself. "Let go of me," she said tonelessly without turning.

He complied, but he didn't move away. "I never expected to care for you."

I am Violet James, she told herself. *I am on top of the world, don't you know? I don't need you.* The words would be her shield, deflecting the pain.

"You know how much I hated deceiving you?"

Her head swiveled so fast it dizzied her. "Why? You're so good at it." He looked awful. She tried to derive satisfaction from that, but it slithered from her grasp. With effort, she straightened. Silently wished him to hell. "You were only doing your job, right?"

"What happened between us was no job, Violet. You felt it, too."

"I feel nothing." *I won't let myself. Or it will kill me.*

He gripped her arm.

She turned to ice in his grasp, staring straight ahead.

He swore, and there was despair in his tone. He released her.

She couldn't care. He hadn't.

"It's your right to hate me. Just know that you can't possibly despise me more than I despise myself."

"I won't think of you at all."

"Well, that's too damn bad. I'll think of you every minute. Every second. And I'll know I had a chance at something special, but I lost it—because I was doing my job, damn it. That's what I do, I protect the innocent by bringing down those who would prey on them, like your buddy Avery. Do you realize what kind of evil he's part of?"

She shook her head. "I don't need to, because you're wrong about him."

"Well, you're going to hear it, anyway." He moved in front of her, six feet of angry, miserable male. "Because I won't let you put yourself in danger."

"You aren't in control."

A bitter laugh. "You're telling me. I've been walking a tightrope, knowing every minute that no matter which way I fell, someone was going to get hurt." He leaned closer. "But I had no choice because people were dying. They still are."

Her gaze whipped to his.

"Yeah. Your pal is involved in a very nasty enterprise, the business of human trafficking. You know what sexual slavery is, Miz James? You understand about women and children being hauled halfway across the world in the hold of a ship, then jammed in the back of trailers and vans for hours in filthy conditions, with scarce water and little food—because they dream of coming to America where gold paves the streets? Only there's a catch. The guys who truck them like cattle then turn around and claim that the women and children owe bills for their transport, bills they can only work off by being sold as prostitutes or sweatshop labor—and they'll never be allowed to work off that debt. Some of them die before they ever make it."

Her stomach roiled. "Avery's a good man. He would never enslave another human being. You cannot convince me of that."

"I won't try to. No, he's not the one stuffing them in container cars or selling them as slaves—but that chain of misery involves many links, and your buddy is one of them. He's weak and he's greedy—he didn't get his lifestyle running a club, I promise you. He uses his club to launder the trafficker's money. As a matter of fact, it's their money that funded the Jag he's driving and the little luxuries he's been bringing you."

Her head whipped to him. "What do you know about what he's been…" Her voice trailed off. "You've been watching me." Oh, God. Somehow that seemed to be the worst violation yet.

"Not me. And they weren't watching you, they were tailing him."

"Was Sophie part of…this?" She didn't think she could stand it if Sophie was involved, though how that was worse than knowing everything between her and JD had been a lie, she couldn't say.

"No, of course not." His shoulders sagged. "She'll be hurt, too, when she finds out."

She would not feel sorry for him.

"Look, Violet, I get that you don't want to believe me, and I don't blame you—it's a big shock. But it's not a lie. You're in danger."

"You've told me so many lies. How am I supposed to know when you're telling the truth?"

The smoky gray eyes she'd once found beautiful were bleak, dark holes now. "Fine, you don't have to take my word on the crimes of your so-called friend—

but you do have to believe this: I want you safe, and I don't care what I have to do to guarantee that. I want you free and whole, able to fly back to your castle, to live your glamorous life. I even want you to forget me, if that will take away the pain of how I've hurt you. But to accomplish any of that—" he bent his head to her "—you have to be alive. That's all I care about, Violet—that you're alive and safe. People close to your pal Avery are dying. Remember his phone call? Remember how frantic he sounded? Right now he's nervous and scared because someone he met with was murdered last night...and it's setting off a chain reaction."

"He didn't do it."

"No one's sure who's responsible yet. Regardless, his world is unraveling and more people are going to die. Avery's in bed with some very nasty folks. The cartel that runs the trafficking pipeline doesn't give one good goddamn who gets hurt in order for them to make a buck.

"Hear me and believe me, if you believe nothing else." He gripped her shoulders. "I will not let you be one of the victims."

Sincerity rang in his voice. Blazed from his eyes.

"Avery would never hurt me."

"He wouldn't mean to, maybe—but this situation is far more deadly than you can imagine, maybe more dangerous than he ever expected. You could simply be collateral damage, but you'd be just as dead. And I couldn't live with that, Violet." He swallowed visibly. "You're important to me."

"But your job was more important." She looked beyond him. "There's my cab. Let me go." She shrugged him off, reached for the knob.

"I wasn't supposed to fall for you, damn it." He stepped in her way. "You weren't supposed to be real and warm and wonderful. You were supposed to be a snotty celebrity."

"I'm not real, JD. And, I realize now, neither was this." Too tired to cry, though the ache in her chest threatened to burn though bone and flesh, still she couldn't leave him so coldly. "It's not your fault," she said softly. "You were just doing your job."

He recoiled as though she'd struck him, but he didn't relent. "I'm not letting you out of here until you promise to stay away from him." His eyes locked on hers. "Now send the cab away and let me take you to Sophie's. Then you're getting on the first plane back to L.A. and away from danger. Please."

"Funny…both you and Avery can't wait to get rid of me."

"Then for God's sake, listen. There's too much going on that you don't understand." He stood very still, but his face bore the strain. "I have to ask you not to reveal any of what I've told you—not for my sake, I don't expect that. But there are innocent people whose lives will be placed in jeopardy if word of this investigation leaks to the wrong ears. I'm counting on the real Violet James and her sense of honor not to endanger them."

Then he let his vulnerability show in his haunted eyes. "You don't owe me anything, but I don't believe the woman who made love with me would ever put other lives in danger."

She wanted to hate him for knowing that. "But what about Avery? Who looks out for him?"

"I'm an officer of the law, not an executioner. I promise I'll do everything I can to safeguard him so that he has his chance to defend himself in court. If he's innocent, he'll go free."

"But you don't think he is."

"That's for a jury of his peers to decide."

It was a decent thing to offer. From a decent man. However hurt she was, she recognized that. "JD, I truly don't believe he's guilty."

"I hope you're right—but I'm still asking you to stay away from him. It's the only way I can ensure your safety. I need your promise, Violet."

She didn't want to give it. If only she could talk to Avery, she could get this straightened out. What JD accused him of simply wasn't possible.

"Look, I could have you taken into custody to make certain you don't contact him. I'm trying to respect your dignity and your privacy."

"You wouldn't." She'd been softening toward him, but the threat got her back up.

"Try me." A muscle in his jaw flexed.

"I won't reveal what you've said." She could promise that. She'd get her own sense of Avery and figure out exactly what was going on here.

"Thank you. But that's not all I asked. You'll stay away from him and make immediate arrangements to go home?"

She didn't want to promise that, but anger and misery and grief were a tangle in her throat, and it would choke her to death if she didn't leave now. "Trust me or lock me up, JD." She tilted her chin in defiance. "Now I'd like to leave."

"I'll get my keys."

"No. I'm taking that cab."

"Violet…" He remained where he was, tall and beautiful and tortured.

Even now she longed for him to take it all back. How pathetic.

"Look at me, Violet. Please." His voice was caress and command. He wasn't going to budge until she did.

Slowly she raised her eyes to his, biting her cheek to keep from yielding to the treacherous yearning she couldn't believe she still felt.

"It wasn't all a lie," he said softly, his heart in his eyes.

"It was only an illusion," she whispered, "and it was cruel." Slowly she dragged her gaze away and fastened it on the door like a prisoner awaiting release.

After a very long pause, he stepped back.

She made her way down the drive on unsteady legs and climbed into the cab.

And stared straight ahead, seeing nothing around her, only the last fragments of a dream drifting away like dandelion puffs.

CHAPTER FOURTEEN

AFTER ENSURING THAT THE KITTEN would be cared for, JD barreled out of his driveway on the way to the station. But however hard he tried to concentrate on his upcoming interview with Candy and the approach he would take with her, all he could think about was Violet.

For the rest of his life he would carry with him the image of her pale, shattered face.

However bad he'd expected his revelation to be... the reality was worse.

She was beyond hurt. And doubting herself again. How could he matter so much—and he had, he could see it in her. He'd blindsided her.

They'd both felt the pull of something extraordinary, no matter what she said now. Didn't seem to matter that their worlds were completely unsuited to each other's. Out of all the universe, that their paths would cross was a massive long shot...that they would form such an immediate bond was little short of a miracle. It wasn't surprising that he would fall for her, but that she would soften in his arms so sweetly, trust him, open her heart to him—

He smacked the steering wheel and swore. He wanted something else to hit, anything that would ease this huge ball of shame and guilt and fury eating away at him.

Something like Avery Lofton, the bastard. How could he allow her to come anywhere near the sordid, nasty tangle he was in up to his neck?

Would she listen to JD's warnings? Had she believed a word he'd said? He should have flat-out refused to let her get in that cab and bodily delivered her to Sophie's himself, then set a watch on her.

He dialed Sophie's number.

"Hotel Serenity."

"Sophie, it's JD."

"Oh! I'm surprised to hear from you already. I guess Violet survived the shock of seeing your place." Her teasing tone only made him feel worse.

"Sophie, I need your help."

"You sound terrible. What's wrong? Is Violet okay?"

"I'm headed to work, and I don't have much time. You have to keep an eye on her."

"Keep an eye on her? Where is she?"

"She should be there any second. She took a cab." He paused. "I hurt her, Sophie. It's the last thing I wanted to do, but…" He couldn't go down that road again, not now. "She's going to need a friend."

"Of course, but…JD, what happened? You two seemed so happy. So good together."

We were. Damn it, we were, in spite of the lies. "I don't know how else I could have handled it, but…" He exhaled. Might as well get it out. "Her friend Avery is mixed up in some dirty business. I was assigned to find out if she was part of it, too."

A very long pause. "And I played right into your hands. JD, what have you done?"

"I've hurt a woman I care about deeply. I'm sorry, Sophie. I didn't want to involve you, but this is an ugly case with a body count that keeps rising. I would never have compromised you by asking you to introduce me to her, but when you came up with your bodyguard idea…"

"Oh, no. Oh, JD, she's so fragile."

"I've never been ashamed of my job before, if that helps any—and what developed between us was as real as it was unexpected. That part wasn't a lie, Sophie, I swear. I care more for her than I have any right to—I mean, she's from a different world, and I realize we have no future, but…" Despair swamped him, and he couldn't let it. He had a job to do. "I have to live with what I've done, but I've got to know she's safe. She doesn't want to believe me about Avery, and I'm scared she's going to get caught up in the same deadly web he is. You aren't too happy with me right now, and I don't blame you one bit, but I need you to promise that you'll stick close to her, that you'll call me if she's getting any crazy ideas about seeing him. If she'd get on a plane back to L.A. pronto, that would be best, but she's so angry with me and so hurt, she's not going to listen to anything I say. You don't owe me this, but please, Sophie, will you watch over her? The one thing I can't handle is her being put in harm's way, and we're short-handed. I'm going to do my best to get her put under surveillance, but in the meantime, I have to know she's safe."

Sophie's voice was heavy when she replied. "Of course I will. I'm not angry with you, JD."

"I can't imagine why not. I'm furious as hell at myself."

"You'll beat yourself up ten times more than I ever could. But poor Violet…"

"Yeah." His own sorrow weighed him down. "Would

you tell her...never mind. She doesn't want to hear anything from me. I'm nearly at the station, Sophie. A thank you isn't enough, but it's the best I've got right now."

"You be careful, JD. Don't get hurt because you're not focused. I'll take care of Violet for you."

"You're a better friend than I deserve. I'm grateful."

"Be safe, JD."

"Thank you, Sophie."

As the station came into sight, JD flipped through his options. He'd talk to Doc first and see if there were any resources Doc could tap for Violet's surveillance. If need be, JD would snag some of his buddies in APD.

Once he was sure Violet was being watched over, he could turn his mind fully to this case. He'd already lost more than he could bear. To let Avery Lofton and his friends swim through their nets would mean all the pain he'd caused was for nothing.

That was not going to happen.

INSIDE THE CAB, VIOLET HUDDLED in the corner of the backseat, refusing all the driver's attempts to converse.

She was all talked out.

She considered herself fortunate that the driver hadn't recognized her; then she realized that she hadn't spared time for even a speck of makeup in her haste to get away from JD. She was a wreck, her features haggard, her eyes red with unshed tears. Seeing any resemblance to the star most people knew would be a real stretch.

Plus, she felt a hundred years older. And broken.

Not thinking about that.

She was an empty husk, dry and lifeless...and she welcomed the void. If she let herself feel...if she let herself remember JD, his teasing, his warmth, his touch…she would, quite simply, die from the pain.

Why a man she'd known only a matter of days could have come to mean this much to her when her husband had never been half so close to her heart, she couldn't fathom.

But now her soul had withered as quickly as her illusions.

If only her mind would do the same.

She had to stop thinking about him. Frantically, she cast around for something, anything that would ease the blistering sense of betrayal, the dull thud of worry over Avery, the dying echo of lost hope that love would ever find her.

"Eight twenty-five," said the driver as he stopped before Hotel Serenity.

Violet didn't move. If she went inside now, Sophie would sense that something was wrong. She would be sympathetic, and her sympathy would make Violet break.

I will not break, not ever again. The time for tears was over…because if she started now, she might never stop.

"Ma'am?"

Maybe she should just head for the airport, as JD wanted. Go back to what she knew. She could ask Sophie to pack her things for her and send them….

No. That would be rude, and Sophie would be distraught enough once she found out how her attempt to help Violet had ended.

Or had the attempt truly been Sophie's? The notion struck her with the force of a blow: had meeting her been JD's initiative all along, whatever he said?

She'd told JD she wouldn't reveal to Avery what

she'd learned about the investigation, but she hadn't agreed not to contact him. Clearly JD didn't want her to, but what did that matter? She didn't owe JD Cameron anything. Avery had been her best friend for half her life. Maybe JD was right and Avery had fallen in with some unsavory company—he'd always had a tendency to look for an angle. Maybe he had financial problems, and that had forced him in an undesirable direction. Or maybe his partner Sage, whom she'd never met, had done something that had dragged Avery into a web he couldn't escape. She couldn't deny that Avery had been tense and uneasy ever since she'd arrived.

This situation is far more deadly than you can imagine, maybe more dangerous than he ever expected. You could simply be collateral damage, but you'd be just as dead.

Avery had been evasive on the phone, and she would get no more information out of him from a distance. She had to be able to look him in the eye, and once she did, she would know if he was in trouble.

Women and children? Sexual slavery? Her mind balked. Could she be that naïve? That blind? Regardless, she was done with all of that. No more blinders on her, not ever again.

She tried Avery's cell again, but the call went straight to voice mail. She didn't leave a message.

"Miss?" the cabbie prompted.

"Yes." She battled her way out of the fog and reached into her purse, tipping him handsomely. "Thank you."

She stepped from the cab and stood at the walk gate, blinking like a cave creature emerging into sunlight. The hotel grounds looked exactly as she'd left them, a welcome refuge, a beautiful retreat.

While she was forever changed.

In the midst of her misery and humiliation, she forced herself to acknowledge that however much JD had wounded her heart and her pride, if any of what he'd said was true, she had to proceed carefully. If there indeed were innocents being victimized, she didn't want to stand in the way of the efforts to save them.

Her focus would be on learning the truth.

Reassured by some semblance of purpose, at last she remembered that she needed a key card and a combination for the gate. While she was scrabbling in her purse to find the card, she heard footsteps and looked up.

Sophie opened the gate for her and held out her arms. "Oh, Violet…" She drew her inside and opened her arms. "Come here."

Gratefully Violet fell into them and dissolved in a river of tears. "I'm sorry," she sobbed. "I just…"

"He's miserable, too." Sophie hugged her. "And he's worried sick over you."

"I don't want to talk about him. I can't."

"Then we won't. Let me take you inside. Would you rather come into the hotel or go to your quarters?"

Violet didn't want to be alone. "I'll go with you."

One arm around her shoulders, Sophie led her along the sidewalk and up the stairs, murmuring soothing sounds in her ear. Inside, she settled Violet on a soft, comfortable sofa.

"I'll get you a glass of water," she offered. "Or would you prefer wine?"

She was far too miserable to be drinking. "Water's fine." She curled into the cushions, exhausted and heartsore, and wished for the sweet surcease of forgetfulness she knew would not be waiting.

As AVERY DROVE TOWARD his house late that afternoon, he was newly grateful that he'd chosen to live outside the downtown—way outside. He was actually past the city limits to the west, a good twenty miles from the center of the city. Since he didn't operate during the normal rush hours, traffic had never been an issue, and to him, the trade-off of quiet after the constant bass thumping and frenetic activity of the club was worth the inconvenience of distance.

He turned off the highway and down a winding road. The houses here were screened from view by the preponderance of trees. In addition, the homes were spread quite a distance apart. In the years he'd lived here, he'd only met one of his neighbors, and that was absolutely fine with him.

He made a right into his driveway, an asphalt ribbon winding through the trees. The house wasn't visible for two more turns. The cedar tree cover was dense except right around the house where he'd had it cleared.

The feel of the place was lonely to some.

Occasionally it was to him, as well, but not today. Right now he was glad that anyone following him couldn't do so easily.

He wondered if Sage already had a tail on him.

He sure wouldn't put it past her, but anyone she sent wouldn't be able to sneak in on foot, plus he had security cameras scattered over the entire ten acres. Whoever it was would have to lurk at the perimeter.

He wouldn't be here long, anyway. He hadn't waited for Sage to return to the club, but he'd told Leslie he was getting a massage and would be back afterward. Since he got massages frequently and had already mentioned the possibility to Sage, no one would think anything of it.

Not at first.

And by then, he'd be on a plane, headed out of the country.

He hoped to God Violet had heeded his message and would be on her way home to L.A. right away. At least she had a bodyguard, though the fact that the guy was an off-duty cop could go both ways. He didn't like having cops anywhere around, especially not now, but he was happy she had one with her.

There was no danger to him from the cop's presence—Violet knew nothing about his situation. He'd kept her in the dark on purpose. If he'd suspected things would hit the skids like this while she was nearby, he'd never have encouraged her to visit.

He pulled into the garage and was about to shut off the engine when his cell rang.

Sage. He groaned. He really didn't want to talk to her, but he needed to allay any of her suspicions. "Hey, Sage. Didn't expect you back already. Get enough sleep?"

"You need to get down here."

Crap. He hadn't grabbed his passports and money yet. "I'm about to go in for my massage. Can't whatever it is wait?"

"Sure, if you don't care that one of Hector's girls went to the cops."

"What? How do you know?"

"I have contacts inside the police department."

"Shit." His mind worked frantically. His masseuse was downtown, not far from Danger Zone. He couldn't

make it back to the club soon enough to make it cred-
ible that he'd been to see her. "But what could the girl
possibly know?"

"Jorge will be asking Hector that."

"You told Lima?"

"Of course."

"But Hector isn't our responsibility." He tossed
some clothing in a bag. His laptop case was already
in the car. He'd buy whatever else he needed.

"I'll remind you that his girls operate out of here
quite often."

And some of them were on the video footage they'd
used for the blackmail scheme.

"Jorge doesn't like mistakes. It doesn't matter who's
responsible," she pointed out.

He opened the safe in his bedroom and pulled out
the cash, credit cards and passports.

"Avery?"

"I'm here. Just thinking. Which girl was it?" he
asked, buying time as he strode back through his
house toward his car.

"The one called Candy."

"I don't remember her—wait, is she the twin?"

"Yes. The one whose sister tried to engineer an
escape."

Avery swore ripely.

"My sentiments exactly. Swearing solves nothing,
however. Hector told me a few days ago that he found
her outside the club the other night with a man who'd
been in here asking questions of Bella."

Avery frowned. "What kind of questions?"

"Hector didn't know. Bella is on the early shift tonight. I'll discuss it with her."

"She talks to a lot of men."

"Hector has a sketchy description that should narrow it down."

"And then we can review the camera footage to find him." He'd made it to the highway, but the clock was ticking and he was nowhere near downtown. "I should go in and pay this woman, at least. She made a special trip for me."

Sage sighed dramatically. "I suppose you could go ahead and get the massage."

Her arrogance grated on him, that she thought she had the right to give him permission. He needed the time, though, so he swallowed his umbrage. "Thanks. I could use it. I'll be back right afterward. Sure you're okay talking to Bella by yourself?"

"I think I can handle it." Her tone was dry as the Sahara.

He managed a sardonic laugh. "Of course you can. Thanks, Sage. See you after a while. I scheduled a long massage, and I have to turn my phone off in there, but I'll check for any messages as soon as I'm done."

He'd no sooner disconnected than his phone rang again. He glanced at the display.

Oh, hell. Violet. He couldn't talk to her, not right now.

Please, Violet, do as I asked. Go home and stay safe.

He rejected the call and sent it to voice mail.

CHAPTER FIFTEEN

JD STOOD IN THE OBSERVATION AREA, looking through one-way glass at the woman who answered to the name Candy.

He nearly wouldn't have recognized her, and the fact that he was seeing her now in full light rather than nighttime had little to do with it. The girl/woman he'd talked to at Danger Zone had been terrified. Cowed. Frantic over her sister's fate and desperate to get away from him, to avoid rocking the boat.

She looked younger now, her face scrubbed clean of the thick makeup she'd worn, her clothing simple instead of provocative. Despite the warm weather, she had her shirt buttoned all the way to her throat, and her jeans were baggy, not tight. Her long dark hair was tied back in a ponytail.

She appeared almost nunlike—but even that wasn't all that differentiated her from her earlier incarnation.

She looked...fierce.

What had caused the change?

"She said you're the only one she would trust," Bob remarked.

Nice that someone does. Violet's heartbroken, accusing eyes were never far from his mind.

"You really fell for America's Sweetheart, huh?"

He hadn't meant to say it aloud. "Doesn't matter.

She can't stand the sight of me now." He shrugged. "It never would have worked, anyhow."

"I'm sorry, kid." Bob clapped his shoulder in sympathy. "Tough position to be in."

"Guess I was due for a fall." But it felt like a dive from Everest.

"I know we rib you, but there's no pleasure to be had, seeing you this way."

"I'm fine." He would be. There was no other choice. "Sure Doc will find someone to cover Violet?" Her safety was paramount.

"He's on it. And I'll go myself, if need be."

"Thanks." JD squared his shoulders. "Okay, showtime." He went back out in the hall then entered the room he'd been observing.

The girl looked up. If she was sixteen, he'd eat his favorite cowboy hat. "Hello."

"Hello," she said, her voice heavily accented. "I wait for you."

"I'm sorry I couldn't be here sooner. Are you comfortable? Would you care for a soft drink? More water?"

"I am fine. Thank you."

"You wanted to see me. What can I help you with?"

Her brown eyes burned into his. "You will kill Hector and his men."

Whoa. "You know I can't simply walk out and shoot them, right?"

"Give me gun. I will do it."

"May I ask your real name? I don't like the sound of Candy. It's all wrong for you."

"I don't answer to it anymore. That time is over." Tears welled, but she brushed at them impatiently. "I am Melis. My sister was Meryem."

Was. "You know about her."

A brusque nod. "She was murdered. My family will blame me. I am elder."

"You're not twins?"

"We are—were. But I am born first. Meryem my responsibility."

"You're not responsible for her death, Melis." His voice was low and harsh with his own fury. "Others are. Many others who have made themselves rich by preying on innocents like you."

"I am no longer innocent." She stared at the table, her hands clasped so tightly her knuckles were white. "To come to America was my idea."

He reached for her hands, but stopped when she flinched. God only knew how she'd been brutalized. He let his hand lie still nearby on the table in a show of silent support. "You wanted to make a better life."

"I thought it would be like the movies." In her broken voice, he heard an echo of Violet's youthful disillusionment. Why did the world so often prey on the female of the species? His gender had a lot to answer for.

"Melis, you have to listen to me. You did nothing wrong. You dreamed, and others victimized you for it."

"I want them to die. My father would kill them." Her voice dropped to a whisper. "I can never go home now. I am...*parya.*"

"What does that mean?"

"It means...how you say? Outcast. Unwanted. If I return, no one talk to me, no one look at me...that is...?"

"Shunned."

She nodded. "I think this is the word."

A pariah. Good God.

JD vowed that he'd find a way to help this girl. He couldn't fix the damage he'd done to Violet, and to the end of his life, her devastated face would haunt him.

But this, he could fix. And he would. Hector and Avery and Jorge Lima would pay, whatever it took. "I can't just kill them for you, but I can make sure they are caught and punished, if you help me. Will you?"

Her nod was fierce.

"Then tell me what you know. Start from the beginning, when you first met a contact in Istanbul."

With a grateful glance, she began talking.

"HERE," SOPHIE SAID, WALKING into the living area with a tray full of goodies.

Violet jolted back from the edge of sleep.

"Oh, I'm so sorry," Sophie said. "Here's your water. I'll just leave the tray here and go. A nap would undoubtedly be good for you."

Everything about Sophie always said *come here, rest your weary head...let me take care of you.* "There's not a hotelier in the world to match you, and I've stayed in many of the best hotels in the world." Sophie's cheeks pinkened with pleasure, but Violet could already see her starting to demur. "I mean it. You're this amazing combination of professional and the best kind of mother possible. I could live here, I swear."

A flicker in Sophie's eyes at the word *mother.*

Oh, dear. "Is everything okay...are you—I mean, did you take a test?"

Everything about Sophie bloomed then. "I didn't really need a test, but...yes. I'm definitely pregnant. Due in January, I think."

"I'm really happy for you." She was, too, even though the news only highlighted that her own dreams of a family had never been further away.

"Thank you. And somehow, once I told Cade, all my fears vanished."

"You told Cade? While he was still on assignment?"

Sophie rolled her eyes. "I know…I wanted to wait until he was home, but then last night he made a video call, and I guess I was just too transparent. Not that he figured out what was different, just that something about me was. The next thing I knew, I just blurted it out. No self-control at all."

"He was pleased?"

"He was thrilled. He could hardly wait to call his family."

"So when's the wedding?"

Sophie looked startled, then smiled. "The day he gets back, if he has his way."

"Will he?"

Sophie sighed. "I…it probably sounds foolish, given that it's a second marriage, but… I never had a real wedding the first time." Longing shone from her eyes.

Violet yielded to impulse and grasped her hand. "It doesn't sound foolish. Romance is important. You have something special with Cade—anyone can see that. You deserve a beautiful occasion when you pledge your lives to each other."

Sophie's fingers squeezed hers. "Thank you." She hesitated. "Would you come?"

Violet froze. Could she ever bear to come back to this city? Especially for an event where JD would no doubt be in attendance?

"I'm sorry." Sophie drew away. "I got swept away

by sentiment. I should have thought…I'm really sorry, Violet. Of course you wouldn't want to be here after…"

Violet was well aware of how private a person Sophie was, how hard she worked to afford that privacy to others. *I have no family,* she'd once said. Violet had no sisters, no close girlfriends who weren't related to the industry—which was basically the same as none at all. In Hollywood, true friendships were extremely rare when you reached a certain level of fame. Everyone wanted something from you.

She would probably be stretching things to lay claim to sisterhood with Sophie, but honest admiration and fondness? Absolutely. Too much of both to risk tainting Sophie's excitement by dwelling on her own heartache. "It's not about JD. I'm a big girl."

She sighed. "These are the times I regret my choice of career. I would love to, Sophie, truly, but…you haven't seen how bad things can get when I'm in the center of the paparazzi storm."

"I've had some experience with Zane's situation," she responded. "And I'm not afraid."

Zane and herself, both in attendance at the same occasion…that was definitely tempting fate. She should say no, but she had a sense of how difficult it had been for Sophie to ask.

"I shouldn't," Violet responded. "But I really want to. You let me know when and where, and I'll figure out something. Maybe a disguise. I'm not an actress for nothing." She found a nearly genuine smile.

"I'm not after a big fancy wedding. It will be very private. All I want are the people who are important to us."

Violet was deeply flattered to be included in that company. She wasn't quite sure how it had happened, but she and Sophie had crossed a boundary from host and guest to friendship in a surprisingly short time.

The best part was feeling that the liking was genuine, that Sophie thought of her as a person and not a star. Except with her family and with Avery, she almost never experienced slices of real life, genuine relationships not motivated by ambition or self-promotion or sucking up to gain some sort of advantage...at least until JD.

Or she'd thought it had been real with JD...then she'd learned it had all been a lie.

I was doing my job, which is protecting the innocent by catching those who would prey on them. That's your buddy Avery.

She had to know. She would try Avery again.

And she would stop thinking about JD.

Sophie was still waiting for her answer, and there could be only one, if Violet cared about her. "I would be honored to come, Sophie. Truly."

Sophie's eyes welled. "I would love that."

"Don't. I can't start crying again."

Sophie hugged her. "It feels wrong to be so happy when—"

"I don't want to talk about JD."

"I'm not happy about what he's done, but I'm sorry for him, too. He's devastated, Violet."

His expression at the end...his eyes gone dark and bleak... If she didn't hurt so badly, if she hadn't flown so high... But she had, and she wasn't ready, might never be ready to acknowledge the untenable position JD had been in. Had chosen to be in, she reminded herself.

She would get past this. She would live. She had a life she needed to get back to.

But first she had to talk to Avery. Look him in the eyes. Decide for herself.

"You're getting cross-eyed from lack of sleep," Sophie noted. "You should take a nap."

"Sounds wonderful, but I'd better pack." She'd focus on that task for now and reach Avery as soon as possible. Then she would remember her real life and return to it.

"I'll walk you over, then."

Violet demurred. "Piece of cake. All I have to do is lie down and roll across the grass on this overstuffed belly."

"Climbing stairs that way could be a challenge." Sophie grinned. "Want me to wake you up at a certain time? Cade's coming home early. Join us for dinner."

"That's very kind of you, but I think I could probably sleep all the way through until morning." She stepped closer and kissed Sophie's cheek. "Give Cade my congratulations."

"I will." Sophie hesitated. "Are you sure you have to leave?"

"Yes, but I'll miss you. Could we stay in touch?"

A bright smile in answer. "I insist on it."

Violet hugged her hard. "Thank you, my friend."

Sophie hugged her back, then escorted her to the door and watched as she made her way across the lawn.

Once inside her room, Violet tried Avery again, only to get his blasted voice mail. *Where are you, Avery?*

She felt grungy and in dire need of a fresh start, so though she wanted to fall face-forward onto the bed, instead she took a long, hot shower. While she was washing her hair, she remembered that Avery had told her that he often went to the club in the afternoon because it was quiet at that time and he could take care of business details.

She emerged and wrapped herself in one of Sophie's decadently thick towels, then used her phone to find the club's number and punched it in.

For whatever reason Avery wasn't answering his cell, but maybe he'd answer the club's phone, or at least someone there could tell her where he was.

"Danger Zone. Leslie speaking."

Leslie? Oh, yes. The manager. "This is Violet James. Is Avery there?"

"He's stepped out, Ms. James." There was a familiar note of eagerness in her voice that made Violet glad for her fame...or should she say her notoriety now? "May I take a message, or would you like to talk to his partner?"

Sage Holland. Maybe she would know where to find Avery. "I would, thanks."

"Just one moment—and, Ms. James?"

"Yes?"

"I'm a huge fan."

"Thank you."

A long pause, also familiar as the other person tried to prolong the encounter.

Violet wanted to nudge her, but she mustered patience and remained silent.

"Well, I'll just..."

"I appreciate it."

The phone was picked up quickly. "Sage Holland here. May I help you, Ms. James?"

"I hope so, thank you. I'm having difficulty getting in touch with Avery, and I'd like to see him before

I leave for L.A. tomorrow. Do you expect him back soon, or can you tell me where he might be?"

"He has an appointment that will take a little while longer. Would you care to come here to wait for him? We'd love to show you around the club, if you have time. He said you were staying at Hotel Serenity, correct?"

"That's right."

"We're perhaps a ten- to fifteen-minute cab ride from you, but let me send someone to pick you up. May I?"

Funny, in her time in Austin, she'd become so accustomed to being Violet the person and not Violet the star that she'd almost forgotten what it was like to have people fawn over her.

It wasn't always a bad thing. "That would be lovely. Shall we say an hour?" She'd have to hustle—she'd gotten out of the glamour habit, as well, and that wasn't a quick process—but she'd find some viable compromise that would satisfy the starstruck Leslie yet remind Avery of how long they'd known each other.

"Perfect," the woman purred. "We'll look forward to having you. I'll arrange for a car right now."

And probably call a contact or two to be sure there would be pictures of Violet entering and leaving the premises, for publicity purposes.

Avery had done everything in his power to keep her away from the club for fear of exactly that happening, and she appreciated the thoughtfulness, but...this was her life. Better get used to it again.

She set down her phone and went to study her closet.

CHAPTER SIXTEEN

AVERY'S FLIGHT WAS BOOKED. He'd limited himself to two bags he'd tossed in the backseat. He had funds waiting for him in several offshore accounts. He'd be leaving assets behind, regrettably, but that couldn't be helped. He had to be alive to spend what he'd accumulated.

His cell rang.

Sage, he saw.

His faked massage wouldn't have ended yet, so he let it go to voice mail and kept driving toward the airport. Once the phone chirped to indicate a waiting message, he debated whether to listen, but it was better to be armed with information.

"Avery, darling…" That superficial tone she took on when she was performing for an audience. "I have a friend of yours here who'd very much like to see you. Let me put her on." He could actually hear the crocodile smile she was no doubt wearing. What friend? Who would—

His stomach was already sinking before he heard the voice he most feared to hear.

"Avery? Your place is amazing," Violet said. "Sage and Leslie have been showing me around, and I'm very impressed. I want to take you to dinner to thank you for everything before I go home to L.A., so I'll wait here until you call."

The phone switched back to Sage. "We're having a lovely girl chat while we wait." Malice coated the glee in her tone, and he wondered why Violet couldn't hear it.

Except that Violet was a romantic. And she trusted him, so she would trust Sage by extension.

"See you soon." Sage clicked off.

Oh, Christ.

Sage had Violet. She'd had a man killed only a day ago.

Violet was famous. Surely Sage wouldn't…

He couldn't be sure. Sage, he'd begun to realize, would do whatever she perceived to be in her best interests, including getting rid of anyone in her way.

At a minimum, Violet was a hostage, though she clearly didn't realize it yet.

Avery didn't want to go back, wanted badly to be far, far away. He wasn't the right person to handle something like this. Where the hell was her bodyguard? What on earth had possessed her to contact Sage?

Think.

He couldn't call the cops until he was safely out of reach. He didn't have his own hired muscle as Sage did.…

Wait. Violet did. What was that bodyguard's name? Why hadn't he paid better attention to what she had said about the man instead of being too preoccupied with his own problems?

The man was a cop, though. Getting him involved… could he work out a deal? He couldn't risk going to jail. *Damn you, Sage, for triggering all this.*

He had to get out of Austin, but he couldn't leave

Violet with Sage for as long as it would take to be safely away.

Then the answer occurred to him. He'd call the hotel. The owner had been responsible for hooking Violet up with the cop, he remembered Violet telling him, and he'd been introduced to the owner on one of his visits… Sophie, that was her name.

Frantically he hit the browser on his phone and looked up the hotel's main number.

JD STOOD IN THE DOORWAY of Doc's office, leaning on the jamb.

"I've got dates, places, some physical descriptions to add to what we know, but these guys aren't sloppy, Doc. They've been doing this long enough to have their system down. Most of the women are pliant— they get threatened with deportation if they leave the protection of the cartel, so they don't take any chances. But these guys don't let it rest there, they hold the women's families over them as leverage. They also get rid of the troublemakers quickly, separate them from the pack."

"That what happened to the twin?"

JD nodded. "She got rebellious early on. She was the younger twin, and this girl Melis's conviction that she was responsible for her sister rendered her less inclined to stir up trouble and more determined to protect her sister." He shook his head. "But all that changed when she learned her sister had been killed. She feels more responsible than ever, but she's ready to come out, guns blazing."

"She has a weapon?"

"Not that I can tell, but she has a powerful thirst

for revenge and something even more dangerous: the conviction that she's got nothing left to lose."

"Bad combination."

"You're telling me. On the other hand, she's eager to help, however we need her to. For now, she's willing to believe that we'll get her the justice she craves."

Doc leaned back in his chair, pondering the next step.

JD didn't feel nearly so patient. He had that itching under his skin he always got when events were coming to a head. "You found somebody to put on Violet, right?"

Doc jerked his attention back to the present. "Should be in place anytime."

JD frowned. He'd hoped surveillance would already be in force. Doc had plenty on his plate, though, and Sophie had promised....

Doc's phone rang. He hesitated. "Anything else I need to know?"

"Not yet."

"Okay. Send out the word. Let's meet in, say, an hour."

"Got it." JD called Bob and passed along the message.

But he was still itchy, worse than ever. He had to be sure that Violet was covered. He would call Sophie and be certain.

Just then, his phone buzzed at his hip. He flipped open the holster and drew it out.

Sophie.

JD's heart took a nosedive. She wouldn't call him when she knew he was working, not just to share good news.

"Sophie, is Violet okay?"

"Oh, JD, I'm so glad I got you. I—I'm so sorry."

His heart stopped. "What happened?"

"She wanted to take a shower, and there was no excuse for me to hang around, but—I was watching her door, I swear, but then a delivery came, and—"

"She left," he said flatly. Just as he'd feared she would.

And apparently their surveillance hadn't been in place yet. He wanted to tear his hair out by the roots. "Do you know where she went?"

"Avery just called me. She's at his club."

His breath stalled. "Why did he call?" If he'd threatened Violet...

"He's not at his club. He sounds frantic, JD. He didn't know how to reach you and was worried you might not take his call, so he asked me to do it. He said his partner Sage has Violet, and he wanted me to tell you that Sage is the one who had the man in Houston killed. Oh, JD, what if—" Her voice faltered, but she kept herself together. "Violet was going to go back to L.A. She said she'd probably sleep until morning because she was so exhausted from..."

From me. From the damage I did to her.

"She never gave me any indication she'd leave, JD. I had no idea this would happen."

"Don't beat yourself up, Sophie. You're not to blame." That was squarely on him. "I should have followed through on my threat to take her into custody. None of that matters now, though. Can you give me Avery's number?"

She read it off her phone.

"Good. Did he say where he was?"

"It sounded like he was driving. He said that he's afraid of what Sage might do. He was very upset that he'd been ignoring Violet's calls. Apparently she called the club when she couldn't reach him on his cell, and Sage told her she could wait there for him."

Friction between partners could be a helpful wedge, but right now it only increased his problems exponentially. "Did he say anything else? Anything at all—every bit counts."

"I...nothing I can think of."

"What time did he call?" JD glanced at his watch.

"I hung up with him then called you immediately. I'm so glad you answered." Once again her voice faltered. "I will never forgive myself if..."

"You did nothing wrong, Sophie. This is completely my fault." He kept his tone soothing and calm, but inside, rage crashed against the bars of his control. If anything happened to Violet...

Don't go there. Just get plans rolling. "I'll call you with an update when I can, but I don't know when that might be. Get in touch if you remember anything else. I'm going to phone Avery now, but if we don't connect and you hear from him again, give him this number. Tell him I'd talk to the devil himself if it meant protecting Violet."

"I will. Is there anything at all I can do?"

He was already running toward his car. "Not right now, but I'll let you know if there is."

"Please. I'll do anything." She was in an impossible position, and he'd put her there.

"I know you will. You've already helped. Thank you."

Violet could be a hostage right this minute. *Hostage.* The word knifed straight to his gut. Fear wouldn't help her now, though. He needed to be cool and calculating, though every cell of him was primed to charge to her rescue without pause.

Going in blind wouldn't help her, though. And a lot more people than him were involved.

He punched in Lofton's number as he ran.

IN HER ACTOR'S TOOLKIT, one prime asset was the ability to observe others closely. To put herself in a character's skin and understand how that person feels, thinks, what forces have formed her, how she would react in any given situation.

Violet was as good at this as anyone she knew.

But she couldn't get a bead on Sage Holland.

Outwardly, the woman could not be more cooperative. The activity level in the club was clearly building, and Avery wasn't here to help, so it would be natural for Sage to be a little distracted, even somewhat on edge because Violet was interfering with the normal flow of an evening.

But the woman seemed to possess an unnatural calm.

There was something almost…robotic about her. No, that wasn't it. She was clearly a force to be reckoned with, a statuesque blonde who appeared to be in superb physical condition. Her arms were strong, her legs long and toned. She was an imposing presence, especially in three-inch heels as she was right now, bringing her to what Violet would guess was six feet or taller.

"Ms. James?" The bartender, who went by the name of Rory, appeared at her side, as much of the staff had been doing since her arrival—cruising by to get a glimpse, maybe an autograph.

"What is it, Rory?" Sage's tone was clearly displeasure.

"I was just wondering if Ms. James would care to taste my latest cocktail invention. Sure wouldn't hurt business to be able to say she likes it." He winked at Violet.

She smiled back.

"Fine," Sage responded. "But send Leslie to me when you see her."

Violet glanced at the other woman, curious at Sage's impatience.

"I'm sorry about him asking for a favor," Sage said. "That must get so tiresome."

"It's fine. I'd be happy to sample the cocktail. Whatever I can do to help Avery—and you, of course—I want to."

Leslie hurried over. "Yes? Something I can get for Ms. James?"

"Violet, please."

A beaming smile. "Violet, then. Thank you."

"Yes," Sage said with little warmth. "You can tell the staff to stop gawking and get to work. We have a club to run."

The manager, whom Violet liked a great deal, paled. "Of course." She turned to Violet. "I apologize."

Violet placed a reassuring hand on her arm. "Don't worry a bit."

Leslie's relieved smile was quickly extinguished by Sage's stare. "Um…it won't happen again."

"This way." Sage gave no acknowledgment to Leslie but simply led Violet away.

Violet glanced back toward the manager and smiled to ease the sting of Sage's dismissal.

The bartender rushed up with the drink. Leslie restrained him.

"No, please. Bring it here." Violet gestured him over and took the cocktail. "Now what is this called?"

"If you like it, it'll be called the Violet James." His green eyes gleamed eagerly.

"Then I'd better like it, right?"

Impatience rolled off the woman beside her, which only made Violet want to dawdle. She took a slow sip. Closed her eyes to better focus. Her eyelids flew open. "Oh, my…that's yummy. What's in it?" She held up her hand. "No, never mind. I don't want to dissect it, I just want to enjoy it." She took a second sip, nearly as pleased to have the too-composed Sage fidgeting beside her. "Yes," she said, meeting the bartender's gaze. "I would be delighted to have this bear my name."

"Awesome—so if I got you a napkin, would you, like, sign it and say something about the drink?"

"Later," Sage snapped. When Violet glanced at her, arching one eyebrow, the woman subsided a bit. "We need to finish the tour I promised her first."

The bartender looked to Violet for affirmation, and Violet had to swallow a grin at the knowledge that this increasingly unlikable woman would really be out of sorts that he was deferring to Violet. "As soon as we're done, I'd love to."

"Great! Thank you."

"Oh, it's my pleasure," Violet responded, then turned back to the woman whose icy composure wasn't quite as solid now.

For whatever reason, the woman really did not like her. Maybe she had a thing for Avery and saw Violet as competition? Normally, Violet would have hastened to ease her mind, but for the moment she took a perverse pleasure in a little needling. "As I said, whatever I can do to help Avery, I want to do."

A faint tightening of those lips had Violet wanting to smile again, but she resisted. "He's very important to me, you know."

Narrowed eyes, then a regal lift of the head. "Of course. Come this way."

They headed toward a set of stairs. "Does this lead to the windowed rooms above?"

"Yes. My office, Avery's office and a VIP suite. I thought you'd be more comfortable waiting for him there."

"That's very kind of you." Though kindness was a stretch to attribute to this woman.

"Don't mention it."

JD PACED OUTSIDE HIS TRUCK as Lofton's phone rang. When it went to voice mail, he swore at the delay required by Lofton's message.

At last, the beep. "Lofton, this is JD Cameron. Sophie Carlisle relayed your message, but we need to talk. If you're half the friend Violet believes you are, call me the second you get this. Don't screw around— if she gets hurt, I will hunt you down, you son of a bitch." He squeezed his phone in white-knuckled fingers. "Call me." He rattled off his cell number and choked down the urge to hit something.

After he disconnected, he got in his vehicle and immediately dialed Doc, trying not to think about his last sight of Violet's face, set and still, steeled against him and the hurt he'd caused her.

When Doc answered, he relayed what he knew, but JD's phone soon beeped for call waiting. When he saw it was Lofton, he switched calls immediately and didn't waste any time on niceties. "Lofton, where are you?"

"That doesn't matter. You need to help Violet."

"I intend to, but I need some answers first. We should meet."

"I…can't."

"What do you mean you can't?" JD's eyes narrowed. "Are you running away? After you got Violet involved in this? You bastard, when I get my hands on you…"

"You don't know Sage, how she is."

"So you'd leave Violet at her mercy?"

"I can't go to jail." He hesitated. "If you could get me immunity, I could help you."

"Unbelievable." JD choked down the urge to leap through the phone and strangle the asshole. "You're the reason she's in this position."

"I never intended for this to happen. I tried to keep her away. Things have gotten out of hand, but it's not my fault." He was practically whining.

"You are some piece of work, you know that?" JD ground his teeth. "All right. I'll talk to the D.A."

"How soon?"

"You expect me to leave Violet in danger while I track down the D.A.? Forget that. Go ahead and run. Just do this one thing for Violet's sake, answer some questions about your setup at the club while you drive off into the sunset, you coward. Then to hell with you." The second they were off the phone, he'd have a bulletin out for Lofton, but the clock was ticking.

"You don't understand."

"Oh, I understand enough. I know that Violet thinks you're the only person in the world she can trust, and you're throwing her under the bus to save your own hide."

A long silence. JD waited him out. *C'mon...show me that Violet wasn't completely wrong about you.*

A sigh. "What do you want to know?"

Besides why I shouldn't shoot your sorry ass? JD forced his mind back to the operation. "Is Violet alone with your partner?"

"No, our manager is at the club, too."

"Name?"

"Leslie Alsobrook."

"So, two females. Give me a description of each one."

Lofton complied.

"Anyone else on the premises?"

"Not when I left, but by now the place will be full of staff getting ready to open."

Crap. "So what's that mean, number-wise?" He cast back in his memory to when he'd been there before. "You have one DJ, a bartender and a bar back, how many wait staff and busboys?"

"You've been in the club before? When?"

"Doesn't matter. How many?" JD snapped.

"Six cocktail waitresses to begin the evening, four more later. Six busboys, two bouncers. Two dishwashers. Lighting and sound guy."

JD shook his head. "A lot of bodies to work around. Doors open at, what, seven?"

"Yeah."

It was now nearly six. "Where do you think your partner would have her?"

"I don't know. They were touring the club when Sage called."

"Take a guess."

"There's a VIP room upstairs. Look, whatever you're going to do should happen soon. Sage expects me back any minute. If I'm not there, she'll get suspicious, and she's paranoid at the best of times."

"Then call her and stop her from getting suspicious. Tell her you're nearly at the club, that it won't be more than ten minutes."

"But—"

"I'm almost there, but I need more time to get backup in place."

"If Sage sees them…"

"She won't. They'll be staged farther away. First priority, though, is to extract Violet. So how do I get inside without attracting attention?" If the club were already open, it would be simpler, but no way was he leaving Violet there one second longer than he had to.

"If Sage senses a cop, there's no telling what she'll do."

A possible gambit occurred to him. "What kind of deliveries would you get this time of day?"

"What?"

"Deliveries," JD barked. "So I could enter at the back without anyone noticing something unusual."

"It's too late for that. Alcohol and food are already onsite. Linens, too. Sage would be suspicious of any deliveries right now."

Crap. "Anyone there you trust? Someone who likes you and not Sage?"

"That would be nearly everyone."

"Pick one."

"Leslie. The manager."

JD searched for a parking spot, though his sense of urgency pushed him to abandon his truck in the middle of the road and haul ass straight for the club. "Can you call her now without Sage knowing?"

A pause. "Yeah. I have her cell. We, uh, we had a thing."

Oh, great. "You're sure she'd be on your side?"

"Yeah. She's solid."

"Is she involved in the trafficking?"

"No. She knows nothing about that. She's a good person."

Like Violet. Someone else who could be hurt by this bastard's use of a legitimate business to make dirty money. "Do it, then. Tell her to let me in the back door and to say nothing to anyone. See if she knows where Violet is." JD pulled in a spot and cut the engine.

"You're not just a teacher at the Academy, are you?"

"No."

"Who are you?"

"I'm the man who's going to see you fry in hell if one hair on Violet's head comes to harm."

"I— Look, I never thought…"

"You thought you and someone like Lima would just have a cozy little tea party? And speaking of Lima, what do you suppose he'll do if he gets his hands on Violet?"

"Oh, God." A pause. "All right. I'm coming back. I'll help you."

"Why should I believe you? And how the hell can I trust you now?"

"Because Violet's important to me. Sounds like she's important to you, too. You willing to turn down help? I can get you inside. You said yourself getting her out of there is critical."

"I can't promise you a deal."

"But you'll try?"

"Help me get Violet to safety, and I'll do my best."

This hesitation was shorter. Lofton exhaled in a gust. "All right. What do you need me to do?"

"How far away are you?"

"Close. I've been circling. Listen—Violet mentioned taking me to dinner when Sage handed her the phone. Maybe I can use that as an excuse to take her away from the club."

JD's heart thumped. "You talked to her? How did she sound? Was she all right?"

"It was a voice mail, but she sounded like Violet—sweet. Sincere. Said she was having a nice time looking around."

"Did she sound as though she was under duress?"

"Not then."

JD thought madly. "Okay. Your restaurant is only a block or so away from the club, right?"

"Right."

JD didn't like involving civilians, and he wasn't sure how far to trust Lofton, but the man could get inside the club with no questions. And JD would be right on his tail. "Okay. Call Leslie the manager first. See if she knows where Violet is and have her keep an eye out for me at the back door—"

"Wait—" Lofton interrupted. "I don't know what you look like."

Impatiently JD rattled off a description. "Call me with Violet's location ASAP. Then you'll phone your partner. Tell her you got her message and that you set up an early dinner at the restaurant so you can be back at Danger Zone not long after opening."

"What if Sage says no?"

"If she balks at all, that's an answer of sorts."

"But then what do I do?"

"You show yourself to be the actor you once claimed to be, and you keep it calm and casual. Reassure her you'll be there in ten minutes, then report back to me on the conversation."

"Got it." Lofton clicked off.

JD phoned Doc. A team was on its way, and they refined their plans quickly. JD donned his earpiece while they were speaking, then checked the transmitter to be sure it was on. He'd like to wire Lofton, as well, but he didn't have spare equipment on him and time was too critical.

Then he spotted Lofton driving his Jag into the parking lot, talking on the phone.

"Gotta go, Doc."

"Be safe, JD."

"Always."

JD shoved his phone in his holster, checked his service weapon and yanked out the tail of his shirt to cover it, then checked the clutch piece fastened to his ankle.

And waited impatiently to hear from the piece of garbage Violet thought had only her best interests at heart.

"AND THIS—" SAGE GESTURED around her like a Vanna White substitute "—is a special suite for VIPs. Everything they could want—the sound from below piped in or their own music played on a state-of-the-art system." She strolled along one wall. "Home theater, a wet bar, catered meals, all manner of cushy seating…"

"Very impressive," Violet murmured. "Is that one-way glass?"

"To a degree, though if the light is on up here, dancers on the main floor can see in. Some VIPs like to keep things private, but others want to be part of the scene below."

"Without actually having to rub elbows."

"Exactly." Sage's phone buzzed and she held it to her ear. "You're still not here? What's the holdup?" She frowned, casting an irritated glance at Violet. "Why don't you ask her yourself when you get here? You're neglecting your guest, and there are things I need to check on." She listened again, a line forming between her brows.

Uh-oh. Botox wearing off, Sage. "Want me to talk to him?" Violet extended a hand.

Instead, Sage hit the end button. "I don't know what's taking him so long." She pocketed her phone and strode to the door. "Why don't you try out the chairs and enjoy your drink while I get back to work? You don't mind, do you?" Her expression said she couldn't care less if Violet minded.

"Of course not." Sage wasn't exactly scintillating company, anyway.

"Fine." Sage was through the door in an instant.

"What did Avery want to—"

The door shut with a click.

Talk to me about? she was going to ask.

Or not. Violet settled into a decadently comfy chair and took a sip of the Violet James cocktail. Then she let her head rest against the back of the chair and tried to relax.

A few minutes later, Lofton called JD back. "Sage isn't going for it. She wants me there now. I'm going in."

"No. You don't have any training for this."

"Look, Sage is getting really agitated. Leslie says Violet is upstairs in the VIP room, and she's ready to let you in. But someone's got to keep Sage occupied if you're going to sneak Violet out. That's what you want, right? To get her out quietly?"

"Yeah." Damn it.

"What? You don't trust me?"

"Should I?"

Lofton's voice went tight. "On this, yeah. I know you don't think much of me, but Violet is all the family I have. I can't leave her in there alone with Sage."

You were ready to do exactly that earlier. JD didn't have a lot of choices, though. Hostage situations could be deadly. Surrounding the club and demanding Violet's release when she was in the custody of an unbalanced woman? The odds were too dicey. If Sage was getting more agitated, waiting would only worsen the situation.

And eyes on the inside would be invaluable.

"Go in, then, but keep your partner downstairs and away from Violet. Make sure there are others around. She'll be less likely to do anything if other people are in sight. Set your phone to vibrate only, and keep this line open. Hit any key when it's clear for me to come in behind you, but stay on the line so I can listen in—that's your best protection until the team arrives. With luck, I'll be in and out fast. As soon as I have Violet clear, I'll text you, which should make your phone vibrate. Then you get the hell out of there. We'll do the rest."

"Got it. I'm going into the club now."

JD moved into position in the parking lot and watched Lofton enter the building.

CHAPTER SEVENTEEN

VIOLET STUDIED HER SURROUNDINGS, thinking of all Avery had created, how nice the people were who worked for him. Okay, not Sage—he had lousy taste in business partners—but everyone else. If this club was being used for nefarious purposes, she couldn't see it. She could not believe Avery was part of anything like what JD had suggested.

Sage, on the other hand… Maybe it wasn't fair to accuse her simply because she'd taken such a dislike to Violet. If she only knew…the only man Violet wanted was a smoky-eyed detective she couldn't trust.

Thoughts of JD wrecked any hope for relaxation. Violet leaped to her feet and went to the window to watch the activities on the main floor. She would not think about JD—not ever again if she could help it.

Oh, yeah, that's gonna happen.

Just then, Avery strode into view below, his head swiveling to scan the premises. He headed for Leslie and spoke to her intently. Sage walked up to the two of them, clearly impatient for Avery's attention.

Suddenly Violet couldn't wait any longer to see him. She would know the truth as soon as she looked into Avery's eyes.

She'd surprise him. She crossed the room in quick steps and grabbed the door handle.

It was locked.

There are things going on right now, serious things. People could get killed.

Violet banged on the door. "Hello?" No one else had been up here but her and Sage. She returned to the window and knocked on it, but no one looked up.

Sage, she saw now, was in Avery's face, apparently reading him the riot act. Avery appeared both nervous and upset.

Suddenly this spacious, beautiful room felt like a cushy prison, and she wanted out.

Things JD had said began to resurface. *People close to your buddy Avery are dying. Right now he's nervous and scared because someone he met with was murdered last night...and it's setting off a chain reaction.*

Unease prickled between her shoulder blades. The locked door no longer seemed like a mistake, and Sage, not Avery, appeared to have the upper hand.

You don't have to take my word on the crimes of your so-called friend—but you do have to believe this: I want you safe, and I don't care what I have to do to guarantee that.

Think, Violet.

Whatever Avery's role, she could not believe he'd let her come to any harm. Surely Avery would come upstairs to get her soon, and when he did, she'd insist on leaving the premises for dinner to get him out of Sage's sphere. Then she would start asking Avery some hard questions.

JD STOOD OUTSIDE THE BACK ENTRANCE, waiting for Lofton's signal.

His phone was also on vibrate for when he went inside. He put his Bluetooth on mute and pitched his voice low on the mic, testing to see if the team had arrived yet. "Doc?"

"It's Vince, JD. Had a holdup, but we'll be there in ten," said Vince. "Where are you?"

"Back door." Suddenly, his phone vibrated. "Got my signal, Vince. I'm going in. Have to get Violet out of there before everything goes sideways. I'll signal when I'm clear."

"Copy that. I'm closer than the rest. Be there in five."

Suddenly JD heard voices through his Bluetooth.

"What do you mean, you locked her in?" Lofton demanded. "Where?"

"I don't believe you're in any position to be making demands," said a sultry voice that, from Lofton's description, must be Sage. "Joe, check Avery's car, tell me what you see inside. Particularly if there are suitcases."

Crap. JD backed away to hide and spoke into his mic. "Do not approach. Someone heading for the back parking lot. Repeat, do not approach."

"Roger that."

A burly guy came through the back door. JD watched him while he listened in on Lofton.

"What the—Sage, what the hell are you doing?"

"That's more a question for you, I believe. Did you think I didn't have someone watching your house? You weren't getting a massage, Avery, you were making preparations to run."

"You're crazy."

In the parking lot, JD watched Joe cast a glance into Lofton's car, then shake his head and return to the club. JD raced for the door as quietly as he could and stuck a foot through to stop it from closing, then replaced his foot with a small stone he eased inside.

"You're a coward," he heard Sage say through the earpiece.

"Screw you."

"Been there, done that." The woman was cool as a cucumber. "Lost your nerve, Avery?"

"We were only laundering money. There wasn't supposed to be any violence. But then you murdered Bately when he decided to stop paying blackmail."

JD stood for a second to let his eyes adjust to the dark hallway. He didn't dare miss a word if he had to speak to Vince, so he keyed the mic, instead. Vince gave an answering click to acknowledge.

"You were setting up a side venture, may I remind you? Cutting me out. That isn't going to happen, Avery."

"What are you going to do, kill me next?"

"Don't tempt me." Hard as diamonds. "Jorge will want to weigh in on your fate when he gets here, I'm sure."

Lima was coming here? Capturing him had been one of the primary goals of the case from the beginning, but JD couldn't risk Violet's safety by waiting.

"Let Violet go. She's no part of this."

The woman's laughter was like nails on a blackboard.

Say something that verifies Violet's location, goddamn it, Lofton.

"Ah, yes, Joe. What's in Mr. Lofton's car?"

JD couldn't hear the words, but he didn't have to.

"A suitcase? My, my. What would we find in your pockets, pray tell? A passport?"

"Up yours, Sage. Is Violet upstairs? I want to talk to her."

"You're not in charge, Avery. You never were. Search him, Joe."

"For God's sake, not here," Avery spluttered. "Let's go upstairs. People talk. Don't create a spectacle in front of the staff."

A deep sigh. "Bring him along, Joe."

"I want to talk to Violet when we get there."

JD ran through the layout mentally. There was no easy way to get upstairs unnoticed. He wouldn't be able to get ahead of them in time to get to Violet. He'd have to let them go first.

"Did I say she was upstairs? Maybe she's in one of the back rooms," Sage said.

If only...that would make extracting much easier, JD thought as he checked his weapon again.

"You won't get away with this, Sage. I—"

Suddenly, the three of them approached JD's position. He flattened himself into a recess as a woman—Sage—preceded Lofton up the stairs, followed by the muscle JD had seen in the parking lot.

JD waited until they were out of hearing distance. "Going up, Vince. I think Violet's upstairs, but I'm checking the downstairs rooms on my way. Lofton, Holland and one guard are on their way up. And apparently, Lima's due in town."

Vince whistled his appreciation. "To snag Lima…"

"I'm not waiting."

"I understand. I'm two blocks away with Trini. Keep your mic open, so we know what's going on."

"Copy that." JD slipped from his hiding place.

Then he heard Lofton yell.

And Lofton's phone went dead.

WHEN SHE FIRST HEARD VOICES and footsteps, Violet moved closer to the door but stayed carefully back, listening.

"Jorge will be here soon, Avery. I don't imagine he'll think much of your travel plans. Joe, take him to his office. Restrain him."

"You won't—" Avery yelled.

The sound of a blow.

A moan.

A thud on the floor outside where she was trapped.

"Stick him in his office and watch him," Sage said coldly. "I have a call to make."

Oh, no. What had they done to Avery? Violet scrambled for her phone, then moved to the far wall and scrolled to JD's number. What if he wouldn't take her call, after what had happened between them?

This situation is far more deadly than you can imagine, maybe more dangerous than he ever expected. You could simply be collateral damage, but you'd be just as dead. And I couldn't live with that, Violet.

Oh, JD... She hesitated for a second. What could she tell him that would help? She didn't have any details, and she didn't want to expose him to danger, too.

I want you safe, and I don't care what I have to do to guarantee that.

She pushed the button. Immediately the call was sent to voice mail. Her heart sank, and she nearly disconnected. Maybe she should just call 911.

But the sound of his voice on the message made her remember how safe she'd felt with him once.

She stayed across the room and spoke softly. "JD, I...you were right. I—"

A text popped on the screen.

Cant talk. Im downstairs. Where r u?

She stifled a gasp. She had no idea what miracle had brought him close, but she was beyond grateful. Upstairs. VIP. 1st door on rt. Door locked. Want me 2 call 911?

No. Help comg. Hide. Stay away fr door.

Avery hurt. In 1st ofc down hall on L. 1 guard. Sage in her ofc nxt dr.

Good. Now hide. Im here.

Her eyes prickled with tears of gratitude. Im sorry. U were rt.

Will keep u safe. Got 2 go.

After how she'd doubted him, accused him…

He'd warned her, and she'd refused to listen, yet still he was trying to take care of her. *I love you,* she wanted to type. But she had no right.

Pls be careful, she typed.

U 2.

Relief mingled with fear for him, but, oh, how glad she was that he was nearby. She searched for a good hiding place, but first she scanned every surface for something to use as a weapon. She didn't like feeling this helpless.

The place was too clean. Then she remembered that they catered up here. She opened the drawer below the counter and found a knife. She knew next to nothing about self-defense, but it had a point and it could hurt. It was better than nothing.

She longed to linger by the door, to hear JD pass by. To reach out and touch him.

But she'd gotten them both into danger by ignoring his warnings to stay away from Avery.

This time she'd listen.

JD CREPT DOWN THE DARKENED HALLWAY.

A figure appeared at the opening into the dance area.

He ducked into the restroom alcove.

The figure passed him. A woman, meeting Lofton's description of the manager, Leslie.

JD crept up behind her and clapped a hand over her mouth.

She struggled against him.

He kept his hand tight and leaned next to her ear. "Leslie, I'm Detective Cameron. Avery tell you to let me in?"

She nodded, tried to speak.

"Can I trust you to stay quiet if I remove my hand? I'm here to protect Violet, not to hurt you."

She hesitated then nodded.

He removed his hand slowly, ready to clap it back on if need be.

She faced him, whispering. "Sage and Avery went upstairs. What's going on?"

Lofton had sworn she knew nothing of the way the club had been used illegally. Since he'd said she liked him and not Sage, JD decided to omit Lofton's part in the criminal enterprise. "Sage is involved in some illegal activities that could bring down the whole club. She's going to use Violet as a hostage."

The woman's eyes went round. "No."

"Yes. I don't have time to explain more. Sage is expecting company, right?"

She nodded.

"Know when?"

"No."

"I need to get Violet out of here now. Do you have a key to the VIP lounge?"

"Yes, but—"

"She's locked Violet in. Give me the key."

"I like Violet." She withdrew a key ring and searched for the right one.

When she put it in his hand, he nodded toward the main area. "I don't want anyone else hurt. Can you get the staff to leave without Sage noticing?"

"Some of them, but her office looks out on the main floor. She'll be suspicious if it's completely empty."

"Then keep a couple of people you trust not to panic. Get everyone else out of here now and warn them not to talk to anyone but my team who'll be waiting outside to take care of them. Be sure the back door stays unlocked and propped open. Are there exterior cameras that Sage can see?"

"We have cameras, but the monitors for the exterior are down here in my office."

"Good. I'm going to go upstairs and bring Violet out quietly if I can. Put your number in my phone, and I'll let you know when I have her safe, then the rest of you get out, too."

"What about Avery?"

He couldn't tell her Lofton was hurt. No predicting what she'd do. "I can only take one at a time, but my team will be coming for him."

"He's a good man."

Not you, too. But he didn't argue. "I'm trusting you to keep things calm down here."

Her gaze was resolute. "You can count on me."

"Thanks. Can you think of something to call Sage about, to distract her while I get Violet away?"

"I'll figure out something. How soon?"

"Spread the word to your people as fast as possible,

then call Sage as soon as you can. Three minutes cutting it too close?"

"I'll manage." She entered her number on his cell then retraced her steps.

JD followed silently, but detoured to the left to mount the stairs.

BEING STUCK BEHIND A SOFA let the mind run rampant to create every possible nightmare scenario. Violet longed to go to the window to see what was going on downstairs, to listen at the door.

Don't be that idiot heroine in the Gothic novel who goes into the darkened basement. You've already created problems enough.

She subsided against the corner wall. She flexed her fingers, realizing that she'd been gripping the knife handle as if it was her one remaining hope.

But JD was nearby. That thought brought her more comfort than she was entitled to, given the lack of faith she'd shown in him.

He'd deceived her, yes—repeatedly—but she could look at the situation with new eyes now, and she realized how difficult the situation must have been for JD. He was an undercover cop—he had to be a convincing actor, too, only the stakes were life or death, not mere box-office receipts.

What happened between us was no job, Violet. You felt it, too.

She had. And if she got a chance to be with him again, she wouldn't squander it.

Please. Give us that chance. Keep him safe.

A noise outside. A moan, like someone in pain. Avery? What if JD was hurt? She wanted to act, to help.

Then a sound, a key in the lock. She edged toward the end of the sectional nearest the door.

Her phone vibrated. Unlockd but dónt come out.

JD. Relieved by his nearness, Violet eased closer. She would be ready for whatever happened next.

JD's GOAL WAS TO SPIRIT VIOLET out without anyone noticing, to send her away before the raid went down. He listened to Sage talking on the phone to what he hoped was Leslie. From the sound of it, Sage wasn't happy, and he knew he couldn't count on her being preoccupied for very long.

Just then he heard footsteps in the office across the hall, the one Violet said was Lofton's. He sprinted to the wall next to that door and flattened himself against it, his weapon at the ready.

The door opened, and the burly man walked out, weapon drawn.

Headed for the room Violet was in.

"Don't move," JD said quietly. "Police. Drop your weapon." *Be smart, please.* JD didn't dare fire because Violet was somewhere behind the man. Bullets could go through walls.

The man whirled, instead. Fired.

JD tried to dodge but there was no time. The bullet slammed into his shoulder, knocked him back against the wall. His weapon tumbled from his grasp.

"JD!" Violet's voice.

The man kicked in that door.

The team would hear the gunfire on his mic and move in, but quickly enough? He scanned the floor to see where his weapon had landed, gritting his teeth against the fire in his shoulder.

While Joe was looking away, JD grasped his weapon in his left hand and braced himself against the wall.

The man yanked Violet out, brandishing her in front of him like a shield.

"You're surrounded. Let her go," JD said. He wanted to look Violet over to be sure she wasn't hurt but couldn't afford not to watch Joe closely.

"I've got him, Joe," Sage said from her doorway.

JD couldn't watch both at once, and the goon was closest to Violet. He could sense Sage nearing and spared her one quick glance. She was armed and approaching.

A form hurtled through the door beside JD and barreled into Sage.

Lofton.

He knocked Sage to the ground.

JD eased back so he could see both Joe and them.

Lofton struggled with Sage for her weapon.

"Avery, watch out!" Violet cried.

Joe raised his arm and fired a head shot. Lofton collapsed on top of his partner.

"No!" Violet screamed and lunged for Lofton.

"Violet, don't!" JD shouted.

But the man grabbed Violet and yanked her in front of him again, one beefy arm around her throat, his weapon rising toward her head.

JD's vision wavered. He couldn't get a clear shot.

Violet's right arm rose from her skirt. JD spotted the gleam of metal.

She jammed it into the man's thigh.

With a roar, he backhanded her into the wall. She collapsed like a rag doll.

JD fired. The goon fell to the floor.

JD staggered toward Violet.

A sound came from his left. He whirled to see Sage's weapon aimed at Violet.

JD threw himself in front of Violet.

The bullet plowed into him.

"Violet—" he called.

But there was no answer as he collapsed.

FOOTSTEPS POUNDED UP THE STAIRS, and Violet stirred. "JD—"

She heard Sage screaming with rage, but the sound was getting farther and farther away. She saw double and closed her eyes, trying to rise.

"Easy now. It's Vince Coronado, Violet. Don't get up. Someone will be here to take a look at you."

"Vince?" She tried opening her eyes again. Blinked hard to focus.

"Yeah. Where are you hurt?"

"Just my head. JD—is he—he got shot. Where is he?"

"He's alive."

But the look in Vince's eyes made her heart stop. "How bad?"

"Don't know yet. He took two hits. Lost a lot of blood."

"Two?" She'd only seen one. "What happened?"

Vince stared at her. "Sage tried to shoot you. JD took the bullet to save you."

"No. Oh, God, Vince." Grief bent her double.

"Sage and her henchman are in custody. JD's in the ambulance now."

"Where are they taking him? I have to go to him." She struggled to her knees but swayed.

"You're not going anywhere yet." Vince caught her.

"He'll be taken to University Medical. It's a level-one trauma center. He's in good hands."

"This is my fault." She wrapped her arms around her middle and rocked herself. "All of it. He told me to stay away from Avery, but—" Then she remembered more. The vision of Avery charging Sage, and his head— She swallowed back the sour sickness. "Avery…."

"I'm sorry."

"He's been my best friend for years." Violet clapped her hand over her mouth in horror at what she'd set in motion. Forced herself to meet Vince's gaze. *Don't fall apart. You don't have the right.*

"I did this, Vince, all of this—if I'd believed JD, none of this would have happened." She gripped his arm. "JD has to be okay. Are the doctors good enough?"

"We have to hope so."

Hope? She wanted a guarantee. "If he needs anything…anything, Vince. I'll give every dime I have if it will save him." *But you weren't willing to give him your trust, were you? You were too busy feeling sorry for yourself.*

Once again, she tried to rise on unsteady legs. Vince assisted her, but she felt the distance in him, saw the looks on the faces of his men.

They knew why JD was hurt. Knew she was the reason he might not make it.

She'd placed her faith in someone who didn't deserve it.

And hadn't believed in the best man she'd ever met.

"You would be right to despise me, but—" She fought to steady her voice. "I want to be there at the hospital to wait until—" Her voice broke. *He has to make it. Please.* "However little I deserve the privilege." Once again she lifted her eyes to the man beside her. To her surprise, his gaze was more sympathetic than judgmental. "Would you—please, Vince...could you get me a cab or...?"

"After you let the paramedics check you out, I'll drive you. If you'll wait right here..."

"I will." This time she'd listen. Do what she was asked.

She made herself straighten when she wanted to huddle, searched for a dignity she didn't deserve.

No matter that she'd set the wheels in motion, could she have prevented JD being wounded so badly or Avery being killed? If she hadn't screamed... If she'd been farther back from the door... If she hadn't let that man grab her, if she hadn't stabbed him or she'd stabbed him somewhere else or...?

Too late, all of it.

Please, she beseeched God and fate and every force in the universe. *I'll do anything.*

But God hadn't done this. Fate hadn't acted.

She had.

She might have a lot of money, possess the world's adulation...

But right now, when the life of the man she loved hung in the balance—

Everything else in her world was empty and meaningless.

Violet stared ahead blindly into a future that was forever altered.

CHAPTER EIGHTEEN

A WEEK LATER, VIOLET STOOD in Forest Lawn Cemetery in L.A. to say goodbye to her friend Avery. He hadn't been able to achieve the acting fame he'd sought, but she could give him this, a final resting place among those he'd admired.

It wasn't enough.

But she wasn't sure what would be. Didn't even know how to feel about what she'd learned about him, the person she'd trusted most outside her own family.

Instead of believing in the man she should have.

But thinking about JD now...she couldn't. He'd nearly bled out, but the second shot had hit him in the right side and missed critical organs. Once the doctors had said that he would live, she'd left.

As she walked toward the waiting limo, she was intensely grateful that JD had survived, that he would recover.

She didn't know if she ever would. For a few days, she'd experienced something beautiful and amazing. A rare gift she didn't expect to ever find again.

And she was the one who'd tossed it aside.

"Violet! Over here!" cried a voice from the crowd outside the gates.

She didn't even care. She was finding it hard to care about anything these days. She simply looked straight into the cameras and let the shutters snap.

"Ready, Ms. James?" her driver asked.

"Yes, thank you."

"I'll get you home in a snap."

"Thank you." Home. *Home is where the heart is.* In that case, she was hopelessly lost.

She'd left her heart halfway across the country, and she couldn't even ask for it back.

"IT'S BEEN NEARLY FIVE WEEKS," JD grumbled. "I'm sick of lying around."

"You're not sitting around, you're doing physical therapy," Jenna, his current babysitter, pointed out. "Maybe you ought to walk ten yards for every time you bitch. You'd have finished a marathon by now."

He had to smile. "Smartass. I'm not that bad."

She rolled her eyes. "Shall I get your mom on the phone and let her give her opinion?"

"Maybe not." His folks had just left a few days ago. They'd been badly shaken by the seriousness of his injuries. It wasn't the first time he'd been hurt on the job, but he'd always bounced back fast. They'd hung around even after he'd been released from the hospital and had done everything imaginable for him. "But in my defense, I wasn't in my right mind."

"Yeah, but what's your excuse after the first few days?"

"Watch it, kid."

She smiled. "They sure put in time on this house of yours. It looks a lot better. You actually have three livable rooms now."

"Hey, I'd have gotten there eventually."

"In this century?"

The kitten he'd named Spot leaped from the floor and landed on his belly. "Oof! Not there, okay?" Gingerly he used his good left arm to shift her away from the healing wound just above his hip.

"You with a cat...who'd have thought?"

Not him, for sure. His neighbor had cared for the cat while he'd been in the hospital, and, as it turned out, no one had come to claim the kitten, so he had. It was pretty pathetic that he wanted her because she connected him to Violet, but...there it was.

He wondered, as he did every day, how Violet fared. If she'd gotten over Lofton's betrayal and his loss. She must hate the publicity that had still not fully abated. The police had managed to keep some of the details out of the press, but the media had had a field day with the salacious nature of Avery's death and Violet's connection to him.

He devoured every picture of her he saw on TV or in the papers or online.

She looked...sad. Weary.

"Thinking about her again?" Jenna asked. "Violet?"

"No point." He glanced over at the TV. "So what should it be today, Judge Judy or Dr. Phil?" He lifted the remote.

Jenna snatched it out of his hand. "Are you just going to sit here and let her go?"

He didn't have the spirit to engage in his usual battle with her. "Leave it, Jenna."

"Why? Because, for the first time in your life, a woman's not falling at your feet?"

"That has nothing to do with it. You don't understand the first thing about what happened."

She settled on the coffee table beside him. "Then why don't you explain?"

He shoved to a sitting position and winced. Slowly he rose and glowered down at Jenna. "I said leave it."

He stalked to the back porch. Stood there and looked around.

Even here Violet haunted him. He could see her, languid in his arms...crouching over the kitten... bare legs beneath his shirt...kissing him with such sweetness...

He'd never had his heart broken before.

It hurt like ten kinds of hell.

"JD, I'm sorry," Jenna said from the doorway.

He glanced back. "It would never work, can't you see that? She's—she's Violet James, and I—I'm... this." He gestured around him. "Nothing wrong with it, but there's no midpoint, no compromise, even if—" Even if she'd ever bothered to contact him since that day.

"She refused to let them admit her to the hospital for her own injuries so that she could stay near you until she knew you'd make it. Does that say she doesn't care?"

He'd been told that, but he had no memory of her being there. "She left town before I ever woke up."

"She told Vince she'd cover the cost of the best specialists available."

"Oh, yeah, that's just what I want, her throwing around money on my behalf."

"I never got the sense that money was all that important to her."

He snorted. "She's one of the richest women in the country. Hell, in the world, for all I know."

As an artist, you don't perform for the money.

He ignored the memory. Easy for her to say—she had buckets of money.

"So your pride is more important than your heart?"

"What else do I have, Jenna? I can't be a kept man. And I don't want to live in L.A., anyway."

"Zane's figured out a different path."

"Zane is the one with the money in that relationship."

"If you weren't hurt, I'd smack you. So you can only love a woman who makes less than you? You are such an idiot, JD. What does money matter compared to love?"

"A whole damn lot." Again he tried to shrug her off with a mock-leer. "You can only spend so much time in bed."

"Ooh!" She glared at him. "Do not be deliberately thick-headed. I saw her at the hospital. She was devastated. She feels guilty, JD, that's why she left. She thinks what happened was her fault."

"It was." Suddenly he was furious in a way he hadn't allowed himself to be before. "It absolutely was. I told her to stay away from him, but she didn't listen."

"So you need a woman who's obedient *and* poor before you'll fall in love?"

"No!" It was too late for that. He'd already fallen. But still… "She didn't trust me, damn it!"

"You were undercover. You lied to her—by necessity, yes, but she'd just gotten divorced from a man who lied to her constantly. You're good at what you do, very convincing…so somehow she's magically supposed to trust you even though you were deceiving her, too?"

"Yes—no—she should have known me, damn it. What we had was real. She felt it, same as I did, but in the end, she didn't trust me. And she walked away from all of it."

He stared out at the trees, at the yard he'd had such

plans for. Had even pictured Violet there in those heady few days, even when he'd known he shouldn't. "It was real. I love her. And none of that matters."

"So you're going to sit around here and mope? Just give up without even trying?"

Her needling didn't bother him this time, not when the pain inside his chest had claws like a saber-tooth tiger.

He wasn't a quitter, no.

But recognizing the truth wasn't quitting, it was simple logic. The chasm between their worlds was too huge to span.

"I can't travel for another week, anyway, the doctor said."

"And then?" she prompted.

"I don't know."

"I think you do," Jenna said softly. "Sit down, JD. You're pale as a ghost." He fell into the porch swing, she sat beside him and they rocked in silence.

"VIOLET, DARLING, YOU'VE LOST WEIGHT." The photographer fluttered around her. "You're delicious, of course, but we have to take in this gown, just like the last three." He sighed. "Someone get the seamstress again."

It was the last outfit of the shoot at the beach house the magazine had booked, and she couldn't wait to be done. She was in more demand than ever for magazine covers. On the heels of a scandal involving adultery, possibly the only thing more tantalizing was being in the midst of gunfire and bloodshed. And when rumors included a knife-wielding star...

Human skin was tougher than she would have

imagined. Her stomach rebelled whenever she thought of it.

So she tried not to.

Not that her nightmares cared.

She stood like a mannequin, eyes closed, while her makeup was refreshed, while hands moved over her body, tucking here, pinning there. Music that sounded entirely too much like that played in Avery's club pounded, and voices chattered at insane speeds, speaking on inane topics...

She wanted to run away.

But the only place she wanted to be was off-limits.

"You can't come in here," the magazine booking agent shrieked suddenly. "We're doing a shoot."

"I came to see Violet."

That voice. She felt her insides quiver. Her eyes flew open.

"Well, you can't. I don't know how you ever got in here. Get out or I'll call the cops."

She swallowed hard. "He is a cop."

JD stood perhaps twenty feet away, gaunt and weary, his arm in a sling but so very beautiful to her.

"I'll wait outside until you're done. Will you talk to me?" He was curiously stiff and formal.

"I will," she managed to say.

"All right." He turned to go.

Fear shot through her at the thought that he would leave and never return. "Wait!" She searched frantically for the photographer. "Franco, please. Can he stay?"

"No!" the booker complained. "He'd be a distraction, Violet."

Violet looked back. He was nearly to the door. "JD, please don't leave. Franco!"

The photographer approached. Framed her face in his hands. "I don't enjoy shooting a rag doll. There's life in your eyes now." He nodded. "For you, precious Violet, he can stay."

"Thank you, Franco." She pressed a grateful kiss to his cheek, then immediately sought out JD again. He was looking at her, but she couldn't decipher his expression. She grabbed her skirt and lifted it, racing to where JD stood.

Up close, his beautiful smoky eyes were unreadable. Once again, fear shivered through her.

But he'd come. That meant something, didn't it?

Her throat crowded with everything she wanted to say. Was afraid to. "Please. Will you wait in here for me, instead? We're nearly finished."

His eyes softened. "Go ahead. I'll be here."

She wanted to touch him so badly, to throw herself into his arms.

To find out how he was feeling, to be sure he would be okay…she couldn't hope for him to tease her or smile at her again, though that would be the best kind of miracle.

But everything had changed. She had changed it. She had no right to her hopes.

"I'll hurry." But she hesitated. She didn't want to leave him.

"Go on, Hollywood," he said gently. "Let him take pictures of you in that dress you're almost wearing."

The nickname undid her. She glanced down and blinked hard so the makeup artist wouldn't have to start over. "It will be all the rage," she said, and her voice was almost steady.

"Tissues held together with pipe cleaners never go

out of style." And there it was, that old twinkle she'd thought never to see again.

She drew a ragged breath. "I've missed you so much."

He nodded. "They're waiting for you," he said softly.

She made herself turn around and walk over to Franco.

She only looked back twice to be sure JD was still there.

"Honey, girl," Franco stage whispered. "You've been holding out on us." He winked. "It might be worth reshooting the other outfits, the bloom he puts on you."

She gripped Franco's arm. "You're not serious."

"I am tempted, precious." He winked. "But I wouldn't do that to you." He clapped his hands. "All right, people, let's get this done."

JD WATCHED VIOLET SPEAK to an assistant, who promptly brought him a chair. Someone else scurried over with a tray of fruits and breads, whispering the assortment of beverages that were available. "But whatever you want, Miss James says. You just name it."

"I'm fine."

"Oh, please. This shoot is costing buckets. We don't want her unhappy. Whatever you'd like, just let me bring you something."

Finally he agreed to a cup of coffee and saw the girl's relief. Seeing how everyone in the place was focused on Violet made him newly aware of just how important she was, how many people fawned on her, how far up in the stratosphere she existed.

Was this trip a fool's errand? Probably. Hopelessly

naive to think he'd glimpse even one trace of the sun-burned, laughing woman who'd shared tacos with him and argued over Jane Austen?

Almost definitely.

I've missed you so much. Haunted lavender blue eyes.

He'd missed her, too—however miserable he'd been, he hadn't truly realized how much he'd missed her until he'd seen her again in the flesh.

But observing her in her milieu, watching the power she wielded...the secret fantasies he'd been daydreaming when he couldn't stop himself crumbled to dust now.

JD, please don't leave.

He wouldn't go, at least not yet, because even being slapped in the face with the reality of her life, being forced to witness the gulf that yawned between them... was better than not seeing her at all.

At last she was done. Violet didn't want to let JD out of her sight, but all her usual detachment at being poked and prodded, stripped and dressed, vanished under the weight of JD's gaze, and she found herself newly modest. "I'm just going to change," she said to him. "Five minutes." She waited until he nodded, then raced for the bathroom, assistants trailing her and muttering.

Once inside, she let them peel her out of the gown. "Where are my clothes?"

Someone shoved them at her, and she donned the yoga pants and hoodie quickly then slipped her feet into her flip-flops, trying not to wish she had something prettier to arm herself with for this conversation.

She raced back to the set. "Thank you, everyone.

Great shoot." She kissed Franco. "I'm going to take him out on the deck, maybe to the beach. How long do you have the place?"

"Take your time, dear heart. We'll pack up, but we've got the property all day. I'll keep security in place so no one bothers you. Just send them home when you're done. What about your driver?"

"Would you tell him I'll call if he has to come?"

"Sure thing. Good luck, sweetheart."

"Thanks." She bit her lip. "I need it."

She crossed to JD, led him onto the deck overlooking the ocean. "We can go down to the beach—that is, are you okay to walk?"

"Been doing it for years."

"I meant—"

"I know what you meant. I'm not back to full speed, but I'm getting there."

He didn't move.

Neither did she.

The waves crashed behind them. The air pulsed with the heat of emotions, the sweet sting of memories, the weight of too much unsaid.

"How are you feeling?" she asked at last.

"I don't know why I'm here," he said in the same instant.

Hope faltered.

She'd wronged him. She should go first. "JD, I'm so very sorry. It was all my fault. I don't expect you to ever forgive me, but—"

"But?" The faintest curve of his lips encouraged her just enough.

"I guess... I wish there were some way to earn your forgiveness, anyway."

"I lied to you, Violet. You had every right to be upset. I just…"

"Didn't have any choice," she finished for him. "I get that now. If I hadn't been pitying myself so much, I would have realized it then. You were in an impossible position. You have nothing to apologize for. I'm the one who can never say I'm sorry enough. None of…*that* had to happen." A lump the size of a basketball lodged in her throat, a ragged tangle of all her regrets.

She forced herself to straighten, to face him and what she'd done. "Sophie tells me you're doing well in physical therapy. Are you in terrible pain?"

"Not enough to justify what a bear I've been to my family and friends. At least, that's their opinion."

She tried to smile, but guilt overrode her ability to see humor. "You're completely justified. You—" Her voice broke. "You saved me. You nearly died doing it." She ducked her head and brushed at her eyes.

He lifted her chin, and even that small touch zinged straight to her soul. "I didn't, though," he said gently. "Are you fully recovered?"

"Yes." Physically, at least.

"You're too skinny. I should have brought some barbecue."

That did make her smile. "That was a fun day."

"All of them were—okay, maybe not the last one."

She dropped her gaze in shame.

"Hey…" he said gently. "It's okay."

"It's not. It won't ever be. Avery died. You nearly did. I live it over and over again. I can't sleep because all I can see is you bleeding and still fighting to protect me. And me doing everything wrong."

His free arm closed around her, gathered her in

to his broad chest. The scent of him wrapped around her, the fragrance of so many dreams, such tortured, beautiful memories. She wanted to cling to him, to stay right here forever.

His cheek came to rest on her hair. "Hold on to me just a second," he whispered. "I need to hold on, too."

She dug her fingers into the back of his shirt. "I thought I'd never see you again."

"I'm not all that hard to chase down right now."

"I wanted to go back." She raised her head, stared into his eyes. "Every day I wanted to, but...I didn't have the right. I ruined your investigation. You almost died because of me. I'm so sor—*mmph!*"

His mouth closed over hers, and the world filled with sweetness. She moaned into his lips and held on tighter. This, this...oh, God, she'd missed this. Thought never to have it again.

His kiss lingered, soothing her, easing her, arousing her to want more, to hang on and never let go.

At last he lifted his head, and his eyes were that warm, smoky velvet she could practically feel against her skin. "I wasn't going to come," he said. "No matter that I wanted you so bad I've been a raving lunatic." His face was serious. "Because I don't have any answers for us. I don't know how to make us work."

"Because there's something wrong with me? I can't blame you. I can't seem to get love right."

"No! There is nothing wrong with you. You're a romantic and you have faith in love, and not everyone measures up to it, but the world is a better place because you believe people are basically good."

"You think so? I'm not just hopelessly naive?"

"No."

"But you're a good person, so why can't we work?"

"Look around you." He gestured. "I don't fit in this world."

"Why not?" She couldn't let him just walk away, not now.

"You stood there in that room, and twenty people were focused solely on you. God knows how much money got wasted in the few minutes you talked to me. You have a wall built around you to keep the world out, to keep ordinary people like me back behind the ropes where we belong."

"But that's not who I am. You know that."

"It *is* who you are, Violet—not all of you, maybe, but…you can't just ignore how different our worlds are. Can't you see it's hopeless?" His brows snapped together. "And speaking of the differences between us, you are not paying my medical bills. I will not be a kept man."

"What?" She blinked. "This is about money? Are you crazy?"

"It's not crazy. It's reality."

She'd never expected to be angry at him. "You'd give up what's between us over money? That's insane."

"That's what Jenna said." He looked insulted. "Face the facts, Violet. I'll never make what you make."

"Did Jenna say you were stupid, too?"

"She might have."

Her anger faded at his truculent tone. She bit back a smile. "So if I gave away everything I make, would that make us fit? You'd be happy?"

"I don't—I'm not saying I don't want you to have it. You've earned every penny."

"But?" She cocked her head. "Have you ever flown first class, JD?"

His brows snapped together. "No. And don't mock me."

"I'm not, not really." She sighed, and for the first time in weeks, something inside her relaxed. "I thought you'd hate me."

He exhaled wearily. "It'd be a damn sight easier if I could."

"I like luxuries, JD, but I don't need them." She arched an eyebrow. "You might like them, too, though."

"Not when I see what you have to go through to get them. I'd never feel right about that. Anyway, I'm a simple guy with simple tastes."

A laugh burst from her. She covered her mouth. "Sorry, but you are the least simple guy I've ever met."

"Watch it, Hollywood. I may not be at my peak right now, but that doesn't mean I couldn't wreak some havoc."

"You already have," she said, patting her heart. "Right here." Then she rose to her toes and whispered in his ear. "Exactly how not at your peak are you?"

"Why, Ms. James, are you propositioning me?" His eyebrows waggled.

"You better believe it, cowboy." She slipped her hand behind his belt buckle.

He stopped her. "Violet, this is no joke. I don't want a fling, and I don't know how we could have anything else. I can't see where we can meet in the middle."

"Do we have to know right this minute?"

"Yeah. Because I'm in love with you. I want to be with you from now on."

Her mouth dropped open. "Seriously?"

"When you come that close to dying, you don't kid about things like this."

She spread her fingers over his chest as if she could

protect him from now on. "I don't want a fling, either, JD. And I don't want you arguing with me or discounting it when I tell you I love you, too." When he opened his mouth, she stopped his words with her fingers. "You came into my life out of the blue. And you saw me, JD, just as I am. You understand the roots I come from. We're a lot more alike than we are different." She shrugged. "Every bit of this—" she gestured around her "—could all vanish in an instant, and I know it. Anyway, I've been thinking about making some changes." She bit her lip. "Since I thought I'd have to live my life alone."

"You never have to be alone again. I'm here."

She wondered if he could possibly imagine what that meant.

"What kind of changes?" he asked.

"I've thought a lot about those women you were trying to save, ones who've been victimized by people like Sage and—" She cleared her throat. "Like Avery."

His gaze filled with sympathy. "He got into something he wasn't prepared for. And whether or not he meant to involve you, in the end he paid for it. Sage and the bastards she was in bed with will have years in a cage to think about what they did. Their deadly pipeline has been severed, so good has come out of Avery's sacrifice." He covered her hand with his. "I'm sorry you lost your friend. Sorry he lost his way."

Her eyes filled. "What he did was so very wrong. And I was more wrong not to listen to you. I'm sor—"

Another kiss, quick and torrid. "I don't need any more *I'm sorrys.* Guess I'll just have to kiss the socks off you until you stop."

Her heart lightened enough to meet his teasing. "Well, then, I'm sorry, I'm sorry, I'm—" He stopped her with another kiss. Tears mingled with laughter, and they embraced for a long, healing time.

He spoke into her hair. "I've been thinking about making changes myself. Truth is, I was getting pretty burned out. I've been doing undercover for a long while. Too long."

"Do you know what you want to do?"

"I've considered all sorts of things—I could be a cop in L.A. as easily as Texas…"

"You don't want to live in L.A. and you love Texas."

"But *you're* not in Texas."

She lifted her head. "I could be, at least part of the time. And I don't have to shoot so many films, one after the other. Seeing someone die makes you stop and reconsider everything you're doing."

"This work with victims of trafficking, do you know how you want to structure it?"

"No…I haven't got that far in the planning. Maybe… Would you be willing to help me figure it all out, if you leave law enforcement?"

His look was considering. "I really might."

"Well, if I'm taking a vow of poverty, I can sell all my worldly goods and start a foundation." When he rolled his eyes, she smiled. "I think the point is that we're both ready for a change. Sophie says love will find a way, and I want to believe that. We have some decisions to make, so why not think about them together?"

For a long moment he stared at her, and she could see their future hanging in the balance.

"Why not?" he said at last.

Violet felt like she could breathe again.

"Spot says hi, by the way," he said.

"Who's Spot?"

He looked aghast. "You've forgotten our furry child so soon?"

"You named that cute little kitten *Spot?*"

"Well, she's young, so she could learn a new one, I guess. But to have any input, you'd have to come see her, get reacquainted."

"I guess I would."

"I have three livable rooms now. My folks stayed at my place while I was in the hospital, and the Camerons aren't all that good at twiddling their thumbs. When I got out, Dad stuck a paintbrush in my hand and called it physical therapy."

"Are they still there? I'm dying to meet them."

"They went home a couple of weeks ago. It's just me and Spot. Place feels pretty empty." He drew her close again, placed his lips on her throat. "Especially the bedroom."

Her head fell back as she tumbled into bliss. "How's the claw-foot tub?"

His mouth cruised over her jaw. "Coulda sworn I heard it cry the other night. Damnedest thing."

Her thoughts kept flitting away as her eyes rolled back in her head. "Um…do I have to fly back economy with you?"

"We'll flip a coin at the airport. Now how far away is your bedroom?"

"Too far. But my driver can get us there fast," she panted. "If I could corrupt you with just one more little luxury."

"I was afraid of that." His lips brushed hers. "Okay, Hollywood…do your worst."

"In a minute. First…tell me again that you love me."

"I love you, Violet. You as you are, inside and out.

And I want to be around to see you at eighty-five, like my grandmother. You'll be beautiful, too."

After all the mistakes, here he was, at last, the man she'd dreamed of and hoped for and tried to keep faith in. "I want to build a life with you, make a family with you."

"Then I think we'd best get started, Hollywood." He bent to her, his eyes warm, his arms strong.

"Me, too. I love you, JD." She sank into his embrace, into the first kiss of their new life.

The forever-after life of her dreams.

* * * * *

HEART & HOME

Harlequin®
Super Romance

COMING NEXT MONTH
AVAILABLE MAY 8, 2012

REQUEST YOUR FREE BOOKS!
2 FREE NOVELS PLUS 2 FREE GIFTS!

Harlequin®

Super Romance®

Exciting, emotional, unexpected!

YES! Please send me 2 FREE Harlequin® Superromance® novels and my 2 FREE gifts (gifts are worth about $10). After receiving them, if I don't wish to receive any more books, I can return the shipping statement marked "cancel." If I don't cancel, I will receive 6 brand-new novels every month and be billed just $4.69 per book in the U.S. or $5.24 per book in Canada. That's a saving of at least 15% off the cover price! It's quite a bargain! Shipping and handling is just 50¢ per book in the U.S. and 75¢ per book in Canada.* I understand that accepting the 2 free books and gifts places me under no obligation to buy anything. I can always return a shipment and cancel at any time. Even if I never buy another book, the two free books and gifts are mine to keep forever.

135/336 HDN FC6T

Name _____ (PLEASE PRINT)

Address _____ Apt. #

City _____ State/Prov. _____ Zip/Postal Code

Signature (if under 18, a parent or guardian must sign)

Mail to the **Reader Service:**
IN U.S.A.: P.O. Box 1867, Buffalo, NY 14240-1867
IN CANADA: P.O. Box 609, Fort Erie, Ontario L2A 5X3

Not valid for current subscribers to Harlequin Superromance books.

Are you a current subscriber to Harlequin Superromance books and want to receive the larger-print edition?
Call 1-800-873-8635 or visit www.ReaderService.com.

* Terms and prices subject to change without notice. Prices do not include applicable taxes. Sales tax applicable in N.Y. Canadian residents will be charged applicable taxes. Offer not valid in Quebec. This offer is limited to one order per household. All orders subject to credit approval. Credit or debit balances in a customer's account(s) may be offset by any other outstanding balance owed by or to the customer. Please allow 4 to 6 weeks for delivery. Offer available while quantities last.

Your Privacy—The Reader Service is committed to protecting your privacy. Our Privacy Policy is available online at www.ReaderService.com or upon request from the Reader Service.

We make a portion of our mailing list available to reputable third parties that offer products we believe may interest you. If you prefer that we not exchange your name with third parties, or if you wish to clarify or modify your communication preferences, please visit us at www.ReaderService.com/consumerchoice or write to us at Reader Service Preference Service, P.O. Box 9062, Buffalo, NY 14269. Include your complete name and address.

HSR11

Harlequin®

American ★ Romance®

The heartwarming conclusion of

CALLAHAN Cowboys

from fan-favorite author

TINA LEONARD

With five brothers married, Jonas Callahan is under no pressure to tie the knot. But when Sabrina McKinley admits her bouncing baby boy is his, Jonas does everything he can to win over the woman he's loved for years. First the last Callahan bachelor must uncover an important family secret…before he can take the lovely Sabrina down the aisle!

A Callahan Wedding

Available this May wherever books are sold.

*After a bad decision—or two—Annie Mendes
is determined to succeed as a P.I. But her first assignment
could be her last, because one thing is clear: she's not cut
out to be a nanny. And Louisiana detective Nate Dufrene
seems to know there's more to her than meets the eye!*

*Read on for an exciting excerpt of the upcoming book
WATERS RUN DEEP by Liz Talley...*

THE SOUND OF A CAR behind her had Annie scooting off the
road and checking over her shoulder.

Nate Dufrene.

Her heart took on a galloping rhythm that had nothing to
do with exercise.

He slowed beside her. "Wanna ride?"

"I'm almost there. Besides, I wouldn't want to get your
seat sweaty."

His gaze traveled down her body before meeting her
eyes. Awareness ignited in her blood. "I don't mind."

Her mind screamed, *get your butt back to the house and
leave Nate alone.* Her libido, however, told her to take the
candy he offered and climb into his car like a naughty little
girl. Damn, it was hard to ignore candy like him.

"If you don't mind." She pulled open the door and
climbed inside.

The slight scent of citrus cologne, which suited him,
filled the car. She inhaled, sucking in cool air and Nate.
Both were good.

"You run often?" he asked.

"Three or four times a week."

"Oh, yeah? Maybe we can go for a run together."

Her body tightened unwillingly as thoughts of other
things they could do together flitted through her mind. She

shrugged as though his presence wasn't affecting her. Which it *so* was. Lord, what was wrong with her? *He* wasn't her assignment.

"Sure." No way—not if she wanted to keep her job. As he parked, she reached for the door handle, but his hand on her arm stopped her. His touch was warm, even on her heated flesh.

"What did you say you were before becoming a nanny?"

Alarm choked out the weird sexual energy that had been humming in her for the past few minutes. Maybe meeting him on the road wasn't as coincidental as it first seemed. "A real-estate agent."

Will Nate discover Annie's secret?
Find out in WATERS RUN DEEP by Liz Talley,
available May 2012 from Harlequin® Superromance®.

And be sure to look for the other two books
in Liz's THE BOYS OF BAYOU BRIDGE series,
available in July and September 2012.

Hoping to shield the secret she carries, Brooke McKaslin returns to Montana on family business. She's not planning on staying long—until she begins working for reporter Liam Knightly. Liam is as leery of relationships as Brooke but as their romance develops, Brooke worries that her secret may ruin any chance at love.

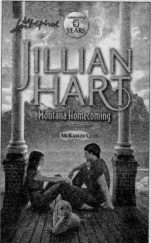

Montana Homecoming

By fan-favorite author

JILLIAN HART

THE McKASLIN CLAN

PRESENTING...

More Than Words

STORIES OF THE HEART

Three bestselling authors
Three real-life heroines

Even as you read these words, there are women just like you stepping up and making a difference in their communities, making our world a better place to live. Three such exceptional women have been selected as recipients of Harlequin's More Than Words award. To celebrate their accomplishments, three bestselling authors have written short stories inspired by these real-life heroines.

Proceeds from the sale of this book will be reinvested into the Harlequin More Than Words program to support causes that are of concern to women.

Visit

www.HarlequinMoreThanWords.com

to nominate a real-life heroine from your community.